The Longest Winter

Kevin Sullivan covered the siege of Dubrovnik in 1991 and the war in Bosnia in 1992/93. He was seriously wounded in a land-mine explosion in early 1993. While recovering, he wrote an early draft of *The Longest Winter*. He now lives in Sarajevo with his wife and daughter.

Kevin Sullivan

The
Longest
Winter

twenty7

First published in Great Britain in 2016

This paperback edition published in 2016 by

Twenty7 Books
80–81 Wimpole St, London W1G 9RE
www.twenty7books.co.uk

A CIP catalogue record for this book is available from the British Library.

Paperback ISBN: 978-1-78577-033-3
Ebook ISBN: 978-1-78577-017-3

1 3 5 7 9 10 8 6 4 2

Printed and bound by Clays Ltd, St Ives Plc

Twenty7 Books is an imprint of Bonnier Zaffre,
a Bonnier Publishing company
www.bonnierzaffre.co.uk
www.bonnierpublishing.co.uk

For Marija and Katarina with all my love

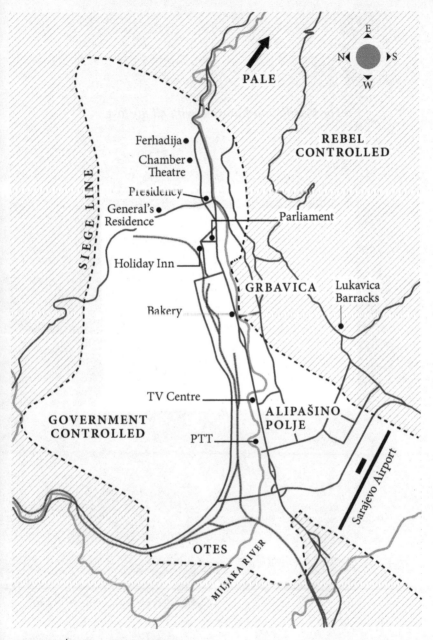

SARAJEVO, 1992-1993

HISTORICAL NOTE

When the socialist system in Yugoslavia collapsed at the end of the Cold War, the country's constituent republics broke away from the central government in Belgrade. Serbs and Croats formed substantial majorities in Serbia and Croatia respectively, but in Bosnia and Herzegovina, which had a centuries-old tradition of diversity and multicultural tolerance, no single community enjoyed an absolute majority. Citizens of Bosnian Muslim heritage, or Bosniacs, formed the largest group, after which there were substantial numbers of Serbs and Croats, as well as Bosnians of mixed origin and other backgrounds. Family names are routinely used to attribute 'ethnic identity' in Bosnia and Herzegovina, and 'ethnicity' is used interchangeably with religious affiliation – Bosniacs are assumed to be Muslim, Croats to be Catholic and Serbs to be Orthodox. In reality there are no ethnic differences among the communities – they are all Slav – and the presumption of religious affiliation does a disservice to those who have no religious affiliation or who believe their religious practice should have nothing to do with politics.

At the start of the conflict, the government in the Bosnian capital, Sarajevo, formally adopted a policy of equal rights for all citizens regardless of which community they belonged to, while a Rebel movement with its headquarters in the ski resort of Pale, just outside Sarajevo, advocated separating the communities into homogeneous statelets. The violent creation of such statelets, with neighbours turning on neighbours, generated the 'ethnic cleansing' that characterised much of the conflict. The better-armed Rebels besieged Sarajevo from April 1992 until February 1996. During this siege, the longest in modern history, thousands of civilians died, including more than 1,000 children, as a result of artillery and sniper fire, and shortages of medicine and food. The United Nations deployed a force comprising troops from France and the United Kingdom as well as other countries, which was tasked with escorting humanitarian aid to vulnerable enclaves, including Sarajevo. With its limited mandate, the UN Protection Force was widely viewed as an ineffectual bystander.

This novel is set in Sarajevo during the first winter of the siege and is based on true events. For narrative purposes two of these events, the battle for control of the western suburbs and the assassination of a government minister while crossing the frontline under UN protection, are described as happening at the same time. In real life they were separated by a period of weeks.

1

The Luftwaffe Transall C-160 made a huge amount of noise; bits of steel and canvas webbing protruded from the metal surface of the interior amid a profusion of buttons and lights.

The three passengers were invited, one at a time, for a spell in the cockpit. Terry climbed awkwardly into a bright space that was airy and cold. The seats were upholstered with shabby and torn leather. Green webbing covered the steel partition that separated the cockpit from the main cabin, with dog-eared maps stuffed behind a matrix of elastic cord.

She looked out of the narrow windows at white clouds as the plane skirted fluffy edges of mist.

The air smelled of tobacco, steel and engine oil.

'What's he doing?' Terry asked the navigator. A crew member dressed in a khaki flying suit and a yellow lifejacket stood on the other side of the cockpit peering through a side window. He held a squat pistol in his hand.

'Missiles,' the navigator shouted over the engine din. The navigator had a huge handlebar moustache, bulging eyes and very red cheeks. He looked like an affable drunk in a state of permanent surprise.

'If we are targeted, he'll fire a flare. Then we get the hell out. The missile follows the flare.' He grinned a round beefy grin. 'At least, that's the theory!'

Firing flares to bamboozle missiles didn't strike Terry as reassuringly high-tech.

There was a burst of turbulence. Terry reached out instinctively and clung to the webbing. After several seconds she felt a crewman take her arm and she allowed him to steer her back into the heaving interior where she was strapped into her seat facing a row of crates covered in heavy tarpaulin.

The other two passengers were UN logistics personnel, a man and a woman. The man, about the same age as Terry, early thirties, had introduced himself as they waited to board the plane. It had been early and cold, and his voice was rather sharp.

'You're a reporter?' he asked.

'A doctor.'

'With which agency?'

'The Medical Action Group, in London.'

'I don't know it,' he said, in a dismissive tone of voice.

Terry would have been reassured if the man had heard of the Medical Action Group. Her own connection with the organisation was tenuous, through a friend of a friend. Yet she had agreed to take on a challenging mission on their behalf. It was a mission for which she knew she was not well prepared. The very fact that the Medical Action Group were willing to send her seemed to Terry now to count against them. Their long-standing associate, a cardiologist with extensive experience of combat medicine, had had to drop out, and they had needed a last-minute replacement. With no conflict training and no military experience, Terry was becoming increasingly conscious of being out of her depth. The bungled exchange with the UN logistics man bothered her unduly.

The man's colleague arrived at the rendezvous breathless. She smiled a short, friendly smile and waited to be introduced to Terry, but no introductions were made. Soon after that it was time to board.

The plane flew in a giant arc, out to the coast and then south for a hundred miles before turning inward and overland again, cruising at 19,000 feet, beyond the range of anti-aircraft fire.

The noise of the engine discouraged conversation. Terry and her travelling companions sat amid the racket like bits of cargo.

When the Transall suddenly banked, the four cockpit crew leaned forward and gesticulated tentatively through the narrow windows as though they were trying to find a parking spot. The navigator pointed to the left and the others nodded vigorously. The plane began to dive.

The passengers sat in their flak jackets and stared at the boxes in front of them. Terry thought about trying to make amends for the abortive conversation with which they had begun the day. She considered a remark about the precipitate descent and the possibility of anti-aircraft fire. But, amid the scream of the plane's fall to earth, she decided to remain silent.

* * *

'Follow me,' the Luftwaffe escort shouted, as the aircraft pulled up on the runway. The rear door opened and Terry saw a snaking line of white forklifts race across the tarmac towards them.

'Let's go!' the escort barked. The passengers filed out obediently behind him.

The terminal was surrounded by armoured personnel carriers, forklifts and jeeps, all painted white with blue UN markings on the side. Blue-helmeted soldiers scurried in front of the long, low building. The terminal had been shelled and burned and was encased in sandbags.

Before they reached the main building the two logistics people nodded perfunctorily to Terry and the Luftwaffe officer and walked away from them towards a sandbagged hangar where the cargo from the Transall was being ferried.

'Someone meeting you?' the escort asked.

'I think so.'

She wondered for the hundredth time if the absence of organisation was normal for the Medical Action Group, or if it was a reflection of the disorder in her own life. The first choice for the mission, someone who had made a name for himself when he rescued members of a vulnerable ethnic group from a hospital in Nouakchott at the height of the Senegal-Mauritania conflict, had withdrawn because of a debilitating toothache. He'd kept quiet about the problem as he was determined to come, but two days before the flight he'd acknowledged that he wasn't fit to travel. When the Medical Action Group put out a last-minute call for a volunteer Terry had agreed to come. Her lack of preparation preoccupied her now. She had no idea where her lift was coming from.

'Go to Movement Control.' The escort pointed to a door behind a long line of sandbags. Then he saluted and began walking back to the Transall. The plane would unload and turn around inside fifteen minutes.

Terry had imagined the bond of flying through dangerous skies might endure beyond the short walk to the terminal, but found herself alone.

'What do you want?' a blue-helmeted soldier asked when she entered the Movement Control Office. The man stood behind a low table looking through a sheaf of photocopied forms.

'I'm going into the city.'

'Yes?'

'Someone is to meet me here.'

He looked up slowly, his expression unfriendly. She saw from his epaulettes that he was from Argentina.

'You can wait half an hour. If no one comes to collect you we'll ship you back. Wait outside please. This office is for UN personnel.'

Terry experienced a moment of panic. She had anticipated difficulty and danger, but not the possibility of being thrown out of the country before she'd even made it into the city.

He looked at his notes again. 'Is there a telephone I can use?' she asked.

'The phones are down.' He concentrated on his forms.

'Your transport not here?' said a man standing nearby. He had an intelligent face and a crewcut that made him look like a soldier or a monk.

'I'm not sure. Where would they wait for me?'

'Here, I guess. You made arrangements?' His accent was American.

'Sort of.'

'We're going into town,' he said. 'If you want a ride, you can come with us. We're leaving now.'

Someone might be on their way to pick her up. What if they came and she'd already gone?

On the other hand she didn't want to be sent back on the next plane.

'Suit yourself,' the man said, and he began to move away.

'OK, I'll come.' She spoke to the back of his closely shaven head. He didn't look round as he walked out. Terry glanced at the Argentinian, but he was pretending she wasn't there.

Outside she hurried past the sandbags.

'The truck's round here,' he said, taking a sharp right when they left the Movement Control Office. 'You got any luggage?'

She showed him her holdall.

'Good,' he said. 'We have to run.'

As they left the shelter of the terminal he began to sprint across a muddy piece of ground towards a sandbagged position fifty yards away. He didn't stop running until he'd reached the emplacement. Terry kept as close behind him as she could. In the distance she heard the sound of machinery. She didn't know which direction she should expect bullets to come from. Her chest tightened – from the exertion of running or from a sudden overwhelming adrenalin spike she couldn't tell. Her holdall swung clumsily in the cold air.

They passed the sandbags, built into a small hut with blue-helmeted soldiers peering at them from inside through slits that served as windows. Then Terry's companion began to run again. She could see a blue Land Rover twenty yards away. It stood by itself behind a long, low warehouse.

'This is it,' he said affably when they reached the van.

The door opened from the inside.

A girl looked down at Terry. 'Jump in,' she said.

Terry squeezed onto the edge of the high seat, swung the heavy door closed and introduced herself.

'I'm Anna,' the girl said. Her face, framed by an effusion of black ringlets, was preoccupied.

Three people were crushed into a driving cabin designed for two. Terry clutched her holdall in front of her against the dashboard as Anna wriggled beside her to find a more comfortable position.

'I'm Brad,' the driver added absently. He switched the key in the ignition.

'Have you got your card?' Brad asked Terry.

'My card?'

'Your press accreditation.'

'I'm not a reporter. I'm a doctor.'

'Shit,' he said. He switched off the engine. 'Do you have a UN card?'

With difficulty she fished her wallet out from the holdall. Inside was a collection of identity cards. She took out the one from the Medical Action Group, with her smiling photo emblazoned across the laminated top.

'How did you get on a plane?' Anna asked.

'I had this.' Terry showed them a letter from the Office of the UN High Commissioner for Refugees in Geneva authorising her to take a UN flight.

Brad started the engine again. 'Let's hope they're not being thorough this morning,' he muttered.

The Land Rover moved onto a track leading to a tarmac road. A white armoured personnel carrier blocked the entrance to the road.

'Hold it up,' Brad told Terry, nodding towards her card. 'They might not notice that it isn't from the UN.' She followed their example and raised her card in front of the windscreen. She could make out the head and shoulders of a soldier inside the APC leaning forward to see them better.

'If he comes out, I hope you can speak French,' Brad told Terry.

'He won't come out,' Anna said. 'There's been shooting today. They never come out when there's been shooting.'

She was right. No one emerged to inspect their credentials. The APC slid back and let them pass.

The Land Rover climbed onto the road, Brad crouching over the wheel.

'When we reach the bridge we enter government territory,' Anna said. 'There won't be any shooting till the second checkpoint.' She glanced at Terry.

Ahead, Terry saw another white APC across the road. 'French,' Anna explained nodding towards the APC. 'Foreign Legion.'

Terry started getting to grips with her fear, and her thoughts, careering wildly, reverted to her boorish behaviour with the logistics officers.

'Is it far to the centre of town?' she asked, trying to keep her voice steady.

'If we get to Sniper Alley with no problems it's fifteen minutes to the Holiday Inn,' Brad said. He glanced at Terry. 'That's our base. It's in the middle of town.'

'Why are you here?' Anna asked.

'I've come to evacuate a little boy. He needs urgent treatment in London.'

The Land Rover stopped in front of the French APC and they waved their cards at the window again. The APC reversed, leaving just enough room for them to pass.

A kingdom of laminated cards.

'This is the scary bit,' Anna said. 'There may be small-arms fire from the other side of the airstrip.'

Terry kept her eyes fixed forward. Ahead there was a fork in the road. Brad drove the Land Rover round a flimsy plywood barricade and onto the left fork. They moved out of the cover of some trees past a disabled tank stuck in a ditch, its cannon pointing towards the sky, and began to move between burned, roofless buildings. There was a small cemetery on one side, gravestones higgledy-piggledy. As they passed the cemetery, approaching a flyover, two bullets hit the side of the Land Rover. A pair of loud cracks.

Anna grabbed a helmet from the floor and put it on top of her ringlets. Brad accelerated. Anna bent down again and produced two more helmets. She thrust one at Terry and placed the other on Brad's head. The Land Rover raced onto the flyover.

Terry began to shake. She was embarrassed by this. She didn't normally respond to pressure in this way. She was normally calm. But everything that was happening to her now was new and strange. She could not know how she would react. All she could process in her untidy thoughts was that she was frightened and she was ashamed because of that.

Once on the flyover they were exposed. She looked ahead. The road led into a depressingly similar district: burned, roofless buildings.

Brad slowed the Land Rover at the bottom of the bridge and turned around sharply, doubling back the way they had come and moving onto the main road.

'Keep your head down,' Anna said gently, fear inducing a sort of intimacy. 'Now we have snipers on both sides.'

'Remind me –' Terry could hear embarrassment in Brad's voice, as though he had forgotten someone's name at a dinner party. 'Which side? Left or right?'

'On the left as far as the barricade and then onto the right! Go fast here!' Anna's voice was hard-edged again.

Brad accelerated. Terry felt the forward momentum. She ventured a sideways glance. On her right was the skeleton of what had once been an office block. It was partially entombed in a vast mountain of shattered concrete, with strips of steel, like congealing spaghetti, hanging from the edges.

'That's the newspaper building,' Brad said, as if pointing out a popular landmark on the road to a resort hotel. 'They're still working in the basement.'

Terry looked at the building again. Then she looked ahead. Two buses were parked across the main road, blocking their path.

'Do I go right here?' Brad asked.

'Right!'

'Just kidding!' Brad said, but Anna didn't laugh.

He swung the Land Rover off the road and onto a cobbled tramway that ran down the centre of the avenue. Then he turned left again, round the barricade. Ahead was a vast white thoroughfare – frozen and completely empty.

2

Milena watched from the bar as the two men who had been arguing suddenly got to their feet. A chair fell over, but it wasn't the clatter that drew the room's attention, it was the sound of safety catches being released. The men stood face to face, lifting their weapons. Milena watched along with the others, transfixed by a scene that unfolded as though in slow motion.

Jusuf stood up and walked almost casually towards the altercation. The slow motion movement of weapons halted. People in the packed room made way for him. When he reached the confrontation he stood, very close and calm, between the two men. He could have reached out and stopped the upward arc of the weapons. Perhaps the fact that he *could* have done this made the action itself unnecessary. Jusuf said nothing, but simply placed himself between the two drunk men. They lowered their weapons. Friends stepped forward, gingerly at first and then with decision, and the weapons were taken away. There was a murmur of conciliation. The standoff ended and the anger seemed to vanish.

When the room had returned to normal, Jusuf came over to the bar and threw a packet of Marlboro on the counter. He put a cigarette in his mouth and Milena held up a match.

They left soon afterwards and began to trudge through the freezing air and the newly fallen snow. It was so cold. Milena wore five layers of clothing. Her best winter clothes she'd left behind in Foča.

She held onto Jusuf's arm tightly. Every step they took was another step from Milena's town. He made her feel the memory of warmth in the deep dark.

'That was crazy … to get in the middle like that,' she said, an oddly gentle indignation in her voice.

They skirted a shell hole, filled with black water and ice.

Two blocks from the presidency they climbed through an ancient stairway, black as pitch. Jusuf struck a match. He led and Milena followed, holding onto his coat. On the first floor he turned the key of a heavy door that opened easily on well-oiled hinges. They stepped inside and Jusuf lit a candle.

This was not Milena's home. The flat where she lived in Alipašino Polje was not her home either. Milena came from a town far away in the east. She would never go back there.

'The guy with the pistol, the one with the glasses, he's caused trouble before,' she said. 'Haris or Hamza, something like that. He started a fight last week, nearly ended the same way.'

'He was a schoolteacher before the war,' Jusuf said, puzzled.

They took off their shoes, fumbling in the candlelight. There were two pairs of leather slippers beside the door. Jusuf lit another candle and set it on a low wooden table between two armchairs in the sitting room. A long sofa filled the end of the room, next to a grand piano.

The owner of the apartment was a colonel who had joined the Rebels at the start of the conflict and decamped to the other side with his family just a few days before the fighting began. Jusuf moved in when the place was commandeered for military accommodation. Milena stayed sometimes.

Jusuf lit an oil lamp and placed it near the door to the kitchen.

The room was filled with an eerie light, the straight lines of heavy dark furniture made soft by shadows and flame.

In the kitchen he began making coffee while Milena opened the piano.

She loved this instrument. On such a cold night every note was clear as crystal, and it was as if the snow and the darkness outside pressed against the walls and sealed the room so that nothing but music could be heard. This piano sounded to her more beautiful than any she had ever played.

She struck one high note and then another, with a soft sure touch.

Jusuf watched. She sat with her back very straight, looking across the room at the dull light from the kitchen where Jusuf, grinding coffee, cast a shadow. The music cut grooves of sound in the snow-cased silence of the big shadowy apartment.

It was necessary to hold the bottom cylinder very firmly where the ground coffee collected and the top cylinder where the beans were crushed. Jusuf's hand hurt. The metal became hot with the friction of the grinder. He watched Milena and listened to the melody she played.

The apartment was filled with paintings. Once, Jusuf would have retreated from the expensive art on the walls, conscious that he lacked the education to admire another man's paintings. But now he lived in the other man's home. His woman played the other man's piano. He found himself assessing the other man's art. Among the figurative scenes was a picture of the city market eighty years before, the men in puttees and red fezzes, the women in shawls and veils. Jusuf liked this picture. It hung between the two large windows overlooking the street. Now it framed Milena's head as she played.

He listened to her play and watched as she bent forward, concentrating on the keys. If he'd spoken she would have looked up and listened. She didn't become so absorbed in the music that she was lost to her surroundings. She was like that in everything. She never seemed to go below the surface. Jusuf had never tried to go further. He didn't know about her past. He never asked her about her family. He only knew *now*. And now Milena was in his sitting room playing music that was beautiful. Perhaps she was a dream. He was aroused by her beauty and by the fact that this beauty was close enough to touch. Yet he did not believe that her soul could ever be possessed.

By the tall windows there were hundreds of books, a handful picked out on the thick shelves by the flame of the lamp and candles.

He had placed two pieces of wood in a small stove and lit a fire with shards of cardboard. When the water on top of the stove began to boil he sprinkled it with ground coffee and stirred it gently. Then he took the coffee into the room and placed one cup on top of the piano in front of Milena. She gave a little nod of thanks and he reciprocated. He liked waiting on her.

He took his own cup to the low table by the sofa and sat down.

She watched, wondering if he wanted her to continue. But who wouldn't want to hear this piano played?

Usually she liked Jusuf's reticence. At the bar, words were even more pervasive than alcohol, a babble lurching between aggression and maudlin good humour.

She wouldn't have chosen to work in a place like that. It was dirty and dishonest and there were killers among the men who came to drink there. Not soldiers doing their duty, but men who liked killing.

She made herself play more slowly, more gently. She listened to the clusters of chords, and then started a different melody, one that reminded her of summer days.

Milena had found a job in a bar because she knew that kind of work. She could maintain a conversation at any level, and she could juggle marks and dollars and dinars, calculating bills for half a dozen tables.

Jusuf wished she would play a particular song, but he couldn't remember the name. She had played it before. It might have been from Eurovision. He could remember the tune, but not the name.

The melody she played now was wistful. Jusuf began to follow the long, lyrical phrases. He knew that in Milena's hands this music would move at its own pace, at the *right* pace. It would set itself down in the candlelight as though it were the sound created at the very beginning of time to accompany their thoughts and feelings in this particular moment. And because she played this assured and beautiful music his thoughts began to rearrange themselves and he considered people and places and faces that had until then been kept from the forefront of his consciousness.

As he listened to Milena play, Jusuf thought about Bakır Mehmedbasić. In peacetime Mehmedbasić would have spent his army days in detention: he was not bright but he was very aggressive – a common combination. At the beginning of the war, he had enlisted with a government militia group put together by a gangster. It was ill-equipped and ill-disciplined, but the boys in Mehmedbasić's outfit were keen to fight. Jusuf had been a major in the pre-war army. Within weeks of the start of the conflict he was promoted to colonel. The designation didn't mean much. There were colonels with next to no experience whose claim to rank was based entirely on having friends in the right political circles. Jusuf's authority stemmed from competence and a natural ability to command – but even he was confounded by the ramshackle chaos of units like the one that had signed up Mehmedbasić. There was no shortage of aggression, no shortage of courage, but a dearth of judgment and an absolute absence of training.

Mehmedbasić was just twenty years old and he already had a criminal record when the war began. In the beginning, he wasn't allowed a gun, since he couldn't be trusted to fire it in the right direction. In wartime, some men discover they are cowards;

others discover they are not. Mehmedbasić discovered that he was *ethical*. The idea of what they were fighting for crystallised in his head and for the first time in his life he gave credence to the notion of right and wrong. He wanted to fight because he believed the cause was *just*.

He was given a job running messages between the lines. The lines stretched through apartment blocks and moved nightly. The fighting was bitter and bloody, street by familiar street.

The day Bakir Mehmedbasić was allowed to join the ranks as a fully-fledged, gun-toting militiaman he was shot dead. He went down to Vrbanja Bridge and stood with his rifle over his shoulder, arms spread wide, and shouted at someone he knew on the Rebel line across the river. Perhaps he was drunk.

'Come and join us over here!'

This wasn't a competition among fans at a football match. It wasn't a day out where you recognised an acquaintance from school and started to trade jokes and insults. Perhaps Mehmedbasić had been seized by the absurdity of their predicament – because they *did* know people on the other side, and they *had* been friends, and they spoke the same language and knew the same streets and bars and rock groups and football teams. It was a family sort of war. There had been a time when being from a different community didn't mean much, when friends were friends regardless. Mehmedbasić grasped that this had changed. Perhaps he simply couldn't accept it.

So he stepped out into the open and like a madman he yelled.

And then he was shot.

Jusuf didn't know why he thought about that boy now.

Yet it was a brave thing Bakir Mehmedbasić did that day. He shouted with indignation, with *righteousness*.

Jusuf looked ahead through the spiralling cigarette smoke and listened to Milena play. He watched her expression, as if she were giving a public recital. He loved the way she pursed her lips in concentration. He wished he could remember the name of the song he wanted her to play.

The coffee had a bitter taste. He stood up, still thinking of Bakir Mehmedbasić's odd and pointless gesture.

When Jusuf had first met Milena in the bar she wore a dark woollen dress with buttons all the way up the front. She was prim and attractive at the same time. That's how he thought of it then. She behaved as if they were being introduced at the house of a mutual friend, and not in a black-market bar. She seemed somehow separate from her surroundings.

Outside now, it was unusually silent, not even the sound of tracer fire.

In the bedroom they undressed. Milena could see his breath in the freezing air. Little tails of cloud in the moonlight. The bed was icy.

Every kiss carried her another microscopic measurement of space from Foča, her town in the east, from the face there that she had loved, from the life there that she had abandoned.

Jusuf's honourable face, hands and body displaced that body, that voice, that look, that touch.

In the light of the guttering oil lamp, she stroked Jusuf's face, running her index finger over the contour of his lips.

Outside there was a detonation, near Gavrilo Princip Bridge.

They lay still. In the morning everything – the bed clothes, the curtains, the furniture, the ancient carpet – would be coated in a layer of grime from the oil lamp. Milena could already feel the residue of oil in her hair.

The banging at the door was more startling than the sound of the explosion. It was sharp and insistent.

Jusuf leapt from beneath the blankets, pulled on his trousers, slipped into his boots and donned his overcoat without shirt or jacket. He extracted his pistol from its holster, eased the safety catch back and walked out of the bedroom.

Milena got up, threw on clothes and followed him into the hall.

He stood away from the door, the pistol pointing to the floor, and signalled her to go back into the bedroom. But instead she stepped forward and stood beside him. He eased her gently against the wall, placing himself between her and the door.

'Who's there?'

'Alija.'

Jusuf relaxed and opened the door.

A dapper-looking man with a bearded, bespectacled face came into the lobby, bringing a blast of cold air with him. Perhaps Milena registered the change in temperature more acutely because Alija's arrival shattered the intimacy between her and Jusuf. When Alija looked at her he did nothing, she thought, to mask his suspicion. In the new scheme of things, her name counted against her. In Alija's eyes it was a Rebel name. And this woman with a Rebel name was the lover of a key government commander.

'You have to come back,' he told Jusuf.

'What's up?'

Alija glanced at Milena and waited.

'Go to the bedroom,' Jusuf said, barely looking at her.

She did as she was told.

'Otes,' Alija whispered when Milena had retreated, closing the door behind her.

Jusuf returned to the bedroom to put on his shirt and jacket. Milena followed him out when he was dressed.

'I'll see you at the bar,' he told her. 'Don't know when.' He went out to the stairway behind Alija.

Rumour had it that Otes might fall to the Rebels within days, leaving the city open to a ground attack from the west.

3

'Why not stay here?' Brad said.

They stood in the lobby of the Holiday Inn, tiles broken on the muddy concrete floor, gusts of wind playing on the cracked glass. Terry was relieved to be inside a building, even a building like this. It was like a giant refrigerator, a science-fiction set, with the inside walls made of dark, peeling plaster, and huge windows smashed and covered with tarpaulin. There was a reception desk, though, which appeared more or less normal and there were people standing around looking relaxed.

She had blown her arrival, but at least she was in the city centre. They hadn't sent her back on the next plane.

From the Land Rover she had peered through reinforced glass at wrecked buildings, some nearly buried in snow, black oblongs on the scarred facades where windows used to be; there were women and children in greatcoats and headscarves pulling water containers across ice on wooden sleds; there were sniper barricades at the road intersections, big steel containers; everywhere there was smashed glass and scorched concrete.

'The phones are down, so you won't be able to call your people,' Brad told her when they reached the reception desk.

She looked lost. 'You'll need time to get hold of them,' he added more gently.

'Check in for the night,' Anna said. 'Someone here might be able to help you find your group.'

Terry looked from one to the other. She was grateful and she wanted to tell them that, but she couldn't find the words. She was generally reticent; expressing feelings didn't come easily to her. There was an awkward silence.

Brad shrugged and said, 'I have to work.' He began to walk away.

'I'm going to have lunch in ten minutes,' Anna said. 'The restaurant's up there.' She pointed to a door near the first of the grid-like balconies rising through the bleak atrium. 'Come and join me.'

Terry watched Anna leave. She noted the black trainers and tight blue jeans. Anna had removed her down anorak to reveal a blue flak jacket.

'Can I have a room for the night?' she asked the middle-aged woman who stood behind the reception desk. The woman had been listening to their conversation. Terry had watched her out of the corner of her eye while she was talking to Brad and Anna.

The receptionist's eyes were magnified by thick reading glasses attached to a fine chain round her neck. 'What is the name of your organisation?' she asked in slightly accented English, well modulated, like a language teacher.

Her grey hair was tied back in a bun.

'I work for a London charity called the Medical Action Group.'

The woman gave Terry a small, unimpressed smile and asked, 'You will pay in cash?'

'How much is it?'

'Eighty-two dollars, full pension.'

She had expected to be speaking to another physician about a patient's condition. Arrangements were supposed to have been made. Now she was asking about room rates. This annoyed her.

She nodded and signed the form that the receptionist placed in front of her. The woman selected a key and handed it to Terry. Then she said, 'Passport please.'

Terry surrendered her passport.

'I will return it to you after lunch.' The woman smiled.

It was just twenty minutes since the Transall had plummeted through winter clouds and landed between armies. Nothing was going according to plan.

'You will have to take the stairs,' the woman said. 'There is no electricity. The lift is not working.'

She walked across the cavernous lobby, climbed the back stairs to the third floor and found her room.

The window had been broken. Shards of glass still clung to the steel frame. The opening was covered by thick plastic tarpaulin. Much of the wall behind the two beds had been peppered by what she took to be shrapnel; there were shallow, elongated gashes in the plaster. The painting above the dressing table facing one of the twin beds was hanging upside down.

Otherwise, nothing was amiss. The two single beds were neatly made. The furniture was standard business-hotel issue.

She went into the bathroom and turned on the shower, but no water came out of the nozzle. She tried the taps at the end of the bath: dry. Nor did water come from either of the taps above the wash basin.

She went back into the bedroom and sat on the bed.

The airport business weighed on her thoughts. Perhaps she'd been wrong to accept a lift. She should have waited. What if someone had made that journey, past those barricades, to fetch her? What if the person who had come to collect her had driven over a mine, or had been shot by a sniper? It would be her fault – because she hadn't waited. She hadn't been where she was supposed to be. She experienced a wave of hopelessness, a huge breaker that hammered the tottering framework of doubt and insecurity. Perhaps the Medical Action Group had been negligent in sending her here, but they were hardly to blame. She'd put up her hand and volunteered and she didn't know why, except for the fact that her life was so difficult, even something as uncertain as this had promised a way out. She was angry with herself because she knew very well that this mission must succeed. A life was at stake. The little boy she'd come to collect needed every ounce of Terry's professional expertise. Self-doubt, she thought, is a weakness that people in her business could not indulge.

Terry was good at her job; she was less good at the other things in her life, like getting on with colleagues, or bonding with strangers on a plane, or making relationships work. This last thought made her chest tighten. She felt the muscles contract more suddenly and more unpleasantly than when she'd made her unseemly dash from the Movement Control Office behind Brad. She was very afraid to dwell at any length on the failure of her marriage. The pain from that wound had not gone away.

She did something she hadn't done for years. She picked up a book of matches from an ashtray on the bedside table and opened it. About half of the paper stems had already been torn off. She'd been told to bring Marlboro, one or two cartons at least. Cigarettes were more valuable than cash here. She took one of the cartons from her holdall, tore it open, extracted a packet, unwrapped it and pulled out a cigarette.

She lit the cigarette and drew on it before she had time to change her mind. It made her feel dizzy and sick. She lay back on the pillows and puffed, gazing round the room, watching coils of thin smoke rise up to the beige ceiling.

The cigarette left an acrid taste in her mouth and she couldn't brush her teeth because there was no water. She put the packet in her trousers pocket along with the matches and went downstairs to the restaurant.

Terry walked past three long tables that stretched from one end of the restaurant to the other; there were several smaller tables in two corners. She felt self-conscious. There were forty or so people in the room, all dressed in a kind of uniform: army boots, jeans and warm sweaters, with arctic jackets over the backs of chairs. Terry noticed flak jackets leaning up against table legs. Her own outfit consisted of wool trousers, winter boots not designed to splash through mud, a sweater with a pattern on it and a silk scarf. She knew she didn't fit in.

The room reminded her of the refectory at her boarding school. She hadn't fitted in there either.

Anna stood up and smiled beneath her ringlets. 'Check in OK?' she asked. 'This is my colleague Sanela.' She raised a small hand and flicked it in the direction of a young woman sitting on the other side of the table.

Sanela gave Terry a weak smile, and then returned to her meal. 'And this is Michael Baring. Michael, this is Dr Barnes.'

Baring was in his fifties. He had a thick grey beard and a lined face. A smoker, Terry could see, or had been once. He was thin. Beneath his wool crewneck he wore a silk cravat.

Terry was generally shrewd. She could spot a phoney from a great distance; she was instantly on her guard with Baring.

'Why are you here, Dr Barnes?' he asked.

'I've come to evacuate a little boy. He will have emergency treatment in the UK.'

'Ah!' Baring chuckled. 'A mercy bid!'

'You're *that* doctor,' Sanela said, looking up from her plate, suddenly interested in the new arrival. Terry nodded. 'My friend was supposed to meet you, but it was impossible to reach the airport,' Sanela continued. 'How did you manage to get here?'

'We brought her,' Anna said.

Sanela looked at Anna and then at Terry.

'I can take you to the State Hospital after lunch if you like,' Sanela said. 'They were worried in case you had been sent back. They're anxious to meet you.'

Terry felt a moment of exquisite relief.

'Yes please!'

'What room?' the waiter asked Terry. He looked at her stony-faced, unblinking. She couldn't immediately remember her room number. He asked again, impatiently.

She found her key and read the number. 'Room 305.'

The waiter moved away without comment.

'You're next door to me!' Baring said. There was triumph in his voice, as though he'd secured an advantage over everyone else at the table.

4

Terry had smoked her second Marlboro. Lunch had ended and the restaurant was practically empty. She was impatient to get to the hospital and she wanted to get away from Michael Baring.

Baring's experience, of the city and of much else, was exhaustive. He enjoyed showing other people the many ways in which his own knowledge was superior to theirs. Terry was unfamiliar with her surroundings, and this seemed to please him. She made the mistake of admitting that her knowledge of the conflict wasn't deep. He wouldn't let this drop.

Anna had begun asking Terry about her mission to evacuate little Miro and his mother to London. However, in a subtly bullying way, Baring had taken over the interview, throwing Anna little bits of praise, which seemed to mollify her. 'Anna's been over to talk to the other side. She knows the score,' he said. 'Anna agrees with me on this. Anna was first with that story.'

'Where's Brad?' Baring asked.

Anna lit a cigarette and said, 'Who knows?'

'Aren't you supposed to be working together?'

She shrugged, but Baring continued snidely, 'I think perhaps Brad would be more comfortable with a less demanding story. Especially after what happened in his last posting.'

'What happened in his last posting?' Terry asked.

'Well, I'm not going to gossip,' Baring said primly. He had been gossiping since she sat down at the table.

'Actually,' Anna said, 'I've never heard the whole story. It was in Sri Lanka, right?'

'You *should* know, because – heaven forbid – you could find yourself in the same position!' He glanced around as though keen to maintain a certain discretion. 'Apparently Brad got a lot of his best stories in Colombo from a local reporter ... used to help Brad clinch exclusives and Brad got the credit. Then – this is what I heard – I don't know the ins and outs, so...' – he raised his hands to show that he was innocent of any slanderous intent – 'Brad's drinking was starting to raise concerns at the paper, and in order to shore up his position he prodded this chap into arranging an ill-advised interview with Prabhakaran –'

'The Tamil Tiger guy?' Anna said.

'That's the one. Hardly ever appears in public. They went up north and when they finally made it to the rendezvous everything unravelled. It turned out there was no interview. Then, when they came back into government territory they drove right into an ambush and the local guy was killed.'

'How did Brad get out?' Terry asked.

Baring shrugged. 'Various opinions. There was some sort of checkpoint and apparently Brad thought he could talk his way through. In the event, it was the Sri Lankan they killed. They left Brad sitting at the side of the road with a few bruises.'

While Baring was holding forth, Sanela continued to sit a little apart, reading her newspaper and smoking Camel cigarettes.

Two men strolled over and began talking to her. Both were in their thirties; one sported a thick flying jacket that made him look comically rotund, like the Michelin Man; he had wiry grey hair and a goatee and he spoke English. The other was more elegantly dressed – pressed jeans and a smart, wool-lined oilskin jerkin – and spoke to Sanela in her own language. He had a wry, almost professorial expression, peering over the top of his designer glasses. The man with the flying jacket began regaling Sanela with a story. Terry couldn't hear everything, just a word here and there in between fits of giggling. The second man took up the thread from time to time before the first brought the tale to a raucous conclusion.

When they reached the punchline there was an explosion of laughter.

Sanela's face was transformed.

She smiled and gesticulated in an animated, deprecating way. She looked young and pretty and her sudden cheerfulness was like oxygen in the room.

Then the two men moved to another table, and there was more laughter. Sanela decided lunch break was over. 'Shall we go now?' she asked Terry.

'Michael Baring is not admired,' Sanela remarked as they walked to the back door of the hotel. 'He understands little, and you must not be offended by him.'

Outside, she said, 'We must move quickly. This is a sniper area.'

They climbed broad steps from the hotel to the pavement and Sanela began to run across the snow.

For the second time since her arrival in the city Terry found herself racing behind a relative stranger across a piece of open ground. Sanela ran faster than Brad had done and the distance they had to cover now was much greater than at the airport. Sanela darted ahead and Terry felt as though she'd been abandoned. As before, she didn't know where the danger lay, the direction the bullets might come from. She became aware of a smell, a kind of rottenness, floating over the whiteness of the snow. To her right she saw a pile of rubbish. She heard the sound her boots made. It seemed to be magnified by the surrounding silence. She counted her steps. She gasped for air as she laboured over the uneven surface. Again the terrible tightening in her chest.

Even if she'd been properly prepared, if she'd undergone some sort of conflict training, she would still have been scared. To be afraid was to respond rationally to danger. She considered this and the thought gave her comfort. Her brain was reasserting itself over animal instinct.

Sanela gained the cover of a building fifty yards from the hotel and waited for Terry. When she caught up, Terry was breathless.

'It is still exposed here, but safer,' Sanela said. 'Come,' she added in a firm, neutral tone. She led the way up a steep hill towards another road.

They walked haphazardly, following a barely delineated path in the snow.

At the road they turned to the right.

'That's the hospital,' Sanela said.

The hospital's facade was wrecked by shell holes. Scars were cut into the concrete; windows hung open; the walls on the top floors had been blasted away.

'We are safe now,' Sanela said. She examined Terry's face for more signs of fear. Then she pronounced, 'You will be fine, I think. You are not uncomposed.'

Terry felt oddly pleased, as though Sanela had given her the one compliment she wished for more than any other.

At the entrance to the hospital, Sanela hurried again. 'This too is a sniper area,' she said and raced towards the main gate. Terry ran after her.

Inside the small compound at the front of the hospital two cars had drawn up and two women were helping an elderly man out of one car. Blood ran from a gash in his head, across his face and onto the dirty white coat he wore over black trousers.

They walked past the injured man into the building. Two men cradling machine guns sat by a small table in the dimly lit lobby. Sanela addressed one of them. Terry wasn't able to decipher even a word of the exchange that followed.

'Dr Jurić is in Casualty,' Sanela translated. 'We may have to wait.' She spoke to the guard again and he replied. Sanela nodded. 'We can enter.'

They walked along a corridor where a dozen people sat on a long bench. Some were bleeding. Terry glanced through an open door and saw the naked body of a middle-aged man stretched out on a trolley. Two orderlies were preparing instruments for surgery. There was mud on the floor.

Sanela quickened her pace at the end of the corridor and called to a man ahead of them about to walk through a set of heavy swing doors.

He turned. Terry assimilated the scene in the operating room they had just passed: the orderlies, the instruments, the mud. It was as if familiar images had been placed together in a weird and very ugly collage. The temperature in the corridor was near freezing.

The doctor that Sanela was speaking to had a capable but weary manner. He replied brusquely and then he looked at Terry and smiled an unexpectedly cheerful smile. He extended his hand and said in English, 'I am Dario Jurić. I was to meet you at the airport, but it was not possible. I am very pleased to meet you now.'

'How do you do,' Terry said. Her voice sounded small. This was not the impression she wanted to make. 'Can we talk?' she added more firmly.

'Yes, of course, but I have surgery all day. We can meet this evening. Where are you staying?'

'At the Holiday Inn.'

He seemed to consider this and then he said, 'It's better. We had thought to put you up with one of our staff but her building was damaged last night. I'll come to the hotel at seven.'

An agitated voice from the other side of the doors called out. The doors swung open and a small, fat man smoking a cigarette looked up at Jurić and berated him.

After several noisy seconds the small man stormed off. 'Our director,' Jurić explained. 'I must leave you now. We have a child – an amputation.'

He walked away. 'See you this evening,' he shouted over his shoulder.

Back in the lobby as a stretcher case was being brought in amid shouts and gesticulations, Sanela turned to Terry and said, 'I have to go to the presidency. Can you find your own way back?'

'Of course,' Terry said, feeling uneasy.

Sanela walked with her as far as the road. 'Don't slow down,' she said. 'Go the same way we came.' She examined Terry's face again and then said, with an impatience that surprised and annoyed Terry, 'Straight to the second road on your left. Turn there and you see the hotel ahead of you.'

Terry said, 'I'll be fine. Don't worry.'

Sanela had already begun walking in the opposite direction.

Terry was adrift, without her routine, without the structure of her hospital at home with its rules and hierarchy. But even there on home ground she realised she was often adrift. Now, she felt as though she had brought her insecurities along with her. Again, hopelessness.

She looked ahead. There were few people on the road. They scurried over the ice. The sky was heavy and she felt chilled. At the first turn-off she saw a man run across the road. She did the same. She moved quickly but found that running made her feel more afraid. At the next corner she experienced a new wave of anxiety. She could see the hotel ahead, but no one was walking on the road that led to it. She began moving down the hill.

She didn't want to die in this frozen waste.

At the end of the road she plunged forward.

'Shit,' she muttered when she realised she was running over fresh snow. Sanela had taken her by a path already beaten into the snow. She spotted the path and made towards it. Cold slivers of ice spilled over the tops of her boots.

And then she heard a sound that was both familiar and alien. It was like the sound of a thick elastic band used as a catapult, a thrumming and humming through the frozen air. Terry had heard the two bullets hitting the reinforced glass of the Land Rover after they left the airport; they made a sharp clatter. This sound was more immediate and more powerful. It was deadly. She understood this in the millisecond it took to hear the thick elastic band scraping and stretching the air around her. She uttered some sort of primordial exclamation as she bowed down and pressed forward. She wanted to vomit. In the corner of her eye she saw a puff of powder snow thrown up by the bullet's impact. She heard a voice. She was no longer seeking the path, but simply floundering across deep snow. She saw the yellow facade of the hotel. She understood space and direction and sound and sight, but only as disconnected elements of terror. The man who was shouting was twenty yards away. He was signalling that she should run faster. Just before reaching him, Terry lost her balance and fell. She hit the concrete beneath the snow hard enough to break bones. She lay for several seconds. From ground level she looked towards the entrance of the hotel and saw a cockroach scuttling away from her.

The man who had shouted pulled her to her feet. He said something Terry didn't understand and then, in English, 'The *other* side! You must use only the other side! Don't you know this is a sniper area!'

5

Sanela's boyfriend, Zlatko, wore a heavy black coat and an enormous red scarf around him, one end thrown over his shoulder. Zlatko believed this made him look like Lord Byron. It did convey a certain elegance.

Sanela, Zlatko and Brad entered the bar – one of the last still operating – on the ground floor of an old Habsburg courtyard. They found a seat near the window, vacant because, despite the sandbags, it offered the least protection should a shell explode in the courtyard.

Sanela and Zlatko had the easy confidence that young people have when things in their world are as they expect them to be. The city was shot to pieces but they weren't. They both spoke good English. They were in demand as interpreters and fixers.

'You are a foreigner, Brad,' Sanela told him with mock seriousness. 'You must learn about us, learn our ways!' She turned to Zlatko and said, 'He's one of *them*, not one of *us*.'

Zlatko put his arm around her. She leaned into him and took hold of his hand for a second. Her fingers were warm. Then she let go again.

'She believes you are a secret agent, Brad!' Zlatko said. 'What can we do to persuade her that you are on the right side?'

'You could pay for the drinks,' she suggested.

'I always do!'

'And that's as it should be!'

They carried on in this vein, and as they joked and drank, Brad tried to match their mood. He had an hour to kill before the evening briefing at the residence of the UN commander.

'It's a waste of time to go there,' Sanela said. 'They know even less than we do, and what they know they won't tell.'

'They have coffee,' Brad said. Sanela pretended to be astonished. Coffee was difficult to come by. 'And central heating,' he added. Her eyes opened wider. Central heating had vanished long ago. People heated their apartments with wood-burning stoves. Except that wood was hard to come by too.

Outside, there were flashes as howitzers in the surrounding hills registered positions further to the north, and then they began to hear the rat-tat-tat of small-arms fire near the river.

'Perhaps we should go with him to see the General,' Zlatko said. 'Perhaps he finds things out and he doesn't share these things with us.' He sipped his beer and screwed up his fine face. 'Weaker and weaker! Soon we'll be drinking lemonade.'

Opposite sat three soldiers, the one in the centre overweight and scowling. The women sitting with the soldiers wore a kind of uniform: leather trousers, tight sweaters, heavy make-up. The men lounged with their rifles piled behind the long, plastic-covered bench. The three couples watched the rest of the clientele insolently, as though the others in the bar were a kind of casual cabaret.

'I despair when I see them,' Zlatko said.

Sanela whispered, 'You should not presume that people do not speak English.'

'They know as much English as Brad knows of our language,' Zlatko said.

Brad asked, 'Who are they?'

'The one in the middle is a deputy to the Special Forces commander. Before the war he ran a nightclub. I don't know about the others.'

Brad glanced at the soldiers. The scowling one stared back.

'How will we win when the high command spend their time here?' Zlatko said. He became suddenly angry. He was struck by the way they lolled there, filled with the smugness of stupidity and power. They were the kind of people, Zlatko thought, for whom the chaos of conflict is congenial, for whom the collapse of order represents a release from irksome obligation. Zlatko didn't like this. That was why he'd used his family connections to avoid being drafted. He didn't object to being exposed to danger. He objected to being exposed to danger by the kind of men who were now sitting on the other side of the bar.

'I think we're attracting attention,' Brad said under his breath. 'Better to change the subject.'

Zlatko was irritated by Brad's timidity. He looked at the soldiers again. They stared back at him.

Sanela now affected unconcern. 'We are a civil society. They can hear if they like,' she said.

She finished her cigarette and stubbed it out. She wished she could brush her teeth. She wished she could bathe. She hated the dirt more than anything. She hated the smell. 'We shouldn't have come,' she added. 'It makes me despondent.'

Brad raised his arm and caught the barmaid's attention.

Milena came over to where they sat. Brad thought she looked somehow older than when they had met earlier in the week. She certainly looked more self-assured. She had come to the Chamber Theatre, to the room at the top of the building where Sanela and Zlatko had lived since the start of the siege. Sanela had arranged the meeting; she said Milena could tell Brad what it was like in Foča at the start of the war. 'She saw everything,' Sanela said. 'You can do an eyewitness story.' Foča had split down the middle; neighbours turned on neighbours; well-armed paramilitaries arrived from outside and for several days in the early summer there was an orgy of arson and murder.

But the interview didn't go the way Sanela had hoped. Milena kept coming back to what life was like *before* things fell apart. She was vague about the mayhem ('There were terrible scenes!' 'Such crimes were committed!' 'Men behaved with wickedness!'). She shook her head and looked into the middle distance with an expression of infinite sadness, but when Brad asked for details, she stuck doggedly to generalities, and then she returned to how nice things were in Foča before the war, and when she spoke about that she smiled and it was as if her entire personality was transformed by the memory.

Brad would have pressed Milena more, but his interest in the events of the summer was not as great as Sanela had assumed. He was happy to write a feature story based on the account of a refugee, but he was more interested in what he hoped Milena could tell him about *current* events in Sarajevo. He'd learned that she was the girlfriend of one of the top commanders and that was the real reason he wanted to meet her. He was looking for inside information.

The interview at the theatre was the closest Sanela and Brad had come to having a quarrel. When he tried to ask Milena about Jusuf, Sanela stopped translating. 'We're not here for that!' she said in a low angry voice. 'I fixed this so you could ask her about Foča! She won't tell you anything about what's going on in the city. She doesn't *know* anything!'

It was a wasted hour. Milena wouldn't talk about the horror she had witnessed, just about what a wonderful place Foča was before the paramilitaries came, and Sanela wouldn't translate questions about whether the government troops were getting the weapons and provisions they required. But at least there was a stove in Sanela's room, and Milena had brought coffee which she produced from the corner of a paper bag. They sat in the warmth and drank coffee and smoked Brad's cigarettes.

Now, as Milena walked through the crowd, she responded to the shouted drinks orders; she soothed away impatience and complaints, firm and familiar. She laughed a lot; she looked as though she was having the time of her life.

'*Bred!*' she said when she reached their table. His name sounded better, he thought, the way she pronounced it. '*How are you?*'

She laughed and then looked at him expectantly. Brad said he was well, and Sanela translated for him.

It occurred to Brad that the two things he could usefully have got from this woman, an eyewitness refugee story and some inside information on the thoughts of a government commander, she had declined to provide. Yet he wanted to know more about her. The violence around them didn't just wreak havoc and destruction on physical things; it imposed itself on the stories of people's lives. Brad wanted to know about Milena's life beyond the war.

Sanela said something and Milena nodded happily and looked at Brad.

'I told her you haven't written your piece about Foča yet but you will,' Sanela said.

'Tell her the interview was very useful,' Brad lied.

Sanela translated.

Milena seemed pleased. Then, with a seamless transition to business that was part of her trade, she asked them what they would like to drink.

In their language, Brad ordered three more beers. Sanela and Zlatko gave ironic cheers. Milena grinned, and spoke very fast in reply. It was part of the joke. She knew that he wouldn't understand the words but he would understand the meaning. She was accepting his order. He nodded and grinned.

'So!' Zlatko said, slapping Brad's knee. 'What news?' He laughed. When he was with Sanela he had the habit of laughing after even the simplest statements. She made him feel euphoric.

Milena returned with drinks on a tray.

A popular rock song had just begun, drenching the packed room with a succession of chords and connecting arpeggios.

The effect, Brad thought, was to slow time down. When he gave Milena a note for twenty German marks, it was as though they occupied a space in the crowd where there were just two people.

She smiled and said, '*Thank you!*'

'Sanela,' Brad said, looking at Milena, 'tell her the interview was really useful but I think I was asking the wrong questions. Perhaps she would talk to me one day about Foča before the war. Perhaps I could write a story about what it was like when there was peace.'

Sanela gave him a surprised look, and translated.

'Maybe we could meet tomorrow?' Brad added.

Milena smiled and spoke rapidly to Sanela.

'She says she's taking a little girl to the children's song festival tomorrow, but she will talk to you again the day after tomorrow. She'll come to the theatre in the morning.'

* * *

'We go this way,' Zlatko said when they emerged into the court-yard. He and Sanela were tipsy.

Sanela kissed Brad. 'Be careful among those foreigners,' she said, and then she and Zlatko disappeared into the darkness.

Brad pulled on his gloves and extracted a torch from the pocket of his coat. Cold air settled on his neck. He drew his scarf more tightly against his skin and buttoned the top of his coat. Then he began walking.

Stars glittered brightly, making dull silhouettes of the tenements near the presidency. He had to switch on the torch to identify shell craters and debris. He kept it lit for only seconds at a time so as to avoid being seen. The corner of Tito Street and Đure Đakovića Avenue, leading to the General's residence at the Delegates' Club, was exposed to sniper fire. The day before, a woman had been shot there.

Brad was afraid a car would race along Tito Street and he'd be caught in the headlights just at the point when he moved out into the open. But no car came. He crossed the street and began walking up the avenue. The road had been lined with trees when he arrived two months before, but now many of them had been cut for firewood. The prospect was bleak, but further to the east was a tall terrace of art deco tenements, a delicate elegant facade where oil lamps flickered.

He thought of oil lamps in Sri Lanka: the faint light after sunset in villages that had not been hustled into the modern world with electricity. This sudden recollection shocked him. He felt an almost unbearable melancholy.

He walked faster across the ice, the last few steps to the gate of the General's residence.

'What's your name?' one of the Egyptian guards asked. They asked this every night, the same words, the same gruff expression and guttural intonation. The routine never changed, not once in the two months Brad had been coming here for the evening press briefing.

One of the soldiers retired to a wind-up field telephone and barked into it. Brad's name was mangled in translation. The soldier stared at him, his face a mask.

After several minutes Brad was allowed in. He walked up the path towards the main house, a soldier beside him.

'*Shukran*,' he said to the soldier as they reached the front porch.

'*Maʾaf*.'

His escort went back to the sentry post by the gate and Brad let himself into the building. As he passed through the front door he was met by an enveloping, infinitely comforting blast of warm air. He unfastened his coat and loosened his scarf before entering a long foyer at one end of which was a staircase.

He took off his coat and the flak jacket he wore beneath it and removed his notebook and pen from one jacket pocket and cigarettes and lighter from the other. He lit a cigarette and sat down by one of two coffee tables to wait.

6

Jim Danby, the UN spokesman, had a rolling gait, as though he had just dismounted from a horse. His pale freckled face was naturally jovial, the mouth turned up as though designed to smile. When frowning, Danby looked thoughtful rather than sullen. He liked *fixing* things, smoothing ruffled feathers, solving problems. He knew how to listen.

Danby also knew how to make optimal use of his Irishness. Small countries have a niche in international relations – they do not represent a threat. Since almost the beginning of his military career, Danby's knack for diplomacy had kept him ahead.

However, as he emerged from the situation room on the first floor of the Delegates' Club he was momentarily overcome by an uncharacteristic feeling of hopelessness. Conditions in the city were deteriorating by the hour, and the situation in some parts of the country was even worse.

There was no international policy, just the pretence of a policy, and that pretence was becoming uncongenial.

Moral tightropes are inevitable in matters of state. Danby could walk the highest tightrope over the deepest philosophical gorge. But he was also sensible to the distinction between pragmatism and cynicism.

He took consolation from the fact that he was at least able to stay above the international bickering. The British and French, who had troops on the ground protecting aid convoys, had become chronically quarrelsome. The General was French. Danby spoke French well, which the General appreciated, but Danby also understood how the British were inclined to think – a real mystery to the General – and the British liked to deal with him because of that.

'Nobody else here?' he asked, advancing towards Brad across the foyer. He looked around as though a handful of journalists might emerge from behind the furniture.

None did.

'I'm the only enthusiast,' Brad said.

Danby took a seat on the other side of the coffee table and felt his hopelessness deepen. If others came later, he would have to give out the same information all over again.

A waiter brought two small cups of espresso, and the journalist and the spokesman crouched on the edge of their chairs and fussily tore open packets of sugar and peeled adhesive tops from miniature cartons of milk.

Danby listed convoy deliveries and aid flights that had touched down at the city airport, and he outlined plans for the deployment of fresh UN troops near the runway.

'The ceasefire is taking hold,' he said, a little more brightly than he had intended. He preferred talking about big issues to reading out cargo manifests. Brad, though, seemed to lap up the convoy details, scribbling every last tonnage figure in his dog-eared notebook. 'Not everywhere, but in many places around the country there's been a marked reduction in fighting,' Danby added, sounding, he guessed, like a bored teacher dictating a familiar lesson. 'The point is, we now believe that placing UN troops along a broad swathe of territory to the west of the city is viable.'

The UN really did see the tiniest glimmer of light. It wasn't spin. Plans were complete for a rapid deployment that could place blue helmets between the armies in a matter of days – but this depended on the will of the political leadership.

'There's a raging battle in Otes!' Brad said, his intonation rising in mild perplexity. Two days of intense fighting in the west of the city made talk about interposing peacekeepers seem unreal.

Danby addressed the fighting in Otes. He was fluent with figures and facts, theories and possibilities. He volunteered information that placed the UN engagement in a positive light. He didn't lie, Brad was pretty sure. He made optimum use of the most unpromising truths.

'Michael Baring had a piece this morning about Otes,' Danby said. 'I suppose it'll be flavour of the month now.' Brad wondered if Danby knew about his own profound dislike for Baring. 'But the fact is,' Danby continued, 'the heavy fighting is limited to one part of the city.'

'The bombardments are bad all over,' Brad said.

'Our monitors have registered a downward trend. The attacks are less intense.'

At that moment there was a loud explosion, three hundred yards away, near the Koševo Hospital.

'So, I'm not saying the problem's solved!' Danby chuckled.

Outside there was now a blizzard, white flakes falling in the darkness, shells falling among houses and factories and empty streets. The two men drank coffee, there in that oddly formal foyer where the air was permeated with cigar smoke, and the old fashioned furniture and heavy curtains reminded Brad of a theatre bar. They could hear cooks chattering in the kitchen.

Then they heard voices at a higher and more urgent pitch. A French officer was speaking to one of the Egyptian soldiers at the front door. Moments later, Alija, bearded, bespectacled and brisk, was escorted into the foyer.

Danby nodded to the escort, who withdrew, and Alija said, with unexpected force, 'There is a problem on the Airport Road!' He looked at Danby and then at Brad, then back at Danby.

There were snowflakes on Alija's hair; he was breathless. He had been standing outside in the snow for ten minutes trying to persuade the Egyptian guards to let him in.

'There are Rebels on the road … one of our ministers … inside a UN vehicle … there's a stand-off!'

Danby rose. 'I can make contact with the airport,' he said.

Brad watched the Irishman take stock of Alija. For several seconds Danby stood still, and some of his calm transferred to Alija. Then he ushered the new arrival to a chair by the other table.

'I'll be back,' Danby told Brad. Then, turning to Alija, 'Give me a few minutes. I'll find out what's happening.'

He moved away quickly, the rolling, easy gait still evident, and climbed the stairs at the end of the foyer.

Brad walked over to the other table and sat down.

'What's happened?'

Chief of Cabinet in one of the ministries, Alija's role and influence went well beyond the parameters of his actual position. He had access to ministers and members of the presidency and he used this to good effect. Alija had a knack for being in the right place at the right time, with the right documents in his leather music case and the right phone numbers etched in tiny well-formed characters on the rice paper of his old-fashioned address book.

'The minister was travelling from the airport in a French APC,' he told Brad. 'The Rebels have a roadblock up. They're holding the APC. That's all we know. I came here to find out more.'

He paused, and then, 'Have you heard anything about this?'

Brad shook his head. 'Why was he on the road?'

'There was a foreign delegation that couldn't come into the city because of the shelling, so the minister went to meet them at the airport.'

'How many Rebels?'

'We only know there's a roadblock.'

'There is indeed a roadblock!' said a smartly uniformed officer descending the stairs from the situation room. He advanced confidently across the foyer and shook hands with Alija and Brad. Alija's arm moved mechanically in the officer's grip.

Major Thomson was one of those people whose judgments are forthright and often wrong. He looked at the two men appraisingly: Alija was agitated; Brad seemed dissatisfied. In the major's view, civilians were a hindrance: they made things harder for soldiers to fix.

'We are resolving the matter now,' he said. He spoke cheerily, his grey head tilted backward as though he was trying to keep Alija and Brad in focus. He had a thin, pointed, handsome face and a slightly too high voice. 'Senior officers have been dispatched to the scene. The latest information we have is that the matter is close to a conclusion. The minister is unharmed.'

Alija sat down heavily. 'When was your last information?' he asked, collecting himself.

'Moments ago.'

They sat in silence, and then Brad asked, 'Do you know how many French soldiers are at the scene?'

Thomson took a short breath before he replied. He had noticed that you can never tell reporters enough. Answer one question, and they ask another.

'Don't know that,' he said with sudden petulance. 'Jim is finding out what he can.'

No one said anything, which Thomson found unsettling, so he said, 'I'll see what he's come up with.' He walked back across the room but then stopped. Danby was coming downstairs.

'The situation is confused,' Danby said, speaking principally to Alija. 'There appears to have been shooting. We do not at this time know whether the shooting involved any of the French troops, or whether the APC carrying the minister was involved.

My understanding is that the APC is still at the spot where it was stopped.'

Alija stood up again.

Danby raised his hands, palms outstretched. 'I'm going to make every effort to find out exactly what's happened over there,' he said.

'When did the shooting take place?' Thomson asked. Five minutes earlier he had been told that all was well.

Danby looked irritated, which Thomson rather resented.

'I have no information on that at this time,' he said, again speaking principally to Alija. 'But I would surmise in the last hour. I think rather than us getting into that sort of detail it would be best to wait till we have a better picture.'

Alija and his people at the presidency had no way of knowing what was happening on the Airport Road. The government's forward lines were too far from the scene.

'Can I speak to one of your officers? You have radio contact.' Alija suggested.

'That's not possible.' Danby registered the surprise in Alija's expression and added quickly, 'The thing is being dealt with from the PTT. I understand the General is already there.'

The pre-war telephone exchange, the PTT, was the main UN compound in the city.

Alija nodded. 'Send news when you have details,' he said. 'I'll try and reach our people at the PTT.'

He began walking towards the door. The other three watched him leave.

Brad said to Danby, 'How many French troops are involved?'

'I'll get back to you on that just as soon as I can.' Danby walked across the foyer and headed upstairs to the situation room.

Brad lit a cigarette.

'This is a pickle,' Thomson said. 'Beats me why we let them travel to the airport anyhow.'

'I guess it's their country,' Brad said.

Thomson disliked when journalists were pious. People are corrupt, he thought, and dishonest and selfish and when things get excessively bad there is apt to be violence. The solution is to be more efficiently violent than the other fellow. In an ideal world there wouldn't be wars, but the world's not ideal. 'Look at the mess they've made of it,' he said.

'I'll go to the presidency,' Brad remarked after a short pause. He had been thrown a scoop. He had a sudden terror of doing nothing.

'Let us know what you find out,' Thomson said affably. He walked Brad to the door.

Outside, Brad waited impatiently for the Egyptian guard to unlock the main gate. As soon as it was open he hurried onto the road and began shambling over the snow.

He would get a comment from a minister and file his story ahead of the rest.

7

Milena sat alone in the darkness listening to the news. She had to place the radio on the windowsill to improve the reception as the battery was weak. The little black rectangle on the white sill was faintly illuminated by moonlight reflected on snow.

She thought about Brad. It seemed strange to her that he wanted to talk about her life. She didn't know why she'd agreed and wondered if she'd made a mistake. Perhaps she'd agreed because she felt she must give a kind of account, to herself and to others.

An account of what she had done and what she had not done.

She would have to leave the apartment earlier than usual the day after tomorrow to go and meet Sanela and Brad at the theatre.

She looked into the darkness and remembered a summer's day in Foča when she watched from her bedroom window. Sunshine on the tall trees near Milena's house, speckled leaves, birdsong in the afternoon, no breeze.

They stood in a circle, Milena's neighbours, around Fudo Omeragić. It was Fudo who kept order at the riverside bar where Milena used to work. He was tall and imperturbable. He

had a large potbelly and equally large shoulders. He did everything slowly and deliberately, and his mouth, obscured by
a very thick moustache that drooped over his lips, tended to
pucker in a half smile. He had a friendly face, bright brown
eyes, bushy eyebrows. He joked all the time, witty observations,
clever remarks – he was inclined towards irony.

That day, Milena saw that Fudo was no longer imperturbable.
He was afraid.

His fear infected the air and with Fudo Omeragić's fear,
Milena's world began to burn.

Fudo was dressed the way he customarily dressed: sloppily.
He was wearing a pale green polo shirt and grey slacks and
sandals. His shirt stretched over his belly.

Fudo kept a good crowd going at his bar, people who'd known
one another all their lives, people who'd known Fudo all their
lives. He ran the place without very much visible effort. He did
most things without very much effort. His aspirations in life
were, as far as anyone knew, unexceptional. He was married to
Amela and they had two small children, a boy called Fadil and a
girl called Snjezana.

But on that sunny afternoon in Foča Fudo Omeragić's fear
polluted the air.

And Milena didn't run into the street to help him.

Because she was shocked. Because she had never believed it
would come to this. Because she was scared.

At the bar, Milena and Fudo were a team. But now she didn't
help him. Suddenly faced with an avalanche of evil, she froze.

Amela and the children had already left Foča by then. Fudo had sent them to stay with his brother on the coast.

The crowd moved slowly along the middle of the street. Fudo gesticulated, tried to argue. He was sweating profusely. His big moustache drooped; his eyes opened wide and his cheeks were drawn. He was taller than the others, but there were many more of them, about a dozen men. Those at the front pushed him. Milena strained to see what was happening. Ordinary men from the town – drivers and builders and shopkeepers and farmers – had become a mob. They had seized a neighbour, a man they once respected, and set upon him because of his name, because of what that meant – that he worshipped differently if he worshipped at all.

Fudo's name condemned him; Milena's name protected her. But she would not accept that protection. She packed her things that afternoon. Clothes, some money, a handful of keepsakes. She left before her husband came home, walked to the bus station and took the first bus out of town.

When she reached the city, just before the barricades became permanent and the siege began, she stayed two nights with a schoolfriend who got her a job. The Rebels had surrounded the city with artillery by then and were about to begin a campaign of shelling and sniping that would terrorise the trapped population. Water supplies and electric power were turned on and off by the besieging troops as a bargaining chip in negotiations with the government. Milena rented a one-room flat in Alipašino Polje from a couple who were leaving for the safety of the coast.

Now, in the same flat months afterwards, she listened to the news and looked out of the large window onto the broad empty boulevard below. She leaned against the lintel, the undulating surface of the cold paint against her cheek.

When Milena had left Jusuf's apartment soon after dawn and begun to make her way to her home in Alipašino Polje, a handful of cars had passed. She tried to hitch a lift, but every car was full. She followed the stream of pedestrians along the winding road past the Holiday Inn and the Tito Barracks to the bakery in Čengić Vila. When she reached the Television Centre, on the other side of the bakery, she walked onto the main road and crossed over to Alipašino Polje.

She had to climb painstakingly the steep steps that cut through the estate between the tower blocks. Frozen snow made the climbing treacherous. At the summit was a terrace with a view of the city. The concrete slabs were scarred by shell craters and surrounded by burned and mangled cars. She walked to her block.

Milena felt safe in her apartment, even though it was exposed to shellfire. The building had been hit four times with one fatality, an old man who remained in his bed during the worst of the bombardments, refusing to go below to the shelter. Yet Milena felt safe. Safe from Foča. Safe from what had happened there.

She did not, however, feel entirely safe from Mrs Hatibović and her nosey questions. As Milena struggled to make her key turn in the frozen lock, Mrs Hatibović emerged from the next-door apartment.

The old woman gave her a look of suspicion and said, 'You're back!'

Milena was inclined to ignore Mrs Hatibović, but the woman was not easily brushed off. 'Did you stay in town?'

'There was too much shelling. I thought it would be safer there.'

'It's more dangerous there, in the town. That's where the shelling is worst!'

Mrs Hatibović waited for a response, but Milena had opened the door and stepped inside out of view.

The old woman shrugged and hurried across the landing to tell Mrs Nurudinović that Milena had returned home.

Snow was falling now, illuminated by the pale white glitter of the moon. No one moved outside. In the distance Milena heard anti-aircraft fire, and further away the thud of howitzer shells, perhaps near Vogošća, but in the city it was quiet.

The snow fell in Marijin Dvor, on the broken concrete carcass of the Parliament building, spreading softly over the ghostly wreck. It fell on the cold grey towers of Alipašino Polje, set on a hill beside the broken railway yards and factories to the west. And it fell in a silent coiling cloud across the tops of buildings in Ciglane where the apartments looked out on a park empty of trees. The blizzard spread an icy shroud over the city. It fell on the Lion Cemetery and on the new graves in the sports field by the Olympic Stadium.

In the cobbled courtyard of the Husref Beg Mosque drifts of snow collected by the ancient stones and covered the little paths between Ottoman halls, and it collected too on the roof of the Islamic University, where the yellowing Austro-Hungarian facade made a bleak and delicate silhouette against the silver storm. On the cathedral, on the Orthodox church, on the synagogue by the River Miljacka, snow drifted downward, silent, white in the black night.

The presidency, a Habsburg palace, stood as a dark mass against the descending tide of white. Nearby, the snowstorm curled silently around the old dome of the Alipašino Mosque.

Snow fell in the courtyard of the State Hospital, freezing in the night. By daybreak the entrance would be blocked with frozen drifts, and stretchers would be carried over ice uncertainly. And in the grounds of the Koševo Hospital too, amid the shell craters and the frozen mud, snow fell.

The cloud engulfed charred timber and broken stones in the great injured shell of the burned-out National Library. In Grbavica swirling snowflakes drifted through the narrow slits of sniper nests, where troops dozed in the freezing midnight dark. Snow fell on the frontlines, on Mojmilo, on Žuč, on Trebević. In Otes snow fell on the ruined apartment blocks where two armies slept just yards apart. It fell on the frozen Miljacka, writhing palely through the battlefields to the west.

Snow fell on the narrow cobbled alleyways of the Old Town, among the minarets. It descended softly on the avenues of the city centre, where a lamp by a window here and there shed a weak light on tenemented streets.

It fell on Bistrik, on the steep decline from the brewery and the Franciscan church to the river. It fell on the shattered buildings where 400,000 people huddled. Hungry children slept in the storm. Men and women lay awake in the icy silence.

At a crossing two miles west of the Koševo Hospital a thirty-four-year-old man lay on his back, arms stretched to heaven, legs spread-eagled, glasses smashed, still on his face, now frozen, engulfed in snow. The man's wife and child waited for him in a basement apartment twenty yards away. The basement was sheltered, but the crossing was exposed. He had been felled by an explosion just seconds from reaching his home and family. He was found the next morning by a neighbour.

8

'Please call me Dario,' Jurić said when they met in the lobby of the Holiday Inn.

They walked across the lobby and climbed to the first floor. Jurić made no attempt at small talk as they walked. In the restaurant they sat at the corner of a small table with a dirty cloth.

'Room number?' the waiter demanded.

Terry gave him the number.

He spoke to Jurić.

'He wanted to know if I'm staying for dinner,' Jurić translated.

Terry turned to tell the waiter that Jurić was her guest, but the man was already walking towards the kitchen.

'It's OK,' Jurić said. 'I explained to him that you are treating me!'

There was an awkward pause and then Terry said, 'I'd like to see Miro tonight.'

Jurić smiled patiently. 'That's not possible. We may go tomorrow if there is less fighting.' He waited to see her reaction. She looked at him steadily and he was prompted to continue. 'We couldn't possibly get into Otes tonight.'

'The fighting's serious?'

'The Rebels may already have taken control.'

'That would affect the evacuation?'

Jurić had removed a foot from a little girl and an arm from an eighty-four-year-old man that day – both victims of shelling. Terry's question struck him as obtuse.

'You see,' he said, trying, not very hard, to speak in a mild, unoffended tone, 'if the Rebels take the settlement tonight, Miro may be dead by the morning.'

The waiter brought soup, a watery consommé with some strands of spaghetti at the bottom. Jurić began to eat.

'Is the district *likely* to be captured?' Terry persisted. She wasn't here to make friends with Jurić but she did need to cooperate with him.

Between mouthfuls, he responded, 'We've been under siege for half a year, doctor. No running water. No electricity. I operate by candlelight. People are dying of cold. There's malnutrition. We're grateful you have come to help us. We admire your courage. Our city is no place for the faint-hearted. But Miro is simply another victim. Otes may be captured and so we may witness one more disaster. Or perhaps our army will hold the settlement. There are many variables.'

Then, more gently, 'I'll collect you in the morning. I can't say what time. I'd be grateful if you'd wait in your room. Probably mid-morning. That OK?'

'Yes, of course,' she said. 'I'm sorry. I'm still getting used to things.'

'I can only tell you that, as far as I know, Miro's condition is stable. His mother sent this to my colleague. It finishes the day before yesterday.'

Jurić reached into the inside pocket of his jacket and took out two sheets of folded A4 paper, handing them to Terry. Each sheet had three columns at the top of which was written, in a neat and educated hand and in English, *temperature, hours of sleep* and *muscle relaxant*, the last unspecified. Down one side were dates, hours and dosages, the numerals traced in the same elegant hand.

'I'm afraid that's all the documentation I can give you,' Jurić said. 'Any records we may have had at the hospital have been destroyed or lost. Miro's mother may have more.'

Terry looked through the list. Without knowing what the medication was, the third column was of little use, though she noted that the dosage had been increased twice during the last ten days, suggesting a crisis. Miro's temperature appeared to fluctuate significantly, which might be a problem when it came to moving him. *Hours of sleep* seemed to Terry little more than a desperate measure by the mother to record any information that might have a bearing on her child's health. Terry couldn't see that it was of any use. She struggled to absorb the fact that two pieces of A4 paper represented the full extent of case documentation ahead of major surgery.

'Which is your field?' Jurić asked. 'Cardiology or paediatrics, or both?'

Terry was startled. 'I'm not a specialist.'

He glanced up from his soup. Terry was beyond trying to assess the meaning of the look he gave her but instinctively she braced herself for a barbed comment.

Miro Pejanović had a form of cardiomyopathy at a stage where a transplant was the only treatment that might save his life. He was eight years old. It didn't surprise Terry that Miro's mother had an educated hand. She must have been very determined to get her child's name onto a case list that was matched against international donors. She had done that a year earlier, and a donor had become available only after the city was placed under siege.

'I've done a good deal of post-operative care,' Terry said. 'They needed someone to supervise Miro's transfer and I was available.'

Jurić had finished his soup. He sat back and looked at her, raising his eyebrows.

The main course consisted of roast beef, potatoes and carrots. Jurić cheered up when this was served. 'Life's not bad in the Holiday Inn!'

He ate with relish, apparently oblivious to the explosions outside, and he took only the faintest interest in the journalists who began trickling into the dining room.

'Did you visit this part of the world before?' he asked.

'I was at the coast twice, in the 1980s, on holiday.'

Until today she'd thought of those excursions as a useful introduction to this mission.

'It's beautiful there,' Jurić said. 'The beaches!' Then he added, 'You should have been *here*, though, when we lived together, peacefully.'

He took a mouthful of roast beef and potato.

'Are you married?' he asked unexpectedly.

'As a matter of fact, no. Are *you* married?'

'Yes, with two children. Two boys. My wife is with them, on the coast. I sent them away in March. I knew what was coming.

Some of my colleagues are less fortunate. Their families are still here. My wife is working now. She's a mathematician.'

'Your English is very good.'

'I travelled all over when I was a youngster. Africa, Asia. I spent a year in the States, in Boston.'

'You speak other languages?'

'German, a little Russian and Italian. Last year I began studying Japanese for my own amusement.'

'You live near the hospital?'

'Our old home was in Grbavica. The Rebels are there now. I live in an apartment near the presidency.'

'Hello again!' Terry and Jurić looked up. Michael Baring was standing over them.

'Sampling more of the Holiday Inn fare?' Baring asked Terry. 'I don't believe we've met,' he continued, extending his hand to Jurić. Jurić stood up and shook hands.

'May I join you?' Baring sat down. 'I've just come from Lukavica. Spent two hours with one of the commanders there, fascinating man. Really has all sorts of interesting things to say.' Baring paused and then asked Jurić, 'Are you a journalist?'

'A doctor.'

'From here?' He sounded sceptical.

'The State Hospital.'

'I know your boss pretty well.' Baring named a director at the hospital.

Jurić said nothing so Baring turned his attention to Terry. 'Been out and about?'

'It's worse than I'd imagined.'

'I don't think anyone has a really clear picture until they've been here.'

The waiter arrived. 'My good fellow,' Baring said. 'May I have a bottle from my stash?'

He turned to the other two and said, 'I'll have to eat quickly. I hope you'll help me with the wine. I have a big story to write.'

The waiter brought soup. Baring addressed Jurić. 'How's the antibiotics situation? I understand you're running out.'

'It's critical,' Jurić acknowledged.

'And you're not getting the cooperation you need from the UN?'

'They have a difficult job.'

'My source told me you weren't getting cooperation.'

'That so?'

The waiter brought dessert for Terry and Jurić.

'How old are your boys?' Terry asked Jurić.

'Six and eight. The older one is a musician, quite gifted I believe, a flautist.' He paused and then, as if this thought had just occurred to him, he added, 'I miss them.'

'Of course,' Terry said. 'But it's better that they aren't here.'

'When did you get them out?' Baring asked.

'Before the beginning of the war.'

'Exceptional foresight. Ah, here's my wine!' He accepted the bottle from the waiter. 'Two more glasses, please.'

Baring's voice droned on while Terry's thoughts raced. Her mind moved into a familiar and painful groove, impelled by Jurić's question about marriage. The immediate circumstances that had brought her to this table involved a last-minute change of plan by the Medical Action Group, but the root cause went further back than that. One bright morning the year before, Terry drove to the university to bring her husband a notebook he'd forgotten. He hadn't called to ask her to bring it but she knew that it contained notes he'd been making for a lecture on medieval symbolism and he'd left it on the hall table. She wanted to drop it off on her way to the hospital: things were going well between them after months of quarrelling. His research assistant was not in the outer office. Terry found her in her husband's office, assistant and lecturer leaping apart when Terry opened the door. She remembered noticing how shabby his office was, and how dull was the view from the little window. They separated soon afterwards. He was living with his assistant now.

Terry took the packet of Marlboro from her bag.

'May I have one?' Jurić asked.

'Two doctors smoking. Whatever next!' Baring remarked.

9

'They have shot him!' the Professor said. He hurried out of his office on the first floor of the presidency building.

He had been nicknamed 'the Professor' by foreign reporters because he spoke impeccable English and had a habit of explaining issues in minute and logical detail, as though instructing anatomy students on the intricacies of the digestive system. He was among the more influential ministers.

The Professor had thick black hair, long enough at the front to fall raffishly over his forehead. Invariably he was well dressed, a bit of a dandy. But the way he now approached Brad didn't encourage a relaxed consideration of the doctor's wardrobe. He was wild eyed.

'Go and tell the world about this!' he said. It didn't sound portentous, maybe because he said it in a low, peculiar voice, struggling to get control of his vocal cords. 'They have assassinated a member of our government!'

Brad wasn't sure if the Professor knew anything more than he himself had already learned. Rumours took on a life of their own in the city. The Professor might have got the wrong end of the story from the Airport Road.

'He is fighting for his life,' the Professor continued.

'Where is he now?'

'At the PTT. The General is there. He spoke to me by phone a few minutes ago.'

The General, though, might also be hysterical, Brad thought.

The Professor started to walk away. Brad followed him. 'What's the government going to do?'

'Emergency Cabinet session. Here. Tonight.' He looked at Brad impatiently. 'I must go now.' He increased his pace along the corridor.

Brad scribbled the Professor's remarks in his notebook and then walked back the way he had come.

A thick red carpet stretched the length of the corridor. The sound of Brad's footsteps was muffled beneath the gilded Habsburg cornices. The walls were cream-coloured and there were heavy red curtains with gold embroidery over the tall windows.

He looked ahead at the three guards standing in the lobby. Two were holding their machine guns at the front, the third had his slung over his shoulder. The soldiers and police in the presidency building were turned out smartly, boots polished, fatigues pressed.

Brad had been the only one at the Delegates' Club when Alija came in out of the blizzard, and he'd caught the Professor for a comment before the Cabinet went into session. Outside, he ran. He hated the stretch of pavement leading from the back door of the presidency round the side of the building towards Tito Street. The pavement was exposed to sniper fire. He was particularly nervous because he was the bearer of important news. He must not under any circumstances let it fall on the frozen ground.

When he reached the main road he slowed down to catch his breath. It was dark and silent and he could hear the sound of his own breathing. He was out of condition.

He began to walk more quickly when he got to the Alipašino Mosque. Someone else might pick up the story in the time it took Brad to walk, run and hobble over the snow from the presidency to the Holiday Inn. Word was sure to get out from the PTT, where the General was.

In the hotel he climbed the back stairs by torchlight and went straight to his room. Inside, he connected the small lamp above his desk to the car battery on the floor and switched on the computer. The satellite equipment below the desk was blinking. There was a message.

As he read the incoming message Brad's excitement began to be displaced by anger. The message wasn't for him but for Anna. The desk commended her on a piece she'd sent that morning – a feature on women at war – and told her to go ahead with the story she'd proposed for the following day. She was going to write about Dr Barnes' bid to bring little Miro to safety in London.

She hadn't told Brad she planned to write about that.

Brad had been in the city for months and Anna had been there just over a week. They were circling around one another. He hadn't made up his mind about her but he didn't like her dealing with the desk direct, over his head.

There was a crate of Carlsberg in the corner by the window. Brad fetched one of the cans and opened it. He began to type.

He wrote that the minister had been shot while travelling under UN escort. He reported that the man was fighting for his life. The incident placed a question mark over peace talks in

Geneva scheduled to begin that week. The Cabinet was about to meet in emergency session.

Finished, he read the piece, made corrections, set up the communications protocol and pressed the 'transmit' option. The signal blinked on the satellite transponder, and he waited for confirmation that the message had been received.

He took his can of beer to the window. Outside it was deathly quiet. A car raced down Sniper Alley, over the snow, headlights on and off. There was sporadic tracer fire in the distance. He lit a cigarette, inhaled, took another sip of beer and moved back to the computer. *Message received.*

He hurried out again and went down to the car park in the basement. Anna had taken the Land Rover. The sedan had a dodgy battery and no rear window and it didn't have armoured plating, but he couldn't make another dash to the Delegates' Club and then the presidency on foot.

He found the car, got in and switched on the engine. It started.

'Thank you!' he shouted at the dashboard. He lit another cigarette and began to ease the car through an impossibly tight geometry of parked vehicles. At the entrance to the car park he gunned the engine. The most dangerous part of the journey was exiting the hotel and turning the corner on the ramp out of the car park, in full view of the sniper nests on the other side of the river.

Brad drove up the ramp at speed. No shots.

It took him five minutes to reach the Delegates' Club. There were no familiar cars parked outside, none of the other armoured Land Rovers, or soft-covered cars plastered with press markings. The story was still not out. 'Thank you!' he told the dashboard again. He swung across the middle of the road and parked on the pavement in front of the guard post.

'What's your name?' the guard asked – the same guard who had asked the same question an hour earlier.

He waited outside while the soldier went through his routine, lumbering back to the guard post and winding up the telephone, then barking into the mouthpiece in guttural Arabic and waiting nonchalantly for a reply. Brad paced up and down. It was well below freezing. He had begun to button up his coat just as the guard invited him to come inside. As they walked through the garden he felt the cold air cling to his body.

Major Thomson met him on the porch.

'Bad news, I hear,' Brad said.

'You hear right.' He grimaced a little.

'Is Jim around?'

'He's gone to the PTT. The minister's in the hospital there.'

'His condition?'

The major gave him a gloomy look and remained silent. Brad guessed he'd been told not to give out any more unconfirmed reports.

'What happened?'

'Where?'

'On the Airport Road.'

'He was shot.'

'Is there anything else you can add?' Brad decided not to hang around. Danby was worth an extended visit, but not Thomson. 'I'm going to the presidency. I'd like to hear your side of things before I send my story.'

'We don't *have* a side,' Thomson said, quickly and with a note of triumph in his voice. After a moment, he went on. 'The General will be back in about an hour. I expect he'll make a statement tonight.'

'Who else has been here?'

'Journalists?'

'Yeah.'

'Only you.'

On the way to the presidency Brad had the option of switching on the headlights and driving fast, or moving slowly in the dark. He kept the headlights on. At the presidency he ran over the snow to the entrance at the rear of the building. As he turned the corner for the last twenty-yard dash to the door he felt nervous and exposed. He was tempting fate making this particular dash twice in one night.

There was a little cubicle just inside the entrance, a glass-fronted box with an opening for identity documents to be passed through, a small table, an oil heater and a chair. Earlier, the guard had sat in the cubicle, protected from the cold. Now he was standing by the stairs. He stopped Brad.

Brad presented his press pass and the guard said something Brad didn't understand. Seeing that he didn't understand, the guard started to climb the stairs, still holding the card. Brad followed. When they reached the top of the stairs the card was given to another soldier.

'Who you want see?' the second soldier asked.

Brad told him that he was expected by the Professor.

'Not tonight,' the soldier said. He looked at Brad, surprisingly confident that the Professor wasn't going to meet any journalists. Brad said again that he was expected. He wasn't expected but he knew the soldier would have to check, and he thought someone would agree to speak to him.

The soldier went into an anteroom and made a telephone call. After waiting several seconds he read Brad's name aloud from the identity card. He made a better job of this than the Egyptian guard had done at the Delegates' Club. There was another pause and then the soldier spoke very briefly into the receiver. Brad knew he'd been told to let him in.

'There's a meeting,' the soldier said. His English was suddenly better. 'You can't see anyone now.'

'I'll wait.'

The man shrugged and returned the card. He pointed to the metal detector at the top of the stairs and indicated that Brad should walk through it.

Through the metal detector he began to move past the three sentries in the lobby, the same ones who had been there forty minutes before, but one of the sentries stepped forward and stood in his way.

'Wait here,' he said politely.

Brad said he wanted to go back to the Professor's office.

'Wait here,' the soldier said again, still polite.

Brad sat on a bench and took out a packet of Marlboro. He lit a cigarette and began to smoke. Then he noticed that the three soldiers were watching him. He proffered the packet. The youngest-looking of the three stepped forward and took two cigarettes. He gave one to his colleague. The third soldier stayed on the other side of the lobby watching Brad morosely.

After a few minutes of silence, during which they smoked and looked around, the soldier who had accepted the cigarettes came over to Brad and said, 'Where are you from?'

'Boston, in the United States.'

'Ah, United States,' he said. He returned to the others. They spoke together and glanced at Brad.

Brad finished his cigarette and looked at his watch. He wasn't sure if it was worth waiting. He was becoming accustomed to the relative warmth of the corridor. He glanced up at the gilt ceiling then looked across the lobby at the red curtains and watched the soldiers.

They stood in a tight knot in the middle of the lobby. The soldier who had not smoked was explaining something to the others, miming a series of events. He removed the pistol from his belt, slowly pushed the second soldier out of the way and pointed his gun at the third. Then he made a sound with his lips, like a child imitating the noise of a gunshot. The other two nodded. That's how it was, they said. The first soldier put the gun back in his holster. They spoke in whispers.

Deciding that to wait any longer would serve no purpose, Brad stood up, but before he had turned to walk back through the metal detector he heard voices at the other end of the corridor. Half a dozen men were speaking loudly. They were moving towards the lobby, coming from the direction of the Professor's office. The guards made a cordon, placing themselves between

Brad and the small procession of politicians who now came into view. The Professor was at the front; several Cabinet members followed.

The Professor saw Brad and came over.

'They've killed him!' he said. 'This is what they do!' he continued with unusually resonant indignation. 'This is their peace initiative!'

He walked away while Brad was still scribbling.

Brad recognised a minister he'd interviewed several times. He called to him over the shoulder of one of the soldiers. 'Do you have a statement?'

The man looked at him absently and then approached. He said something to one of the soldiers and then to Brad in English, 'Say nothing. Report nothing. His family must be informed first.'

The minister spoke again to the soldier, who looked at Brad and then nodded to the minister, who turned abruptly and walked away. Brad started to leave, but two of the soldiers moved quickly between him and the metal detector.

'You wait here thirty minutes,' the English-speaking soldier said.

'No, I have to go now!' Brad tried to walk round, but the soldier moved quickly and placed himself in the way again.

'Sit down,' the soldier said. He looked at his watch. 'Thirty minutes,' he repeated.

The minutes were silent and slow. Brad had the news but all he could do was wait. Twenty minutes went by before he saw Alija coming along the corridor towards the lobby. He shouted to him.

'These guys have been ordered to keep me here,' Brad said, listening to the whining tone of his own voice. 'They've been told to keep me here for thirty minutes.' Alija looked at him, expressionless. 'I can understand the need to inform the minister's family first,' Brad went on quickly, 'but by the time I get back to my office thirty minutes will have passed.' Brad spoke into the vacuum of Alija's expression. 'You've got to tell them to let me go.'

There was a moment of silence and then Alija nodded and spoke, almost diffidently, to the soldier.

'You can go,' Alija told Brad.

Outside on the stairs Brad realised that he hadn't offered the least expression of commiseration or condolence.

He left the building and sprinted to the corner, turning sharply and moving away from the river. When he reached the main street in front of the presidency he saw a small crowd on the main steps of the building. The General stood in the middle of a huddle of reporters.

The story was out.

But Brad had already sent his initial report. He knew he'd beaten everyone. He was sure he'd been first.

'It is a tragedy,' the General was saying. 'No one can deny that, but we must ensure that this does not lead to further tragedy. We appeal for calm.'

'Is this a failure on the part of your troops?' Brad asked.

The General shrugged, a short, sharp rise and fall of his epaulettes, and looked down at the ground. His face screwed up a little, as it did when he was exasperated.

'I will make a full statement tonight at ten o'clock,' he said. 'Please excuse me.'

He turned and walked up the steps into the presidency building.

There was a general rush towards cars. Brad was pleased. He'd already beaten them.

He followed the pack back to the Holiday Inn. They made a small convoy of armoured vehicles, Brad at the back more vulnerable in his soft-covered car.

He was soon left behind. The four-wheel drives moved faster. When he reached the basement car park his competitors had already left their vehicles and hurried upstairs.

As Brad climbed to his room he met Michael Baring. Baring was descending through the ice-cold darkness, shining an expensive miniature torch – with a very narrow body and a very concentrated beam – in front of him. He shone the torch on Brad and said, 'Brad, what's up?'

Baring spoke in a chummy way. Brad sensed his concern. Something was on and Baring didn't know what it was. 'How do you mean?'

'Saw people leave the building at speed.'

Brad told him what had happened on the Airport Road.

'When?' Baring snapped.

Brad related what he knew and then continued climbing the stairs.

'I see,' Baring remarked.

'The General's giving a press conference at the Delegates' Club at ten,' Brad added.

10

The more she thought about it, the more Milena regretted agreeing to speak to Brad. She didn't think that what she had to say would be interesting, at least not to someone who made a living the way Brad did, covering wars.

And in any case she wasn't sure she could put her own memories into words. She wasn't even sure that was something that she *wanted* to do. What was dear to her was in her heart: it couldn't just be brought out and shown to the whole world. Yet she thought about her past more and more now.

When Milena was twenty-two she visited Sarajevo with her friends Jasmina and Mira. The world was there, for the Olympic Games. Jasmina had got hold of tickets and Mira had an aunt and uncle who lived in Čengić Vila and who had agreed to put the three girls up.

They left Foča at six o'clock in the morning. Immediately before departure they began to bicker over whether to take their bags into the bus or stow them with the luggage. Jasmina believed they would be stolen if they put them with the rest of the luggage. 'There are professionals that live off travellers,' she said. 'They steal people's bags when the bus stops at really small places.'

'We're not going to the South Pole!' Milena said. 'It's only an hour and a half!'

The driver shouted at them. 'Are you girls staying there? Or are we all going to get on the fucking bus?'

He looked like somebody's uncle. He was short and fat and he wore a big blue anorak. They took their bags onto the bus. The inside smelled of frost and cigarettes and metal. Mira and Jasmina slept. Milena listened to the sound of tyres humming on asphalt and watched the dawn, dull and distant over woods. She felt the chill window on her forehead.

When Milena was very small, her mother took her to the coast. They travelled for a whole day, on a bus, among strangers. Milena wanted to see the sea. She knew that it was blue and big and beautiful. Her mother said they would play on the sand and they would eat ice cream.

It was a long day's journey. In the seat in front of them were two men with oily hair. They were thin-faced and preening, like the men who came to the coffee shop where Milena's mother worked.

Milena never knew her father. She imagined him like one of those thin-faced men. Her mother remarked once, of a handsome man with a moustache, that he was 'like your daddy'. Milena could tell her mother hadn't meant to say that. Her father didn't come into ordinary conversation. She knew that he'd gone away because he couldn't get a job, and he hadn't come back. That's what her mother said.

Her mother said her father wasn't a bad man, which was a strange thing to say, Milena thought. Why would she say that her father wasn't a bad man, unless other people thought he *was* a bad man? Sometimes her mother had boyfriends. Milena didn't mind. She thought most of them would be OK as fathers. She imagined her real father, though. She imagined how it would feel to be with him. She imagined how it would feel if her father lifted her up and held her very close, like her mother did sometimes. It was how she imagined the sea would make her feel. She imagined somehow that her father would dress in stylish clothes.

That year they spent weeks and weeks on the coast, but Milena only saw the sea from a distance, when they descended from the mountains and when they took the same road back to Foča. They stayed in a room above the restaurant where Milena's mother had a job for the season. It smelled of disinfectant. They sat on the bed when they arrived. It felt springy.

'When are we going to the beach?' Milena asked.

'When I have time off.'

Nothing her mother promised ever happened exactly as she said it would. Sometimes nothing happened at all. They stayed for a whole summer but they never went to the beach. Her mother worked every day from early in the morning until late at night.

When Milena complained, her mother told her she hated working in the restaurant but they needed to earn money otherwise they wouldn't eat. At night Milena lay in the bed, waiting for her mother. Her mother would come in, undress and lie down beside Milena. She remembered the shiny touch of her mother's petticoat and the smell of perfume and the weight of her mother's body changing the contour of the bed so that Milena rolled close and felt the touch of her mother's fingers running through her hair. Sometimes her mother fell asleep straight away. Other times they lay awake and talked. Milena wished the two of them could stay that way forever.

And when they left at the end of the summer and took the bus to Foča, Milena looked back and saw the sea, far away behind them. Her mother said they couldn't go to the beach on their last day because the bus tickets had been bought and there was nothing she could do. They had to get on the bus and leave. Milena knew her mother wanted to take her to the beach and sit on the sand and help her make sandcastles. She knew her mother wanted to go down to the water with her and splash in the sea and swim and look up at the sun. She knew that these things would have happened if her mother could have made them happen. But her mother wasn't lucky, or clever, or strong.

Milena imagined the sea. She imagined afternoons at the beach with her mum and dad. One day she would live in afternoons like that.

Now, years later, on the bus to Sarajevo, she looked out at the trees by the side of the road and the ragged walls of white left by a snowplough. She lit a cigarette. The taste was of metal and smoke.

Milena was more excited than she'd ever been. She was excited about going to the Olympics; she was excited about going to Sarajevo with Mira and Jasmina. Yet she was excited because of something else too. On that early morning travelling from Foča she knew that fate waited at journey's end.

The bus stopped in villages along the way where groups of people in brightly coloured anoraks and woollen hats and scarves climbed aboard. The sound of the wheels was subsumed in a hum of expectant conversation. They moved through deep valleys dissected by black tunnels, and edged along the side of narrow, fast-flowing rivers and crept to the tops of hills from where they could see, spread in the pale clear light of winter, stark snowbound meadows stretching towards Sarajevo. Trees traced black patterns on the snow; smoke coiled from houses sketching grey wisps of cloud in white air; the countryside was crisscrossed with hedgerows and tracks.

Milena saw this geometric prettiness as God's overture to their adventure.

For a short time Milena and Mira and Jasmina would belong to Sarajevo. They would be at home there. It would be *their* time. In these days it would be *their* city. She peered ahead to catch her first sight of rooftops.

11

In the cold candlelit bedroom above the theatre Sanela pulled on her jeans, a sweater and thick socks. She dressed with characteristic concentration, not forgetting to tie her silk scarf and tuck it inside the crewneck of her sweater. Anna had arrived with word of the minister's death on the Airport Road. She wanted Sanela to go back with her to the Holiday Inn and translate the radio bulletins.

Sanela greeted news of the assassination solemnly, almost imperturbably. Zlatko, by contrast, was consumed by nervous energy. As soon as he was dressed, he had hurried off. He didn't say where he was going.

Before Zlatko left, he had asked Sanela to take a message to Dr Barnes, so when she got to the hotel she knocked at room 305. The sound of her knuckles on the door was swallowed up by the vast cold atrium. She knocked again more loudly and stamped her feet to restore the circulation. There was silence inside. She knocked a third time and then tried the handle, but the door was locked. Then she heard the sound of movement inside. Terry opened the door and smiled.

'Put the safety chain on the door when you open it,' Sanela said. 'There are thieves in the hotel. May I come in?'

Terry moved back into the room and Sanela followed. The air was smoky. Sanela had noticed earlier the way Terry smoked. She held her cigarette away from her body, like a schoolgirl trying out her first puff.

She should have been nice to the doctor, she knew, but she wasn't in the mood.

'I had to come back and work,' she said. 'I have a message from a friend of Dr Jurić. They have arranged transport for you to go to Otes tomorrow morning. You will leave at nine o'clock. The car will be here then. The driver's name is Zlatko and he will meet you in the hotel dining room.'

'Sit down,' Terry said politely. She wanted to talk to someone. 'Would you like something to drink?'

'I can't. There's been an incident. A member of the government has been killed. Brad is writing a story now. I have to go.'

Terry looked disappointed, and Sanela guessed it was because she wanted company rather than because a man had been killed. 'After you've visited Otes you will have to go to the PTT, the UN headquarters,' she added. Terry gave her her full attention. 'You need to make sure they will take the boy on a plane.'

'I have a letter from Geneva giving permission.'

There was something inexcusably naive about this woman, Sanela decided. She was out of her depth here if she believed letters would get a civilian and a sick child on a plane.

'I don't know anything about that,' she said.

After Sanela left, Terry sat on the bed. The room was illuminated by two candles which she had placed on the bedside cabinet. She watched the flames flicker in small pools of wax. The candles lit up a fraction of the room. The rest was darkness. She listened to the faint sound of gunfire outside, a sound like pebbles being thrown against a piece of steel. Rat-tat-tat. Not like the sound she had heard when she came back to the hotel from the hospital, the murderous sound of the elastic band. She now had a livid bruise that stretched from her thigh to her hip to remind her of that sound and the panic it had brought with it.

Lying back she listened to the fighting, and then she blew out the candles, smelled the caustic smell of singed tallow, which reminded her of church, and went to sleep.

She woke hours afterwards. It was cold. She slid under the covers still in her clothes and went back to sleep. She remembered the insect scuttling away from her when she was nearly killed. She dreamed about the airport where no one met her, and about the officer with blue epaulettes who said, *We'll put you on a plane.* He had hundreds of photocopies. Some documents could get you out. She remembered the white APC making space to let them pass when they held up their laminated cards.

* * *

Terry wasn't *physically* scared. Sanela had been impressed when they went to the hospital. She had seen people arrive full of bravado and then when the time came to go out of the hotel they were desperate not to show how frightened they were. Dr Barnes, on the other hand, looked as though she could keep her cool. Her fear was deeper than physical fear.

Sanela was wary because of this nearly existential fear. It was the kind of fear that could endanger the people around Dr Barnes, she thought, the people who were trying to help the doctor and the people she was trying to help.

Brad's room was just along the corridor. He looked up from the computer when Sanela came in. His expression was grim. The room was smoky.

She lit a cigarette and said, 'I'll get the news.'

It was two minutes before the hour. She switched on the radio and waited for the slow sad music that preceded the evening bulletin. It was music that made her think of Zlatko. He used to hum the melody when they sat and listened to the news. Brad tapped on the keyboard, transcribing her translation – minister shot on the Airport Road.

He had not been first with the story.

When he returned from his second visit to the presidency, arriving at the hotel minutes after the competition, there was a newsdesk message waiting. They were holding his piece.

The words were so unexpected that he had to read them twice, and it took some time before he accepted their awful significance. They were holding his story because he hadn't said *who* had shot the minister. He had simply reported that the minister had been shot. They wanted clarification.

'The fucking Rebels shot him!' he screamed at the computer.

He sent the clarification, but it was too late by then – he had not been first with the story.

When Sanela had translated the radio news bulletin he sent another story, adding background.

Zlatko would learn more than Brad or Sanela. Sanela worked as an interpreter and translator: Zlatko did more – he was an all-round fixer. Zlatko could interpret and translate, but he could also secure petrol on the black market, arrange interviews with ministers and come up with bits of news that were completely unknown to everyone else. He had gone off to talk to half a dozen people in and out of government – and they would all have something to tell him. When he was in the city at night, Sanela feared for him.

Brad left her at a quarter to ten. She was to sleep on the spare bed in Anna's room.

He brooded on his scoop – consigned to the newsroom wastebasket – as he gunned the engine and drove up the ramp and out of the hotel. The battery was feeble. The car moved off the ramp and onto the road. He accelerated and changed gear and felt the power drain away. The engine stopped and he heard the tyres grind into the snow and thought for the third time that night, *I am in view of snipers; there is a clear field of fire.* He swore, put the gear into neutral and rolled back down the hill onto the ramp and into the basement. At the bottom of the ramp he tried the reverse gear; the engine didn't even cough.

Brad arrived at the Delegates' Club on foot at twenty past ten. The Egyptian guard let him into the garden without asking his name this time. The press conference was ending as Brad entered the foyer. Anna was standing at the back.

'What have I missed?'

'Just about everything!' she said, looking at him with disappointment or annoyance – or both.

He had run most of the way from the Holiday Inn. He was dishevelled and sweating, and the foyer was crowded and very warm.

Standing in the glare of television lights with reporters jostling around him the General put on a calm front. 'This is a tragedy,' he said, repeating almost word for word what he'd said earlier outside the presidency. 'I appeal to all those who would seek revenge ... do not make this tragedy worse.'

His face broke into a pattern of fine wrinkles. He grimaced. His steel-rimmed spectacles flashed in the television lights. He was smoking a small cigar.

'General,' Michael Baring made himself heard. 'I'm sure I speak for the press as a whole when I say that not one man jack among us believes you or any of the soldiers under your command bear personal blame for what has happened. However, I'm obliged as a journalist to seek from you an assurance that this event will be investigated in such a way that the world's media,' – he made a sweeping motion with his hand – 'whom we represent here tonight, will be able to assess with whom responsibility rests.'

'Everything will be done to find out what happened,' the General said. 'Now, if you will excuse me –'

He began to move towards the stairs.

Jim Danby shouted over the babble of questions and irritated cameramen trying to secure a clear line of view to the General. 'There will be a full briefing tomorrow morning at eleven o'clock at the PTT. Thank you very much, ladies and gentlemen. That will be all for this evening.'

KEVIN SULLIVAN | 89

'I've got it,' Anna told Brad. 'I'll file as soon as we get back.'

'Brad!' Baring swept past him on his way to the door. 'Wherever *were* you? That was a *crucial* briefing!'

'Crucial?' Brad asked, catching up with Anna.

'More curious than crucial,' she said. 'It wasn't the UN's fault. That was the gist.'

'Anything else?'

'Very little in the way of explanation. Very little in the way of apology.'

12

Terry sat on her own at one of the smaller tables. She had placed her coat on the back of the chair next to her and her black acrylic holdall on the floor. There was a cup of coffee in front of her, but Zlatko could tell that she had finished drinking the coffee long ago. She looked sad, he thought, and bewildered.

There was hardly anyone else in the restaurant. The journalists had all gone to the morning press briefing.

She looked up as Zlatko approached, and he noted the uncertain expression on her face.

He smiled a broad friendly smile and extended his hand.

'Dr Barnes, I am Zlatko. I am to drive you to Otes.'

He sat down.

'Let's have a coffee first,' he said. 'And a cigarette.' He beckoned the waiter over and ordered two more cups of coffee. 'You are just as Sanela described you!' he said.

He is very young, Terry thought.

He wore cowboy boots under blue jeans, a black sweater, red scarf and an elegant woollen coat.

'Dr Jurić isn't coming, then?' she asked.

He carried on smiling his wide, getting-to-know-you smile. 'He's been detained at the hospital. I've just come from there. There are many casualties today, I'm afraid. There was a heavy bombardment this morning, and some of the wounded are coming from Otes.'

Terry had awoken to the sound of explosions. Her first reaction had been to leap out of bed and lie on the carpet as far as possible from the window. She jumped onto the floor so violently that she hurt her ankle, which compounded her existing injury. The pain from her bruise of the previous day had not receded. She lay beside the bed for a few seconds and then decided it was too cold to stay there. The explosions continued so she pulled her coat on and went into the loo. No windows. It felt safer. But the candle used up the oxygen and she started to get a headache, so she came back out and tiptoed to the window as if some artillery officer miles away might be waiting to hear the sound of her footsteps before directing his next round of fire. She peeped through the space in the tarpaulin. The noise was very loud but she couldn't see smoke or fire or sparks flying. She had hurried downstairs to the restaurant long before breakfast.

Zlatko picked up Terry's packet of Marlboro. 'May I?'

She took the packet and extracted a cigarette and offered it to him. He took the book of matches, nearly finished now, and lit the cigarette.

The waiter brought coffee.

'I will interpret for you,' Zlatko explained. 'It's dangerous today – a lot of shelling – but we'll manage. Shall I call you "Doctor"?'

It was not clear to her whether he intended this to be funny. Perhaps it was some sort of Central European courtesy. Everything was odd, from explosions and small-arms fire to conversational eccentricities.

'Yes, if you like,' she said.

'We will manage, Doctor. We will manage. Are we to take the little boy to the airport immediately?' Zlatko hadn't been given any details.

'No. Today I'll examine Miro, and we'll evacuate him tomorrow.'

'And you have already arranged this with UNHCR?'

'Not yet.'

'We must visit the PTT on our return from Otes, then.' He guessed that she imagined others would make allowances for Miro, but he knew that they wouldn't. 'We'll get the necessary permission, the papers to enter the airport and board a plane,' he continued. 'And after that, I'm going to take you to a concert!'

She looked at him with astonishment.

'Dr Jurić asked me to bring you to our annual children's song festival. We'll meet him there this afternoon,' Zlatko said. 'The festival is to take place near the TV Centre and the doctor will be in that part of the city. Anyway, you should have an opportunity to see something positive when you are here, and the song festival will be a contrast to everything else. It was supposed to have been cancelled – it didn't seem right to hold such an event in these conditions – but there was a contrary view that this is something that we hold every year and we must not let the gentlemen on the other side of the frontline stop us from holding it this year.'

He spoke in a wry, engaging tone of voice, as if the carnage around them was a disagreeable inconvenience. He was dressed as she imagined he might have dressed in peacetime. His winter clothes were stylish and he wore brown leather brogues, a contrast to the heavy boots and arctic jackets and greatcoats that were in universal use.

'Who is it exactly that you work for?' she asked.

'Today, I'm working for you!' he said. 'Until the start of this year I was a student.'

'What did you study?' She expected him to say philosophy, or literature or languages – something in line with his rather bohemian appearance.

'Accountancy.' He smiled. 'I'm a tax specialist. Taxes are not a strong suit with the people in these parts. We believe they are best avoided! But then the war started. So now I'm a taxi driver. I interpret a little, too, and I do some reporting – I was a reporter on our university paper.'

He stubbed out his cigarette. 'Tell me, Doctor, what made you come here?'

'I was asked,' she said, knowing this was an unsatisfactory response, but entirely unable to find the words for a reply that would have been more truthful. 'Look, just call me Terry,' she said, without understanding why she suddenly felt impelled to dispense with formality.

She stood up, slipped the cigarettes into her trouser pocket, put on her coat and picked up her holdall. Zlatko led the way out of the restaurant.

The car had no windows; the window frames were covered with opaque plastic. The cover of the boot was missing. 'Damaged by mortar,' Zlatko said. Two bands about five inches broad had been cut into the tarpaulin where the windscreen used to be. These bands were covered with clear plastic, allowing driver and passenger to see where they were going.

'Is this part dangerous?' Terry asked, peering ahead at the piece of waste ground in front of the hotel, where she had been shot at the previous afternoon. Perhaps she wanted him to tell her it was the most dangerous place in the city – then she would have experienced the worst. He revved the engine, engaged first gear and swung the car round onto the pavement in a sharp U-turn.

She thought he wasn't going to answer, which would have made her feel awkward, but he said, 'It's *all* dangerous, Terry. This part a little more than the next part, a little less than the part after that.'

She looked for the seatbelt, but there wasn't one. He drove very fast.

At the main road they turned left, moving in the opposite direction from the State Hospital towards the west. The road was narrow. On either side, people dragged sledges piled with firewood and plastic water containers. The pedestrians wore dark trenchcoats, woollen hats, scarves wrapped around their necks and faces. There were old women and small children among them.

On either side of the road she saw people cutting down trees.

From time to time the thin traffic built up behind a UN aid convoy escorted by APCs, and they had to slow down.

'That's the TV Centre,' Zlatko told her as they passed a giant grey concrete building. It would have looked ugly even if it hadn't been pockmarked with shell holes. Parts of the discoloured concrete facade were covered by snow and ice, obscuring the totality of its ugliness.

'Coming up,' Zlatko went on, 'is the PTT, where the UN headquarters are.'

He spoke like a tour guide.

The PTT was a flimsy glass and cement structure, just as ugly, but with more windows than the TV Centre. The roof had an assortment of antennae and satellite dishes. There were sandbags all around the building and Terry saw blue helmets behind little fortified emplacements, like guards on a medieval battlement. Across the main entrance there was a barricade of coiled razor wire.

Near the PTT was a guard post manned by government troops. Zlatko stopped the car, opened the door and shouted something. Terry could see black army boots in the snow, and part of a brazier, and she smelled smoke from the fire. She couldn't see who Zlatko was talking to, but he was shouting, his whole manner different from before, and whoever he was shouting at shouted back at him.

When he got back into the car and closed the door he said, 'We are OK to continue.'

Zlatko swung the car round a barricade and they started along a narrower road completely devoid of cars. This continued for half a mile, after which they entered a derelict factory district. There were long sheds with corrugated iron roofs, open spaces where the land was unused and street lamps defining roads with no buildings on either side. There were abandoned cars and trucks everywhere, some of them overturned, the factories fire-blackened and the walls and roofs with shell holes. The car moved along an uneven track across snow.

Terry felt sick.

'The Rebels are on our right,' Zlatko said. He could see that Terry was scared. He was scared too.

When they got to the end of the track there was another guard post. A soldier in uniform came out of a low shed and walked towards them.

'We should get out here,' Zlatko said. He took a book from the dashboard, a black diary in which he'd put a letter. He opened the door and left the car.

Two more soldiers emerged from the shed. The first soldier took the letter from Zlatko.

'It's from Jurić,' Zlatko explained to Terry. 'It authorises us to enter the area.'

He showed the soldier his identity card. The soldier was an officious-looking little man, with a round face, unshaven. 'She's come from London,' Zlatko told him.

'Give me your passport,' Zlatko said to Terry. He kept his eyes on the soldier.

Terry opened her mouth to speak, but she had nothing to say. She had committed a grotesque oversight.

Finally, Zlatko looked at her. 'What's the matter?'

'I gave my passport to the hotel receptionist yesterday and I forgot to take it back.' She glanced at him, shamefaced.

The officious soldier stretched out a chubby hand and barked, 'Passport.'

'Have you got anything else?' Zlatko asked.

They watched her open her bag. At first, she couldn't find her wallet. When she found it at last she extracted her card from the Medical Action Group. She held the acrylic bag in one hand and the card in the other.

The soldier took the card and started to shake his head. Zlatko spoke to him, very calmly, but insistently. The man walked back towards the hut, studying the card.

'I'm sorry,' she whispered to Zlatko.

He didn't say anything and she felt like a fool. They waited until the soldier came back. He returned Zlatko's identity card and then Jurić's letter and finally, after a pause in which he seemed to be making up his mind, Terry's card.

He shrugged. 'You go in at your own risk.'

'What did he say?' she asked when they were back in the car. Zlatko told her. She nodded and sat back in her seat and looked ahead.

The soldiers moved a steel barrier from the road, and Terry and Zlatko drove through. There was fresh snow on the track and Zlatko couldn't see the potholes. The car went straight into one, deep enough to bring the bottom of the vehicle into contact with the ground. There was a loud scraping sound and then they bounced out of the hole again.

'Do you know the road?' she asked.

'I only came this way once, before the war,' he said, looking carefully ahead. 'I hope I remember it well.'

13

When Milena was ten her mother left Foča and never returned. Milena came back from school one afternoon and found two men in the house and her mother gone. She had never seen these men before, yet she recognised their oiled hair and slick clothes and leather shoes; she recognised the way they lounged in the front room as though it was *their* front room.

'Where's my mama?' she asked, looking from one hard face to the other.

'Who are you?'

'I'm Milena,' she said, screwing up her face and trying to screw up her courage too, standing on one leg then the other, glancing through the window and back at the door.

'Your mama's gone away,' the other man said. He spoke as though her mother's absence was Milena's fault.

Her mother owed money and couldn't pay it back. She guessed that much.

Milena's Aunt Jasna lived on the other side of town, near the police station. Sometimes her mother went there in the afternoons so Milena thought she might be hiding there now.

Neither of the debt collectors rose to stop her when she hurried back out of her own house. She listened for the sound of them, but they just sat there in the front room, smoking, as though they owned the house already.

She ran out onto the street and put some distance between herself and the men. Then she walked more slowly because she was afraid she might reach her aunt's house only to find that her mother wasn't there. For twenty minutes she could imagine that her mother would be sitting at Jasna's kitchen table smoking Kent cigarettes and that she would look at Milena with the expression she used when they were in big trouble – she would raise her eyebrows and tell Milena brightly and unconvincingly that everything would be all right.

Milena turned onto the main street leading down to the river and walked past the supermarket with her head down. She wondered if her mother had gone away in order to be with her father. She thought that, if her mother went to be with her father, they would both come back together. Her father would pay the men whatever it was they were owed and then Milena and her mother and father could live together again.

She imagined walking down the street with the two of them and ran the last two hundred yards to Jasna's house.

Jasna opened the door and looked over Milena's shoulder as she ushered her inside. Milena knew then that Jasna knew.

'Your mama had to go away,' she said, sitting down at the kitchen table with Milena opposite her. Jasna had been crying, Milena could see.

That night Milena slept on the sofa in the sitting room. She was relieved that Jasna didn't invite her to sleep in her bed. That would have made Milena feel awkward. She didn't want to pretend that Jasna was her mother, she didn't want Jasna to hug her or cry or tell her that everything was going to be OK. Jasna wasn't that kind of person. She spoke to Milena as though they were the same age.

The next day they left together for school, ten minutes earlier than Milena usually left, because Jasna said she had to come and speak to the headmaster before going to her work at the bottling factory. Milena waited outside the headmaster's office. After a few minutes he stepped out. Milena looked at his waistcoat and jacket: she didn't want to look him in the eye. She noticed the shininess of his grey suit, and heard an unusual and disconcerting warmth in his voice.

She knew by then that her mother would not be coming back. She had accepted – in a deep, dark way – what in years to come she would begin to understand. But the uncharacteristic warmth in the headmaster's voice was another thing. She understood from this that from now on people were going to set her apart because she had been abandoned by her parents. She wanted to cry, but she stared hard at the headmaster's suit, listening to him telling her to go to class. She walked away with dignity and determination.

'Come to our place again this afternoon,' Jasna called after her. 'I'll be there.'

When Milena went home to Jasna's in the afternoon, her clothes were there, and most of her toys and books.

'When's my mama coming home?' she asked Jasna.

'As soon as she can,' Jasna said.

But she never came.

Jasna didn't have any children. Her husband, Željko, worked in Dusseldorf. He came back to Foča every two months for a week. When he was home he drank a lot and sang in the sitting room, even when he was on his own, and told jokes to Milena and Jasna. His jokes were funny because of the way he told them. He used to start laughing before he got to the punchline. His laugh was a sort of muffled explosion, rumbling up and down. When he stopped laughing he would sigh, as though the joke he had just told had come as a bit of a surprise even to himself. Like Jasna, he spoke to Milena as though she was grown up. He told her about life in Germany. He told her about people, about Hans his boss, Clara his landlady, Alex his foreman. He told her stories about their lives, as though Germany was a kind of cheery soap opera in which he had had the good fortune to have landed a role.

He used to bring presents for Jasna and Milena. He would turn up at the door with his suitcase – a tiny white gentleman traveller's case from the 1950s – and one or two big cardboard boxes. He used to smile guiltily when Jasna opened the door as though he had done something naughty. The cardboard boxes would contain dresses, skirts, shoes, blouses.

In the spring of 1971 Željko brought a piano home. It was the most remarkable import from Dusseldorf ever recorded in Foča. It was a 1948 upright Hummel which Hans, Željko's boss, was throwing out. Željko got it for nothing. All he had to do was transport it more than 600 miles to Foča. The Hummel arrived on the roof rack of a Mercedes, although it hadn't come the whole way from Dusseldorf like this. It had travelled as far as Munich in the back of a furniture van that was carrying a consignment of filing cabinets. Željko knew the driver, who agreed to carry the extra cargo for the price of a night out when they reached Munich. From Munich to Sarajevo the piano travelled in a van carrying workers. It was charged at the rate of one human being. It took up the space of three, but it was wedged alongside the luggage in such a way that two boys travelling back from their first-ever paid work were able to lie comfortably on top. From Sarajevo it travelled slowly in Mirko Milutinović's Mercedes. They were stopped twice by the police, and the second time they couldn't talk their way back onto the road and had to pay an instant bribe of twenty marks. That added a third to the total cost of the piano.

Jasna opened the door, and Željko gave her his guilty look, smiling sheepishly. She looked over his shoulder and said, 'What the hell's that?' And his eyes opened wide as though she had expressed approval in a particularly delightful way.

People came from all over town to see the piano.

No one could play it.

Milena knew that the piano was for her. Željko and Jasna never said that, but she knew that they meant her to play it. She knew too that she *would* be able to play the piano. Others marvelled at its long journey from Germany but it seemed to Milena only natural that the piano had come to her. The morning after it arrived, when Željko was still upstairs snoring, dead to the world in a deep sleep induced by brandy and barbecued meat, and while Jasna was down at the shops, buying beer for Željko and humming as she surveyed the meat counter with her wallet replenished by German wages, Milena entered the sitting room and approached the piano.

Her feet dangled when she sat on the piano stool. The leather was cold and soft and comfortable, and she could feel the thumb-tacks around the edges press against the skin on her thighs. She lifted the heavy lid of the piano. The white keys were yellow at the edges, and some of the black keys were chipped. Milena ran her fingers across them without pressing down. She listened to the click-click of her nails on the spaces between the keys. She put her hands on her knees and contemplated the keyboard.

Then she laid the index finger of her right hand on Middle C, the key in front of the lock. The sound was just as she had anticipated: clear, round and pleasing. She pressed D and moved slowly up the scale, giving each note the same measure. When she reached High C she paused and then began to go back down again.

When Jasna came back from the shops half an hour later, Milena was able to play 'Three Blind Mice'.

'Knew you'd be good at this!' Željko said, his eyes wide open as if he was astonished by his own acuity. 'I told Hans,' he went on, speaking to Jasna who was standing listening to Milena, 'I told him, our Milena'll be great at the piano!'

Milena had to wait for three months before there was a place for her in the school music class. Four girls received piano lessons, on Tuesday evenings and Saturday mornings. Milena could already play by ear by the time she started lessons. During the three months she had to wait, she sat at the piano for an hour each day when she came home from school and 'Three Blind Mice' developed into other recognisable tunes. She never played one note that didn't have a good chance of fitting usefully with the others. She was a natural.

The piano teacher quickly saw that the girl had talent. Milena touched the keys with a delicacy and sophistication that, as it became more assured, transformed lessons from a chore to a delight.

When she sat at the Hummel in the sitting room of Jasna and Željko's house, Milena stepped onto a sandy beach. She looked at the ocean and walked barefoot on white sand.

By the time she was fourteen, she could sight-read. She accompanied the school choir. That gave her a certain renown, that and the fact that she lived with her aunt because her mother and father had run away. Milena played the piano the way other people speak. It was the way she articulated her fears and her hopes.

She was no happier at school than any of her friends. As soon as it was legally possible to leave, she did. Her first full-time job, when she was sixteen, was in a dress shop, where she worked for three years.

She came home from the dress shop one afternoon and found Jasna in the kitchen looking awkward and glum.

Milena sat by the table and lit a cigarette. Jasna lit a cigarette of her own and said uncertainly, 'Milena, I'm going to live in Germany. Željko's been promoted and he wants me there with him.'

Milena didn't see why Jasna should feel bad about that. 'What about the house?' she asked.

Jasna blew smoke out quickly and stretched a hand towards Milena. Milena saw a tear in the corner of Jasna's eye, threatening to breach a mascara-illuminated embankment of quivering skin. 'Of course, we're not selling. The house is here for you to live in,' Jasna said.

Now Milena felt bad. The question seemed selfish; it had just popped into her head.

Jasna didn't leave immediately. Preparing to move to Germany took her months. Željko was back regularly, and each time Jasna returned with him and stayed longer, until finally she went off with Željko and didn't come back to Foča.

Milena paid rent into the bank every month, looked after the house, lived in it as she had always done. She stayed in Foča because it was as good as anywhere. She thought sometimes about going to work in Sarajevo. She could not have said why she never did – perhaps because she believed her mother and father might come back one day. They would not find her if she left Foča. Or perhaps she stayed for the very opposite reason. Sarajevo was where her mother and father had gone, at least at first. Perhaps she was afraid that she would meet them there. In the street, in a café, in a shop. She would not know what to say, how to speak, how to convey her thoughts.

Or perhaps she stayed simply because she liked Foča.

When she stopped working in the dress shop, soon after her twentieth birthday, she got a job in a café-bar beside the river. She sometimes played the piano there in the evenings. For a while it was one of the most popular meeting places in the town. Milena had the temperament for that kind of work. She pretended cheerfulness when she didn't feel it; she learned how to chatter inanely to drunken customers; she learned how to spot trouble – looming arguments, bad blood – and nip it in the bud, with drinks on the house, or a friendly warning, or a word to Fudo, who ran things from his perch behind the bar.

14

There were more than forty journalists at the morning press conference in the PTT building. Danby sensed danger, especially since he knew the General believed the situation was under control.

The General thought the minister's assassination could be treated as simply another tragedy in a long line of tragedies. He would not address the question of the UN's responsibility.

Yet the deceased had been under UN protection. They had escorted a man among his enemies and had allowed him to be shot.

He might as well have been gunned down in the lobby of the General Assembly, the Professor remarked.

The minister had been travelling in a French APC. When it was stopped at a barricade the door of the APC was opened. Officially the UN refused to allow its vehicles to be inspected. Unofficially they were flexible.

On this occasion flexibility had led to murder. The door to the APC had been opened and a Rebel soldier had stepped forward and shot the minister who was sitting inside.

The reporters wanted to know why the door had been opened. Danby knew the briefing was going to home in on this single point and stay there. He also knew that there would be no satisfactory answer.

'The General will be here in a moment or two,' he announced. Bulbs were already flashing and television-camera lights started to come on. 'He'll read a statement first of all and then you'll be able to ask questions.'

The air was adversarial when the General entered the room followed by the UN commander in the city and the colonel who had been present at the incident.

The General read out a statement in French and then in English. He condemned violence and called for reason and calm. Danby knew that his boss was thoroughly unprepared for what was about to happen, unaware that his obdurate refusal to address the issue of his own troops' responsibility came over as fatuous and arrogant.

But it was worse than that, Danby realised. It was *immoral*.

The UN was not accountable. That was what the General was saying.

When he finished reading his statement, some of those who were present shouted questions, and some shouted abuse. The General blinked behind his spectacles, surprised. Danby let the mob shout for a few seconds and then he stood up and raised his arms and said, 'One at a time!'

He pointed to a wire-service journalist and nodded amiably, as if they were in the middle of a regular briefing.

'Who ordered the door open?' the man asked.

It was the first question and the second and the third. It was at the core of the matter and the General didn't want to talk about it. As the minutes passed, he pressed on, trying to charm, and then trying to be firm, and finally sounding petulant.

'Did you order the back door of the APC to be opened?' Brad asked the colonel, who had been sitting impassively as the General struggled beside him.

'The door was already open when I arrived,' the colonel said. 'I was on the point of closing it when the shooting occurred.'

'Why was the door open?'

'I don't know, but this is not an issue. I would in any case have ordered it to be opened,' the colonel replied smoothly.

'Where were you when the shots were fired?'

'I had placed myself between the minister and the soldiers outside the vehicle. A soldier fired over my shoulder at the minister. The assassin was immediately pulled away by his comrades.'

'Why did you not order your men to fire back?'

'We were outnumbered. I ordered the APC to the field hospital here.'

Brad turned to the General. 'At what time was the door of the APC opened and who ordered it to be opened?'

'That is not something I can answer. This is not an inquiry! You don't have authority to ask this!'

A wave of indignation rolled across the room and over the General.

'*You* are the commander!' Brad said. '*You* are in charge! These are questions you *should* be able to answer! If *you* won't answer, you shouldn't be sitting in that chair!'

The General glared at him.

'When was the door opened?' Brad asked again, getting his voice under control.

'General,' the familiar voice of Michael Baring intoned, 'on behalf of the entire press corps I have to ask that you bear in mind that everyone here is sympathetic to the difficulty of your position, and there is no question of an inquisition, but at the same time, with representatives of the world's media here it would seem to me, and I believe to my colleagues that –'

Brad interrupted and shouted at the General, 'Why don't you answer?'

'If I could continue,' Baring continued.

'Be quiet!' someone told him.

'Nothing will be served by a shouting match,' the General said. 'We will investigate this entire matter and I can assure you that we will try with every means at our disposal to ensure that such an incident is never repeated.'

The focus of interest now switched to the planned investigation. The General had no idea what he was going to do about that and he spent the next five minutes improvising. They asked him what kind of pressure he would exert to have the killer handed over and he had no answer. They asked him if he planned to resign and he expressed incredulity. They asked him if new orders regarding APC inspections had been issued and he refused to respond on the grounds that he couldn't talk about operational details.

Then, with his own and his organisation's reputation in tatters, he stood up and said, 'Please excuse me. I have another appointment.'

15

There was a competing narrative that challenged the French officer's account. A contingent of British troops had arrived at the place where the APC was surrounded. They advanced along the road and the Rebels gave ground, allowing them to reach the vehicle. The commander of the British unit climbed up onto the APC and spoke to the occupants, including the minister, through the hatch on the roof. When a larger French force arrived, the British were ordered to leave. According to this account, the door at the back of the APC was still closed when the British withdrew, which meant it must have been opened after the French arrived.

The French, it was believed, had tried to reason with the Rebels. The door at the back of the vehicle had been opened as a confidence-building gesture, as part of a negotiation – a negotiation that ended in the minister's death.

'They should have known better!' someone said as a crowd made its way across the car park of the PTT building after the press conference.

Brad looked round abruptly to see who had spoken. There were three correspondents. He didn't recognise them. They wore stylish kit and there was a sort of collective self-confidence about them that struck Brad as being almost repellent.

It was bitterly cold. When Brad turned to look at the men he felt a sharp blast of frigid air on the side of his neck. One of the men looked at him with an expression that was inquisitive at first and then challenging. Brad guessed this was the man who thought the French should have known better.

Brad didn't fully understand the sudden fury that engulfed him. He turned away again and walked quickly to his car. When he started the engine he jerked the steering wheel so that the tyres screeched. He had to make a U-turn to drive back into the city. Once he was headed in the right direction, he accelerated, but almost immediately he slowed down again. The road was potholed, and the ice and snow above the portholes made the surface even more treacherous. There were men and women labouring over the snow on either side pulling sledges. He didn't want to skid into the crowd.

Looking ahead at the bleak winter landscape he thought about a tropical evening eighteen months before.

Wikram was in his mid-twenties, shrewd and popular. He wore his hair in short spiky cords, truncated dreadlocks. He dressed well – linen suits, shirts immaculately pressed – and he spoke with a public school accent. His mother was Sinhalese and lived in Colombo in a rather fine house that was not quite a mansion. His father was Tamil and lived in London.

It was Wikram's idea to pursue the possibility of an interview near Kalpitiya with the reclusive leader of the Tamil Tigers.

'Are you really going to put him at risk?' someone asked Brad before he and Wikram set off. 'Are you really going to put *him* at risk just so that *you* can get a good story?'

But Wikram wanted to do it.

They left Colombo in the early afternoon in Wikram's many times made-over 1964 Zephyr. The seats were big, the suspension industrial-strength. At the first checkpoint leaving the city, the soldiers waved them on; they sailed through the checkpoints after that. They took turns to drive. Along the highway, lorries and buses spilled black smoke into the air, and in the fields boys rode oxen. On the outskirts of towns there were tree-shaded terraces amid the poverty of thatched huts and the polluted urgency of the road.

Before the Puttalam checkpoint they swung off the main road and travelled on the causeway over the salt flats at the south of the lagoon. It was just after three when they reached Palakudawa. They parked behind a coffee shop near the police station. Inside the coffee shop they ordered string hoppers, vegetables and Coke.

After eating, they drank tea and smoked.

Shortly before six, a man about Wikram's age came into the coffee shop and sat down at their table. He spoke to Wikram in Sinhala and Wikram handed over the keys of his car. The man stood up, and Wikram said, 'We are to follow him.'

There was a piece of waste ground on which half a dozen trucks were parked. Their escort led them to the back of one of the trucks, which was covered in brown canvas. He said something short and sharp and the canvas flap opened. The man indicated to Brad with a hand signal that he should climb in.

Two men were sitting beneath the canvas. The back of the truck was dark, and smelled of earth and sweat. Wikram climbed in after Brad. One of the men pointed to a spot directly behind the driving cabin where there were sacks on the floor. Brad and Wikram stepped forward and sat on the sacks, facing towards the back. Their guards sat on the other side of them.

They could not see out. The truck began moving and they drove for fifteen minutes before stopping. The guards lit cigarettes but made no move to go outside. No one spoke. They sat like that for an hour. A stream of air entered the stuffy enclosure through a vent behind Brad's head. He breathed in. The air smelled of Palmyra bark. Then the truck started again. It was almost completely dark now. They drove for another half an hour and when the truck stopped and began a complicated set of manoeuvres, Brad sensed that they were near the sea.

They sat in silence, this time for five minutes, until there was a soft tapping at the back of the truck. One of the guards opened the flap. They had reversed onto the edge of a short jetty. At the end of the jetty Brad made out the silhouette of a fishing boat.

They climbed down from the truck and walked along the jetty.

The journey across the lagoon lasted forty minutes. There were no lights on the boat. They could see very little, no silhouette of land on either side after they cast off from the jetty. There was no moon.

The skipper sat on a plastic chair in the wheelhouse and peered up at the stars from time to time. Brad watched him. It was hard to tell his age. He could have been thirty or fifty. He wore a *longee* and a dark T-shirt, and didn't acknowledge his passengers when they came on board.

The two guards sat at the stern on a low bench. Brad and Wikram perched on coiled rope that made a sort of platform at the front of the wheelhouse.

To the north they saw the pinpoint lights of government patrol boats. As they moved into the middle of the lagoon, the stars became more prominent. It was cool now. Brad felt the sea breeze and looked up from the darkness of the sea to the sky where the stars were coming out one by one, and for a moment he believed himself to be where destiny had placed him, between the sea and the stars.

At the other side there was no jetty. The guards whispered to the captain and then they climbed into the shallow water. Brad and Wikram followed, and the four of them moved quickly up the beach.

He felt cool water flood into his canvas shoes, and then the rough touch of wet sand beneath his heels and toes. His trouser cuffs were wet.

His mouth was dry. Wikram moved more efficiently than Brad, keeping up with the two guards.

The beach smelled of rotten leaves. The last little stretch before the trees was steep and they had to scramble up the incline, on their hands and knees in the sand. Then they were in the jungle.

The guards moved ahead quickly. It was almost pitch black. Brad lost sight of Wikram and tried to catch up. When he emerged onto an asphalt road, Wikram was already talking to a group of men who were standing by a pick-up truck.

'Brad,' Wikram said in a small, emotionless voice, 'we have to go back.'

'What?'

He looked from Wikram to the other men. He couldn't make out which were the guards who had brought them there, and which belonged to this side of the lagoon.

'They are taking us back now. Don't argue.'

Brad felt obliged to argue. This was absurd. There must be an explanation. They could speak to another commander. They could press on. They couldn't go back with nothing.

'What do you mean?' He smelled metal and oil from the truck and the metal of the guns that the men carried. His shoes and trousers were wet and he was frightened and felt foolish.

'Let's go,' Wikram said, walking past Brad towards the path that led to the beach.

'We're not going back just like that!'

As he spoke, Brad felt the barrel of a rifle at the side of his right knee. He recoiled and started to stumble after Wikram.

They got wet again climbing back onto the boat. The two guards came aboard with them. The other men stayed in the jungle. The vessel turned and headed out to the lagoon.

Brad and Wikram contemplated their predicament.

They had passed through all the checkpoints on the road from Colombo and had been stopped at none. It had been so easy to cross the lagoon: the government patrol boats had stayed away. Now they were dependent on men whom they had no reason to trust. This could go badly now.

They sailed through the darkness to the western shore. Brad listened to the lapping of choppy waves on the wooden hull. Wikram was silent.

Brad knew then that they would not reach Colombo together.

Or perhaps he didn't know.

This had been a life-affirming friendship, fuelled by youth and ambition and wit and easy understanding. Only on that night did it shatter.

They jumped onto the jetty at the other end. The Zephyr was parked by the side of the road.

The guards stayed on board. When Wikram and Brad were ashore, the boat turned and sailed out to the lagoon again.

'We should check the car,' Brad said. 'There might be explosives underneath, or contraband in the back.'

'What's the point? Neither of us knows what a bomb looks like,' Wikram snapped.

'What the fuck happened, Wikram?'

Wikram's face formed a humourless smile. 'Someone decided the interview wasn't a good idea,' he said. 'We wasted our time.'

They stopped in front of the car and then Wikram said, more calmly, friendliness trickling back into his voice, 'Let's get back to Talawila. There's a place there where we can sleep on the floor. It won't be comfortable, but it will do until dawn.'

Brad climbed into the driving seat. Wikram didn't object. He walked round to the passenger door.

The key was in the ignition.

'I don't get it,' Brad said.

But Wikram remained silent.

Brad swung the car onto the road and began to drive south through a scrubby area of palm trees and thick shrubs. It was like any other secondary road leading from a beach. The headlights were dipped. Brad could see clearly enough. He peered ahead looking for the access to the highway, driving slowly.

He saw the junction when they were still twenty yards away.

An army jeep was parked in front of them, but the road wasn't completely blocked. There was space to drive round and Brad's first thought was that the jeep had simply been abandoned in the middle of the road. Then he saw soldiers in the bushes to his left, and another jeep parked behind the first.

Wikram sat up in his seat and said quietly, but very firmly, 'Brad, drive round. Don't stop!'

They were moving at fifteen miles an hour. Brad looked closely to see if oil cans or tyres had been laid across the road. The way was clear.

Then a soldier stepped out from behind the first jeep and raised his rifle.

'Drive on!' Wikram shouted.

Brad could have accelerated. They might have reached the main road. There was a turn there. They would have been out of the line of fire. They could have got away.

The soldiers had not had time to prepare the barricade. They were not ready. If Brad had done what Wikram told him to do, they could have escaped.

But when Brad saw the soldier begin to raise his rifle, he saw a scared expression on the boy's face. He saw hesitation.

He stepped into that hesitation and took command.

Brad stopped the car.

'What the fuck are you doing?' Wikram snapped.

Two soldiers walked from behind the jeep. The soldier on the road had his rifle trained on the car.

The soldier in front was an officer.

'Don't get out of the car,' Wikram said.

Brad was exasperated. He wanted this finished quickly. He was very calm. He knew what to do.

The expedition had been a fiasco, but he could write it off. Now, he wanted to get back to Talawila and have a cold beer.

He opened the door and climbed out.

'Good evening,' Brad said to the officer.

There was a blow to the back of his head that crushed his thoughts. His legs buckled. He smelled petrol fumes and asphalt.

Brad heard screams. He felt blood on the back of his neck. He heard shots and then the jeeps started up and he heard them driving away. He didn't hear voices.

He did not remember how long it took him to stand up.

Wikram lay on the other side of the car. The back of his head had been blown away. Blood poured a river.

Brad sank down against the car and gazed at the red dust.

16

'It's terrible,' said Mrs Nurudinović. She shook her head. She had the habit of shaking her head and frowning, sometimes for a long time. 'It's terrible, terrible.'

'It is,' Milena agreed. She wished she could say something more. Mrs Nurudinović looked as though she had been personally bereaved by the minister's death. Milena wanted to make the old woman feel better, but no words came.

They remained silent for several moments. Milena liked sitting in Mrs Nurudinović's kitchen. It was old-fashioned, well kept, comfortable and bright. There were two very worn armchairs with white doilies over the backs. The table took up most of the space in the room. It was covered with thick brocaded cloth. At the end of the table was a window that looked onto a small closed-in balcony where Mrs Nurudinović kept her supplies: some firewood, some onions and garlic and beans, and some tins of food. The outer window had been smashed. It was covered by a tarpaulin that flapped in the freezing wind.

Mrs Nurudinović was tired. She had no energy left to remember how they had once lived in this place. Often she *stopped* herself from remembering because the contrast with the present made her heart ache.

She sighed and said to Milena, 'Let's have coffee.'

Milena sometimes brought cigarettes and coffee. At the bar she could get things like that. Mrs Nurudinović admired Milena for the way she was able to take care of herself. She had never told Mrs Nurudinović her story – how she came to be in the city. She didn't wear a wedding ring and she never spoke of a husband, but Mrs Nurudinović could tell, of course, that Milena was married: such things are clear to those who observe the world carefully.

Mrs Nurudinović could tell that Milena had never had children. She showed the sort of awkward tenderness with other people's children that is distinct from intimacy with your own.

The old woman set water boiling on the stove and worried about how little wood she had on her balcony.

'The concert will be good for you,' she told Milena brightly, changing the subject. 'You'll enjoy yourself.' She was pleased that Milena had agreed to take Nina to the children's song festival. Nine-year-old Nina and her older brother Stanislav lived on the sixth floor. Their mother was in a town in Central Bosnia, stranded there when it became impossible to get back into Sarajevo. That, at least, was what was said. Mrs Hatibović was of the opinion that the woman could have returned to her two children if she'd really had a mind to, but that the man she was living with had objected. Mrs Nurudinović didn't want to believe that this was true, but she was obliged to acknowledge, from what she knew of Nina and Stanislav's mother, that it was a possibility. In any case, Stanislav, who wasn't yet twenty, had looked after his sister, as well as making himself indispensable to neighbours, including Mrs Nurudinović and Mrs Hatibović, running errands, fetching water and firewood, and bartering his services for money and cigarettes. He'd been drafted into the civil defence. Mrs Nurudinović could see that the boy was struggling to do right by his sister, and when he told her that he wouldn't be able to take Nina to the song contest because he was on firewatch duty she had suggested Milena.

Mrs Nurudinović knew that Milena wanted to *belong*, and she also knew that this would take time. When Mrs Nurudinović first encountered Milena she thought, *here's a complicated story.* She moved into the apartment next door with practically no belongings. She earned her living at a bar that Mrs Hatibović said was an unsavoury place. She spoke with a country accent and kept to herself at the beginning. And there was that sadness about her. It wasn't the sadness of bereavement; it was some other kind of sadness.

Mrs Nurudinović placed a brass salver with a coffee pot and small brass cups on the table and fetched coffee from the recess at the end of the room opposite the balcony. She poured a handful of beans into the grinder, sat down again and began to grind.

'How they could just shoot him dead like that, in the street,' she said, returning gloomily to the earlier subject. 'It doesn't bear thinking about.'

Milena shook her head.

Sometimes it's hard to talk to someone when you don't know the most important things about them, and Mrs Nurudinović didn't know the most important things about Milena. She used to wonder, when certain topics came up in conversation – things to do with the war – whether she ought to be silent. She didn't want to hurt Milena unintentionally by speaking about politics, or places and people on the other side.

'What were those UN soldiers up to?' Mrs Nurudinović wondered. 'They were supposed to protect him.'

She was becoming very warm because of the grinder. These days, even grinding coffee exhausted her. On the radio they reported that citizens weren't getting enough to eat – as though they didn't know that already – and that one of the first signs of malnutrition was tiring easily. Mrs Nurudinović had never imagined that one day she would suffer from malnutrition, not in her worst nightmare.

Milena offered to take the grinder, and Mrs Nurudinović gratefully handed it to her. She lit a cigarette and listened to the short whirr and click as Milena turned the grinding arm, rhythmically and more regularly than Mrs Nurudinović had done.

Sitting there smoking, Mrs Nurudinović looked at the other woman's face, watching Milena as she concentrated on the grinder, her nose a little wrinkled as she worked the tricky turn at the top of the device, her lips pursed. Her cheeks were pale and she had shadows under her eyes, but she was still pretty.

Mrs Nurudinović wore a heavy velvet skirt with a hem that reached nearly to the floor. Above this she wore shirts and cardigans, and a brightly coloured headscarf. Her face was deeply lined. Her eyes were brown.

Mrs Nurudinović had never tasted alcohol. She prayed at the mosque in Čengić Vila every Friday and observed Ramadan and Kurban. She communicated with her son in Zenica by means of telepathy and she had twice seen the ghost of her late husband, once in the kitchen of her apartment and once while walking by the Miljacka a year and a day after his funeral.

She was celebrated as a reader of cups. She could interpret the meaning of curls and twists in the intricate pattern of coffee residue drained onto a saucer.

Mrs Nurudinović believed that a length of red thread when prayed over and worn on any part of the body would ward off evil. She believed that a verse of the Koran attached to a person's clothing would have the same effect.

She regarded all politicians as dishonest and incompetent, with the exception of Marshal Tito, who was wise even if inclined to vanity. From her twelfth birthday until the year after her marriage, when the garment was banned by the same Marshal Tito, Mrs Nurudinović wore a *feredža* and *zar*, covering her face and head.

She married in 1948 at the age of twenty-five. Perhaps that was another reason she liked Milena. Mrs Nurudinović had married late. She remembered the fear that tormented her as a girl when the years passed and no suitor came. There was a sweetheart in her youth, Izet, but he was killed in the war. Mrs Nurudinović knew the burden of loneliness.

There are no words sometimes to speak about sorrow.

Then came Emir, who had energy and confidence and a sense of fun – enough for both of them for half a dozen lifetimes.

Mrs Nurudinović was glad her husband didn't live to see what had become of his city and the people he loved. It would have been more than he could bear, even with his optimism and his appetite for life.

Her dowry consisted of two pillows, one set of woollen blankets and five white doilies embroidered by her grandmother on her mother's side. One of the doilies remained now at the bottom of the long wardrobe drawer, in the bedroom where Mrs Nurudinović no longer slept for fear of being killed in her sleep by an artillery shell. She slept in the hall, placing an extra wall between herself and the frontline five hundred yards way.

When she entered her husband's home on her wedding day she was given a loaf of bread wrapped in red cloth and a copy of the Koran. These symbolised a married life of integrity and wellbeing.

Her son was circumcised on his third birthday, and her husband made the Haj the year before his death, a fortuitous piece of timing that comforted Mrs Nurudinović. She believed that marriages that began between the *bajrams* of Ramadan and Kurban were ill-fated and that those who died during Ramadan were blessed.

But now she was tired. Perhaps, she thought, this was why that man's death on the Airport Road affected her. She was tired of death, every death; she was tired of the dying that now went on around her. She was afraid that one day her compassion would be used up.

She thanked God her only son was safe with his family in Zenica. His wife was a good woman. She had earned Mrs Nurudinović's confidence. Mrs Nurudinović had two grandsons, teenagers now. If those boys were taken to the army she would stop breathing.

Mrs Nurudinović and her neighbours had to organise and they had to be sharp, just to survive. A man from the fourteenth floor brought her firewood. His name was Mido. He usually came on a Tuesday. Mrs Nurudinović paid him and served him a glass of brandy. She could imagine her husband and Mido sitting at the table chatting. But now it was an effort. He was a kind man, Mido, but she thought of all the kindness in her life, she thought of sixty years of kindness and kind people and she knew that she was too old and tired to make conversation with Mido. It was the same with Amela, who collected Mrs Nurudinović's twice-weekly ration of humanitarian aid from the community centre. Mrs Nurudinović paid her a little, which she knew Amela needed because she had three children and no husband. She wished she could be kinder to Amela. She wished she could like her more, yet she didn't have the energy, she didn't have the reserves of tenderness and care.

But Milena. Maybe God had sent Milena to them. Milena needed her neighbours, Mrs Nurudinović knew.

And today her neighbours needed Milena.

Stanislav arrived as they drank coffee. When Milena used to see Stanislav, on the stairs or in the street outside when he was coming home from work, she wanted to cheer him up. He had such a sad face. He was slightly cross-eyed, which didn't make him look any more cheerful. He had a round face and drooping heavy cheeks. Milena supposed that most girls would be put off by that hangdog air.

Stanislav was very polite. Mrs Nurudinović was amused because she could see that he was in awe of Milena. He was grateful to her too.

'Shall we go now?' he asked Milena nervously.

She gave him a charming smile. Mrs Nurudinović liked the way Milena put Stanislav at ease.

Milena and Stanislav walked down to Stanislav's apartment almost in silence. The stairs were dark and in several places the thick glass had been smashed and it was possible to see far below to the car park, full of wrecked cars. A small child could have fallen through one of those holes in the glass. It made Milena shiver just to think of it. The stairs were dirty and filled with a sharp, icy odour.

Sometimes she was scared on the stairs. She hated looking through the holes in the glass.

Stanislav unlocked the door of his apartment and they stepped inside. The hall was cold, but the kitchen was warm.

'Hello, Nina,' Milena said brightly.

The little girl wore a blue velvet dress with a white collar, and her hair had been tied up at the back, with a handful of ringlets curling around the side of her face. She was beautiful. Milena knew that Nina was nervous about going to the concert with her. They had only spoken once before. She wanted Nina to enjoy herself. She wished she'd had some chocolate or sweets to bring, but chocolate was harder to come by than cigarettes.

Nina said a shy and ladylike hello.

'Ready to go?' Milena asked.

Nina nodded and stood up. Milena helped her on with her coat and she went out and put on her shoes.

'I'll be there for your song,' Stanislav said.

They went into the freezing stairway. Outside it had begun to snow. 'Do you know the way?' Nina asked. She held Milena's hand, their gloves meshing.

'Yes I do.'

They walked together across the icy ground.

17

When Terry saw and heard a tank shell explode she was shocked. It was like a giant hammer hitting the side of a building, fast and vicious and indescribably loud.

They could see where the impact occurred, on the side of a farmhouse. That morning she had peeped out of her hotel-room window, in vain, trying to identify where the sounds of explosions were coming from. Now she saw clear and close what she'd been looking for.

For a long moment she dreamed. Nothing in her life had prepared her for this. Her senses and her thoughts took an age to catch up with what she witnessed through the plastic windows of the car. She wasn't prepared for the noise, and she wasn't prepared for the overwhelming sense of force.

She glanced at Zlatko: he was frightened too, she could see. She turned away and looked through the clear plastic at snow and trees and low buildings. She didn't want to look for long because she thought that gazing out of the car was tempting fate and she didn't want to be shot in the face.

Zlatko feared the car would come off the road and get stuck in the snow. He had an idea where the garage was, the point he'd been told to try and reach. He pressed on, thinking that if the gunners directed their fire at the car then he and Terry would die.

She was clearly scared, but she was calm and he was grateful for this. Whatever happened now, it would happen to both of them.

Zlatko, his thoughts sliding with the uncertain movement of the car over new snow, didn't fully understand why he was there. He hadn't *chosen* to be here, but he hadn't avoided it either. When he was asked to bring her he agreed. Partly he was there simply because he was curious – he had a passion to know what was going on.

They passed close to the house where the tank shell had hit. Smoke rose from the wall; debris was still falling from the eaves. Then, with the same unspeakably loud crash, a second shell exploded against the same wall. There was a sighing in the air. Shockwaves hit the car.

Zlatko leaned over the steering wheel and accelerated, but the car still seemed to both of them to move over the snow very slowly.

'It's half a mile further down the road,' he told her. 'We have to carry on. There's nowhere to turn.'

He must have considered turning back, she thought, and this brought her very close to panic.

Then they heard bullets.

Zlatko accelerated again. He didn't do this because he judged that it would give them a better chance. He did it out of instinct. Getting up speed wouldn't make them any safer from small-arms fire. In fact it might increase the danger. They began to slide off the road. He slowed down and speeded up again, creating a skid that he managed to control. He was holding the steering wheel very tight. They'd been foolish to try to drive into Otes.

A bullet spun across the bonnet of the car. They could hear it drone, like an insect. They could hear mortar explosions where they were heading.

'Shit,' Terry said.

'They're shooting at us!' Zlatko remarked, as if this surprised him. If they were going to be killed then they would be killed, he thought. If they were going to survive, they would survive. There was little he could do other than drive as fast as possible towards the centre of the settlement.

The road became less potholed. They began to put more distance between themselves and the house where the tank shells had exploded. Terry looked ahead and tried to breathe steadily. Zlatko was under a greater strain. He had to focus on the road. She glanced at him again. He was crouched over the steering wheel, peering ahead bravely, like a little boy driving a dodgem at a summer fair.

He had put himself in this danger so as to bring her here. She had not properly considered this before now.

Then Terry's rational meditation was interrupted by terror.

A bullet flew towards them and – quite abruptly – stopped droning.

It tore through the chassis above the front wheel and hit the engine.

The car lurched forward. Zlatko pushed himself away from the wheel and pressed his foot down, as if that would compensate for damage to the engine. He gave up thinking about the road and the snow and the possibility of skidding, and raced the car towards a cluster of buildings fifty yards away. The engine whined.

There were more bullets, like a swarm of wasps, Zlatko thought. There were explosions ahead.

'Get your head down!' he shouted.

She hated that he shouted. If he loses his nerve, she thought, I'll lose mine. But then he added – and she was immeasurably reassured by this – 'Please.'

She cowered in the front seat. The car skidded. She sat up again and looked ahead. They were hurtling towards the open door of a low garage at the bottom of an apartment block.

The car plunged into the darkness of the garage and skidded. Terry heard men shouting on either side as her face hit the dashboard. She felt a dull pain and pulled her head back.

'Are you all right?' Zlatko asked.

'I think so.'

The doors of the car were opened from the outside.

18

The first shells landed on the morning of Sanela's twenty-first birthday. Within days there was no electricity, no water and no means of getting into or out of the city. At that time Sanela lived high up on the side of a hill in Bistrik. Now she was with Zlatko in the centre of town, in a big empty room on the top floor of the Chamber Theatre.

There was a very large, very old bed that had no mattress. When Sanela came to stay, Zlatko found blankets to put on the wooden bed board. They laid more blankets and coats and towels on top for warmth when winter set in. There were three high windows along one wall. Two had no glass and were covered by tarpaulin. The glass in the third window was broken and the cold air poured in despite the masking tape that they had used to cover up the cracks. There were thick curtains over the windows, but the room was always cold.

Sanela sat on the bed and looked at her dirty feet.

She had just enough water to make a cup of coffee *and* wash her face and hands. She calculated that she could possibly do something about her feet as well. Sanela bore the absence of electricity with fortitude, but not having water was much more of a trial. At the Holiday Inn there was sometimes running water.

Brad let Sanela take a shower there once. She had just arrived in the hotel lobby when she saw a friend running towards the stairs. He whispered over his shoulder, practically giggling, 'There's hot water!' Sanela hurried on up to Brad's room, which doubled up as his office. She could hear pipes rumbling. Everyone in the hotel was taking a shower. He stepped out of the bathroom in a towel and told her to take advantage of the running water while it lasted. The oddness of this didn't occur to her until later. She didn't know him well at that time, and he was inviting her to take a shower in his room and all she could think about was how this was a stroke of unexpected good fortune.

That was weeks ago. Now she put her tiny allowance of water into a small pot and placed the pot on top of a burner that ran on lighter fluid. The burner stood on a table in a corner of the room. There were some tins on the table, half a loaf of bread and two onions. The onions were the last fresh things they had to eat.

The ceiling was very high. There were old-fashioned plaster cornices and along the walls a narrow ledge to hang pictures. From the floor to the ledge the wall was covered by fading yellow paper; above the ledge was white plaster. The table with the stove stood against the yellow wall. On the bare floorboards beneath the table was some firewood. Sanela was endlessly pleased by this room, the big old-fashioned bed, the table with the wood below it looking tiny beneath the high ceiling. It was another world.

She made coffee and took a sip, then she placed the tiny amount of remaining water in a basin and washed her hands, face and feet. She didn't manage to make the entire surface of her feet completely wet but they felt cleaner. They quickly began to feel icy too. She dried her toes and put on two pairs of socks. Then she sat on the bed again and drank her coffee.

She could hear shelling very far away in the west, where Zlatko had taken Dr Barnes. She listened to the explosions for some time and then she brought her thoughts back into the city. She tried replacing her fear with images of snow, falling steadily, softly beyond the curtains of her room.

Sanela had met Zlatko on Ferhadija Street in the winter before the war. He was relaxed and charming and they went for coffee, upstairs at a café near the cathedral. He was carrying books, and he wore his scarf in a striking way, loosely thrown over his shoulder. He was two years older than Sanela. When they left the café Sanela didn't want to go home. She wanted to be with Zlatko in that place, with those beautiful buildings on either side, Zlatko speaking to her in the darkness.

Her recollection was interrupted when the door opened suddenly and Jamila, a tall and strikingly beautiful girl, came in and said, 'We've got a car!'

'Whose?'

'A friend of Edis. He's due to pick up some officers at the Viktor Buban Barracks. He'll take us there. We can come back with Zlatko.'

Edis, Jamila's husband, was a director at the theatre.

'Come and help me,' Jamila continued. 'One of the sets has been damaged.'

Melted snow had flooded through a hole in the roof during the night, seeping down onto the stage two floors below. The theatre had been putting on the same show for months, a sixties musical. It was hugely successful. It had become a symbol of the city – art against barbarism. Correspondents came and reported on a miraculously sophisticated performance in a city without electricity, water or enough food. Every show was packed.

When they had climbed through the blacked-out clutter in the wings Sanela surveyed the damage. A large rectangle had been discoloured by water. The matinee was due to begin in an hour, and the clapboard wouldn't be dry enough to paint before then.

'Get some newspapers,' Sanela said.

Jamila went off obediently and came back with papers.

In a corner of the auditorium just below the stage were a nearly empty tin of yellow paint and two mouldy brushes. Sanela fetched these.

'We'll make newspaper bees,' she told Jamila, 'and glue them to the set with paint.'

The scene was a garden filled with sunflowers. Half a dozen large bees hovered above the flowers. Two bees were water-logged. Sanela and Jamila recreated them with newsprint stripes.

When they had finished they stood back and admired their work. The new bees were better than the old ones, Sanela said. Triumph in adversity.

Soon after the show began, they went downstairs with Edis' friend to drive west to the children's song festival at the Viktor Buban Barracks.

19

Jusuf looked around the table. These men weren't experienced. None had been a commander before the war. They weren't on Jusuf's wavelength. They were looking for something from him that he knew it was worthless to give. They wanted him to be tough, like Sylvester Stallone. Two or three, Jusuf knew, would be difficult when they were ordered to display pragmatism rather than heroics. But he considered this with the calmness that characterised everything he did. The stillness in his manner began to impose itself on the meeting.

On the table, among the maps, there were automatic rifles and overflowing ashtrays. Things ought to have been arranged here in the same way they would have been arranged at a military academy – with order. None of the men had been to military academy, however, and now wasn't the time for basic training. It was like commanding a whole battalion of men in the Bakir Mehmedbasić mould. There wasn't much fear in the room. Probably there wasn't *enough* fear, and there was more bravado than could possibly be useful.

'No additional units can be deployed from the city,' Jusuf said.

He spoke softly. It was the best way to get their attention. There were eight men, all exhausted, all angry. The oldest was above fifty; the youngest in his mid-twenties. There were two gangsters, Jusuf knew, and the rest came from a range of professions – an engineer, a schoolteacher; one had been a dress designer before the war. These were the field officers responsible for keeping Otes in government hands. They had performed with extraordinary initiative and courage. Jusuf was their leader and they had followed him until now. He could only wonder if they would follow him through the final act.

Zdravko, the youngest, reacted predictably. He slammed the table with his fist, nearly knocking over one of the rifles, and shouted, 'Fuck them!' Then he glared at Jusuf.

The others were impressed by Zdravko. He was fearless. If he hadn't been so very undisciplined Jusuf would have been impressed by him too. But now Zdravko irritated him, though he made sure his irritation wasn't visible. He waited till Zdravko withdrew his fist from the table. The others watched.

'It can't be done,' one of the older men said. He was fat, unshaven, as unmilitary as everyone else, but he seemed to have a firm grasp of what was happening. 'Without more men, we have to withdraw from Viktorija – and if we withdraw from Viktorija we have to withdraw all along the line. We can't hold on.'

Zdravko mumbled, 'If Viktorija goes –' but he didn't finish the sentence.

The room was choked with cigarette smoke.

Jusuf stood up and said, 'Let's take a look.' He pointed to Zdravko and said, 'You come with me.'

They went outside. He was glad to be out of the room. It was now a question of saving an impossible situation. He wanted to get on with it.

Anti-aircraft rounds slammed into the building across the street, a jerry-built eighties apartment block with paper-thin walls. Pieces of concrete showered down to the frozen earth mingled with smoke and ash and a fine snow of asbestos particles.

Nearby there was a crack of small-arms fire. Zdravko paid no attention. They walked, keeping close to the wall, as far as the end of the building. There was a sandbagged emplacement there. They crouched behind the sandbags and looked ahead: a large square, with an L-shaped apartment block on one side; on the other side some lock-ups and a couple of two-storey houses. The road passed in front of the emplacement and then made a left turn past the houses and on towards the river and the enemy line.

Zdravko stood up and began running across the road towards the apartment block. Jusuf waited ten seconds and then followed. They ran in a straight line, across the road and then across the waste ground in the middle of the square, following a track past deep shell holes and piles of steel and rubble half buried in snow.

Jusuf reached the apartment block thirty seconds after the younger man, who was doubled up in the entrance to the building getting his breath back.

The entrance was covered in rubble. There was smoke in the air. Jusuf looked past Zdravko and saw a soldier on the landing of the stairway. The soldier put a finger to his lips and indicated that they should follow him. They stood up and clambered over the rubble, making more noise than they wanted to, and began climbing the stairs. There was broken glass on the landing.

They followed the soldier into a first-floor apartment, clothes and furniture strewn on the floor, broken glass everywhere. Haris, the unit commander, knelt by the window. He turned and indicated silently that they should join him there. He waved his hand in a keep-your-heads-down motion. They lumbered over to where he knelt.

Through the window, on a corner of the street below, less than thirty yards away, Jusuf saw what it was that held Haris' attention – the cannon of a Rebel tank protruded from a narrow lane. Half a yard of green metal was visible.

'It came this morning,' Haris whispered. 'It covers the distance between here and Viktorija. As long as that stays, we can't reinforce Viktorija, or withdraw – whichever you've decided to do.'

'Anti-tank?' Jusuf asked.

He was annoyed. If the tank had been sitting there since this morning he should have known about it. The men under his command couldn't – or wouldn't – follow the simplest procedure. Communications between the forward units and the command centre were thoroughly inadequate.

'There's a unit in Viktorija,' Haris said, and from the way he spoke Jusuf grasped that Haris believed the game was up. 'They have no ammo.'

'I'll take it out,' Zdravko whispered. 'We have ammo for this one.'

'How many guys do we have here?' Jusuf asked Haris.

'Forty.'

'In Viktorija?'

'Maybe a hundred.'

There was a crash. It sounded like a mortar exploding on the ground floor. They could feel blast pressure on the concrete and the three of them fell back from the window.

'Shit!' Haris muttered, landing on broken glass. He lifted his hand and stared at a deep cut between his thumb and his index finger. Blood poured across his knuckles. He used his other hand to tear a piece of cloth from a child's dress lying on the floor beside him and tied it over the cut.

As he was doing this they heard shouts from the apartment above. Then there were two short bursts of automatic fire. More wild lack of discipline, Jusuf thought, beginning to share some of Haris' sense of hopelessness. They were responding to the mortar impact with small arms. There was a long answering volley from the building across the street. There were enemy troops on the corner, where the tank waited.

Zdravko helped Haris to the back of the room and the three of them settled behind an upturned dining table.

'We have to take out that tank,' Haris repeated. 'They'll finish us off otherwise.'

Jusuf unclipped the walkie-talkie from his belt. It had no cover and the metal was frigid. He spoke into it, trying not to hold it directly against the side of his head. He ordered two men from the anti-tank unit to be sent over with two shells and a launcher.

'I'll go with them,' Zdravko said.

'You will,' Jusuf agreed.

The two men arrived less than a minute later. The younger wasn't more than twenty-one. He wore a bandolier over his camouflage combat jacket and a red pirate scarf over his helmet. The other had an earring in one ear; he wore a brown raincoat and a brown trilby with a feather in it, the hat sitting on his head at a jaunty angle. He had a gold filling in one of his front teeth. The men scurried up the stairs and joined the others behind the upturned table.

They stayed there for several seconds and then followed Zdravko to the window. Jusuf watched Zdravko point towards the tank. Zdravko looked at each of the men as he explained what they had to do. Jusuf liked the way Zdravko was operating now. He was clear-headed and systematic; he had subsumed his anger, he was engaged in the operation and he looked as though he was still capable of discipline and efficiency.

Zdravko pointed down the street, to a position in front of the area designated as Viktorija, a collection of low-rise buildings on the edge of the village.

From there they could unleash their two rounds with a clear line of fire. They'd have to get out immediately. The enemy would bring down artillery on their firing position within seconds of the assault.

Zdravko led the two men out of the room and down the stairs. Haris and Jusuf moved back to the window. They waited more than five minutes before anything happened. That was as long as they should have waited, Jusuf judged. Zdravko appeared to know what he was doing. They'd found their firing position and coordinated their sights properly. They had to make this attack count. They wouldn't have another chance.

Two explosions, about ten seconds apart, rocked the little lane where the tank was sitting. Jusuf and Haris saw smoke and heard shouting from the enemy infantry in the building next to the tank. There was more small-arms fire and then about twenty seconds later, mortar shells started slamming down on the position from which Zdravko and his crew had fired on the tank.

'It's a hit!' Haris whispered. He was peering at the corner, which was obscured by smoke. 'It's a hit!'

They saw the cannon as the smoke began to clear. It wasn't level, but raised a little. It started to disappear as the tank rolled back down the lane. Jusuf swore. They hadn't eliminated it altogether.

'Could be on an incline,' Haris whispered. 'Could be rolling back without any power.'

'It's moving back,' Jusuf allowed. 'Let's get on with it.'

He switched the radio frequency and said into the cold receiver, 'Viktorija. Viktorija.'

Read you.

'One turtle stunned. You ready to come home?'

Ready.

He recited the withdrawal codes and listened as the Viktorija commander ordered his men back to the reserve line.

Haris and Jusuf waited for more than ten minutes. They returned to the cover of the table. Haris sat as though in a trance. He was close to collapse.

Then the radio crackled. *Everyone home.*

'Let's get your men out of here,' Jusuf told Haris.

Haris moved out to the stairway, holding his left hand in front of him, the flower-patterned bandage covered in blood, and began ordering the withdrawal. Jusuf climbed down to the ground floor and walked to the edge of the entrance. He scanned the lock-ups on the other side of the square for any sign that the attackers had begun to move forward. Then he lunged out into the open and began running on the path between the shell holes and the piles of rusting steel and broken masonry. Above the sound of his own breathing he heard bullets.

20

Even if there had been no Olympics, Sarajevo would have presented a spectacular and intimidating proposition to three young women from Foča. It was a real city, a place where everyone didn't know everyone else.

That morning, on the bus with Mira and Jasmina, Milena was elated. The skyscrapers in Alipašino Polje gleamed at the entrance to the city. The buildings went up and up in ragged rows. The impression of precipitous, grand, confident concrete was magnified by their location on top of a hill. They looked beautiful in the early morning. Milena gawked. Then she caught herself doing this and reined in her excitement. She didn't want to look like an awe-struck country girl, particularly in front of the other two awe-struck country girls.

When the bus pulled into the terminal opposite the Tito Barracks and Milena, Jasmina and Mira climbed sleepily down to the platform the driver shouted, 'Enjoy yourselves, ladies!' and all three started giggling again.

The bus station was full of people. It was half past seven on a February morning. Cold enough to make the straps on a sports bag stiffen. They walked into the main terminal beneath a grey corrugated roof. The steel pillars holding up the roof looked newly painted. They were navy blue, bright and shining. The whole terminal shone. Snow was piled high on the dividing bays between the platforms, making white stripes on a field of water-black concrete.

Milena had never seen so many foreigners. There were people of every colour.

Tired, excited, uncomfortable from the long early-morning journey propped on a hard seat, Milena was seized by an unfamiliar joy.

There were tour guides with little flags organising groups of visitors. Small parties of brightly coloured anoraks and hats set off from the terminal like explorers. They had guides, or maps, or pieces of paper with addresses and instructions.

Mira's uncle was supposed to meet the girls. But he was not there. They waited for twenty minutes. Then Mira went in search of a phone. Milena and Jasmina sat on the bags, looking out at the white stripes of snow, listening to foreigners chatting and laughing in their incomprehensible languages.

'No answer,' Mira confessed, crestfallen, when she returned. 'Shall we walk there?' she asked in a tiny voice. 'It isn't far.'

So they picked up their bags and instead of travelling by car as they had expected, grandly, like visiting princesses, they trekked in single file over snow-packed pavements to Čengić Vila.

It took them nearly half an hour, and when they reached Mira's aunt's house there was no one at home.

The apartment was on the first floor, up a double flight of steps. It was cold in the stairwell, like standing in a deep freeze. It was dark. The walls were grey.

Mira knocked on the door and rang the bell.

Milena put her bag on the floor and sat on it. She rummaged in her handbag for cigarettes. The packet was almost empty, bashed out of shape. She took one of the two remaining cigarettes and lit it. Exhaling, she looked ahead through the semi-darkness at the grey concrete.

Mira started to cry, because she had let the others down. Jasmina started to cry because she had been let down. Milena smoked.

They had been in the narrow, cold stairwell for more than five minutes when the door of the apartment opposite Mira's aunt's opened and a young man looked out.

Later, Milena told Jasmina and Mira that when she first saw Miroslav she saw her future, laid out like a piece of sheet music. She was already humming the melody in the time it took her to stand up and stub her cigarette out on the grimy tiles.

Miroslav looked a little like a rock star. He had just got out of bed and his hair stood up at the back; he was handsome if dishevelled.

He looked from one girl to the next, Milena last.

'We are supposed to be staying here,' Mira told Miroslav, pointing to the other apartment. 'But my aunt and uncle didn't come to meet us.'

'You must be Mira,' he said.

The girls let out a sigh like a gentle breeze, balmy on the frigid stairs. That Mira was known to her aunt and uncle's neighbour augured well.

'This is Jasmina and Milena,' Mira said, relieved.

Miroslav looked from Mira to Jasmina and then to Milena. He put his hand out, open palm pointing down like a theatre usher showing patrons to seats in the front row. 'They went to collect you at the bus station,' he said. He had a pleasant voice, a light baritone shaded by amusement. 'The car wouldn't start so they left late. They probably passed you on the road. Come on inside and wait.'

They didn't say anything, just trooped past Miroslav. Milena wanted to look at his face again. They almost touched in the doorway. She wanted to take his outstretched hand. He closed the door.

In the small, bright sitting room Mira and Jasmina sat on the sofa against the wall facing a teakwood and glass display cabinet that took up the opposite wall. There were crystal figurines – dogs and swans and elephants – in the central section of the cabinet. Milena sat on an armchair facing the door. Light streamed through the window behind her.

'My name is Miroslav,' he said.

He went into the kitchen, separated from the sitting room by a partition wall with a large opening. The girls looked at one another.

'Coffee?' Miroslav asked.

They said yes at the same time, a staggered chorus that made them start to giggle again.

He looked through the opening in the wall. Milena thought he would ask why they were laughing, but he didn't. He looked at her, then turned away and began to grind the coffee. When it was ready he poured it into a small copper jug and brought the jug with four copper cups on a tray. He sat on a low wooden stool, facing Mira and Jasmina, and poured. Then he had to stand up again because he had forgotten to bring sugar. They watched him walk back into the kitchen. He wore faded blue jeans and a T-shirt bearing the name of a Yugoslav pop group. His hair still stood up at the back.

He told them he came from near Foča. He was in his second year studying mechanical engineering in Sarajevo; he rented a room in the apartment.

They were finishing their coffee when they heard the sound of an engine shutting off in the street outside. Miroslav went to the window and stood very close to Milena.

'That's them,' he said, pleased. They heard voices on the stairs.

Mira's uncle was short and effusive. He looked up at everyone and shook hands vigorously. Mira's aunt was large and excitable. She was talking when she entered the sitting room and still talking minutes later when they moved out of the sitting room and across the hall. Her husband carried the girls' bags, walking briskly. He turned sideways to exit Miroslav's apartment and then tried to enter his own apartment face on, perhaps feeling that a sideways approach was undignified. The bags hit the doorposts and he paused for a moment before turning hesitantly sideways in order to edge into his house. The bags appeared to engulf him.

Once he was alone Miroslav checked the boiler above the bath. The thermostat showed a tiny amount of hot water. He brushed his teeth and undressed and stepped beneath the shower. By the time his hair was properly wet, the water had turned lukewarm, and by the time he had finished applying shampoo, it was cold. He splashed himself in a heroic frozen flourish beneath the shower. He wanted to be clean. He stepped out and dried himself quickly. In his room he found socks and a fresh T-shirt. He combed his hair and put on his jacket, checked his pockets for cigarettes, money and car keys, and stepped out.

When he knocked the door of the opposite apartment, it was Milena who answered. She smiled. She too had changed her clothes and combed her hair. Miroslav liked the jumper she wore, a brown crewneck with a narrow blue line around the neck.

'I wondered if you would like a lift into town,' he said. 'I have a car.'

The girls went with Miroslav in his car to Zetra Stadium and when they got there a complex and efficient rearrangement of aspiration and desire took place. The conclusion was that Jasmina and Mira would stay at Zetra to see the ice skating, while Milena and Miroslav went off to explore Sarajevo together in Miroslav's car.

They were among hundreds of thousands of visitors, and yet they were cocooned inside an intimacy that settled on them the moment they were together.

Sleek, brightly coloured tour buses ferried visitors to the day's events, creating traffic jams. There were jams on the pavements too, huge numbers of pedestrians waiting at intersections. At every corner people studied maps, looking this way and that. There were visitors from all over the world. Milena and Miroslav developed a game: how to tell Germans from Americans, and British from French. The Americans were badly dressed and self-confident. The British were just badly dressed. The French were better dressed.

The Germans were just German, showing no apparent intention of having fun.

Miroslav knew a student restaurant in Marijn Dvor. Milena waited on the pavement while he parked the car. He had to step over a low wall of ploughed snow to reach her. She held out her hand and he took it. He smelled of soap and his hair looked untidy though he'd combed it. They walked slowly through the cold, people all around them speaking languages that Milena and Miroslav didn't understand.

The restaurant was busy and they had to wait in a queue. They ordered sandwiches and Cokes. Milena and Miroslav spoke about the Olympics and about Sarajevo and Foča. Milena told him about the time she went to the coast with her mum. Miroslav had three brothers and two sisters. They all still lived near Foča. He liked Sarajevo but he liked Foča more. He felt at home there.

They held hands and laid out for one another a complete and faithful account of their lives.

Like many others who were there, they remembered those Olympics as a time of hope and happiness.

21

Jim Danby spent the morning not answering one question: who opened the door of the APC?

Reporters insisted that the information they wanted would serve the public interest. The minister's murder was being depicted as a powerful symbol of UN incompetence. But much of the media frenzy was fuelled by voyeurism, Danby thought.

His formal comment was evasive, incomplete and unsatisfactory. He didn't know.

He didn't know because he wasn't being told.

And he didn't know because in some part of his normally dispassionate brain he didn't *want* to know. He was pretty sure the answers to half a dozen questions concerning the minister's murder would not be palatable.

Yet he was angry because he had been cut out of the information loop. Danby was one of nature's insiders. He had enjoyed the confidence of the French and the British. Now the French were circling the wagons and Danby was on the outside.

He had been sitting with Michael Baring for a quarter of an hour. This hadn't improved his mood, so he was relieved when

Brad came into the foyer, unfastening his flak jacket as he walked from the door. Brad would want answers to the same unanswerable questions, but at least he'd be straightforward, in contrast to Baring, who was irritatingly circuitous.

'Afternoon,' Brad said, nodding towards Baring and then, with slightly more enthusiasm, towards Danby. 'Been out west,' he added. 'Looks like government troops are pulling back.'

'I've been onto the city command,' Baring said, looking first at Brad and then at Danby. 'They tell me it's a storm in a teacup, nothing to worry about.'

Brad shrugged. 'They've withdrawn from the western edge of Otes. The Rebels are pressing hard. They've brought in more tanks. Wouldn't say the government can hold on much longer.'

'I was told the number of tanks has been exaggerated,' Baring insisted.

'The government side is well dug in, but they have no more supplies coming from the city, and the road can be cut at any time.'

'What's the civilian position?' Danby asked, envisaging a new humanitarian catastrophe, and more blame directed at the UN.

'About 1500 people still in the settlement,' Brad said. 'They'll have to run a gauntlet on the road out ... I did and it's not something I want to do again.'

Baring wondered if Brad had been in Otes to report on Dr Barnes' mercy mission. He had thought Anna was covering the evacuation.

'What made you go there today?' he asked.

'There's a battle on.'

Danby smiled.

'Yes, but today?' Baring persisted. 'The battle's been going on for weeks.'

Brad and Anna had agreed to travel across the airport together in the afternoon to talk to the Rebels. Brad wanted to see the situation in Otes at first hand before that.

'Just doing my job,' he said. 'Not as brilliantly as you, of course. But I thought I might have a shot at finding out what's happening.'

Baring noted that Danby's smile had broadened, and he resolved to visit Otes at the earliest opportunity. He wasn't about to be made a fool of by a drunk with a dubious reputation. He dropped the name of a senior commander and asked Brad if he'd spoken to him.

'Who's he?'

Baring smirked. 'The man in charge of government forces in the west of the city. I've had a chat with him. He gave me a full rundown. His assessment is at odds with what you've told us; not that I am for a minute suggesting you haven't given us an accurate eyewitness account, but he's a pretty smart cookie. I'd tend to put my money on a soldier when it comes to military matters.'

'Any progress on the assassination?' Brad asked Danby.

'You were there this morning,' Danby said. 'Nothing new.'

'Thought you were supposed to be launching an inquiry!' Brad hadn't intended to be confrontational. Baring's put-down didn't help – Brad thought the other man probably *did* have good contacts in the military. But once exasperation had spilled into his line of thought, he was unable to recover a steadier tone. 'Has it started? Who's conducting it? Who are they going to speak to? What's going on? Where's the General?'

There were no real answers, at least no satisfactory ones. He knew that. He'd asked himself the same kind of question a thousand times about that seaside road in Sri Lanka.

'Let me see if there's anything new,' Danby said. Withdrawing to the Situation Room offered time out. He stood up. 'I'll be back in a tick.'

Major Thomson passed him on the stairs. Danby considered the major to be a walking liability, and he would not have chosen to leave him alone in the same room with Brad and Baring, but he couldn't order the other man back upstairs.

The major ambled across the lobby and sat down. 'These buggers won't give up,' he said. He had been giving out *no comments* on the phone for an hour.

Baring smiled sympathetically.

Thomson liked Baring. He was, in Thomson's view, a cut above the other hacks.

'Which buggers?' Brad asked.

'The lot of them, particularly the locals.'

'You mean the press?'

'Well, yourselves excluded, of course,' Thomson said, 'but more particularly the locals.'

'All of them?' Brad asked.

'Yes, all of them! I honestly don't know why we bother. I mean if the people in this country are determined to kill one another, if they really want to slit one another's throats why don't we just let them get on with it!'

'Sterling sentiments,' Baring remarked.

'Yes, but you see, as far as this murder on the Airport Road is concerned, he was travelling under *your* protection,' Brad said. 'If you planned to withdraw that protection you might have let him know beforehand.'

'I don't think that's fair,' Baring said.

'I don't think it's fair either!' Brad snapped. 'I think it's damned *un*fair! It's a breach of contract. In this case resulting in death.'

'We didn't start this war,' Thomson said. 'We're here to do some good, and we've got a lot to be proud of. This incident is beginning to obscure the positive side of UN operations.' He looked at both of them. 'And to demand the General's resignation!' the major continued, getting worked up. 'It's impertinent. None of this is the General's fault.'

'Who's demanded the General's resignation?' Baring asked.

'The government. The Cabinet sent a note,' Thomson said.

'What's that?' Danby had returned.

'The Cabinet has called for the General's resignation,' Baring told Danby, as if he'd known this for ages.

'We received a message earlier,' Thomson explained to Danby in a tone now shaded with petulance. 'While you were out.'

'What's the General's response?' Brad asked. He and Baring looked from Danby to Thomson and back again to Danby.

Thomson opened his mouth to speak but Danby had recovered his composure. 'I can tell you that the General is committed to carrying on his work here for the sake of the civilian population, and the tragic events of the last day will not alter the basic commitment of the UN. That's all for now.'

22

When Terry stepped out of the car and saw Anna she felt as though she'd been friends with the other woman for years. A familiar face was infinitely comforting.

Anna stood at the other end of a long concrete garage that was filled with soldiers. Men milled around smoking and arguing, or sat sullenly beside their rifles on the cold concrete floor.

Zlatko and Anna greeted each other with kisses on both cheeks. Anna's black ringlets moved from side to side, her face tilting upwards to avoid grazing Zlatko with her helmet.

After he had kissed Anna he said to Terry, 'I forgot!'

He returned to the car and took two steel helmets from the back seat. He put one on and handed the other to Terry.

'We were supposed to wear these on the way here! Sorry!'

The helmet was heavier than she would have imagined. If she moved her head abruptly, she would sprain her neck. Zlatko still had his coat unbuttoned, the scarf thrown over his shoulder foppishly, and now the helmet perched on his head in an incongruous, inelegant way. He looked utterly unmilitary.

'You're going to meet the little boy?' Anna asked.

'I'm going to examine him, see if he can travel.'

'May I come with you?'

'Of course!' Terry said, a little surprised by how enthusiastically she agreed.

Zlatko took the letter he'd shown at the checkpoint and walked over to the corner of the garage, where two men seemed to be issuing orders. One of the men took the letter and read it; then he spoke to Zlatko and at the same time signalled to a soldier who had been standing beside the car. The soldier and the man conferred with Zlatko. Then the soldier and Zlatko joined Terry and Anna.

'Shall we proceed to the rendezvous?' Zlatko asked. 'This is our escort.'

The soldier was about ten years younger than Terry, three or four years younger than Anna. He was very big, with a shaved head, blue eyes, a boyish smile and a complete military uniform except for his white training shoes. He nodded amiably and addressed them in a deep voice, slowly and seriously like a teacher addressing a class of teenagers.

'Stay close behind him,' Zlatko translated. 'It's dangerous and we have to move fast.'

They left the garage by means of a shallow concrete tunnel that led into a nearby street. The soldier's jacket made a rough scuffing sound; his training shoes crunched in the snow and he gave a little cry as he lunged into the cold air. Anna followed. Then Terry, then Zlatko.

Terry glanced at the broken windows of buildings on two sides, sharp shards of glass reflecting white snow against the black backgrounds of wrecked interiors; the walls were grey and white and beneath the snow the outline of grass verges could just be made out in front of the ground-floor windows. There was a smell of burning rubber.

Anna was about twenty yards in front. Terry could hear the sound of the camera bag chafing the back of Anna's waterproof jacket. It was like a steady sigh floating among the devastated buildings. Anna ran in a tentative, rather unathletic way – not at all as Terry would have expected: the way she moved made her look somehow vulnerable.

And then she fell.

Terry watched in astonishment and then she heard Anna swear.

The soldier stopped and came back to see what was wrong. Terry and Zlatko caught up.

'Move on!' the soldier told Zlatko and Terry.

Terry didn't understand the words but the meaning was clear.

'Are you all right?' she asked Anna, who was getting to her feet again.

The soldier shouted again. He had taken Anna by the elbow.

'I'm all right!' Anna said. 'Let's keep moving!'

It took Terry several seconds to realise that Zlatko was pulling her forward. 'We can't stay here!' he shouted.

She wrenched her arm away. The soldier and Anna had moved ahead again. Terry and Zlatko ran side by side along the front of the building opposite the tunnel and then across a piece of wasteland towards another, taller building.

There was small-arms fire very close, and the building at the end of the street was on fire. Broken glass and piles of masonry were strewn across the floor of the bombed-out shop that they were running towards. The other side of the shop opened onto a narrow road.

The soldier stopped at one end of the building and looked ahead, then he launched himself again into the open and the others followed. They ran down the middle of the road towards a large apartment block. Anna and the soldier entered first.

'Is it very painful?' Terry asked. Anna was leaning against a concrete wall. Water from the building above trickled down the concrete on either side of her.

'It was a piece of metal,' she said. 'I didn't see it.' She lifted her right foot. The side of her boot had been gouged.

Terry crouched down and began to unlace Anna's boot.

The soldier said something.

'We can't stay here,' Zlatko translated.

Terry slipped off the boot. 'Does it hurt?'

'A little.'

The soldier spoke again.

Terry pulled Anna's sock down far enough to examine her ankle and the side of her foot.

'Move it in a circle,' she said.

Anna did as she was told.

'Does it hurt?'

'It's OK, I think.'

Terry pulled the sock back up, let Anna push her foot back inside the boot and then tied the lace so quickly that Anna didn't have time to bend down and do it herself.

Terry stood up and nodded to the soldier. 'We can go.'

He led them to the end of the corridor over an uneven surface of fallen masonry and broken glass. Terry watched Anna step among the debris. She would have a bad bruise, but it wasn't more serious than that.

At the end of the corridor there was a steel door. The soldier hammered on the door and shouted. The heavy metal swung open almost immediately and they were shepherded into a pitch-black space. Terry heard male voices.

'There are steps here,' Zlatko said. 'Please be careful.'

Terry felt around her until she found the top of a metal banister and then she began to climb down. The basement was illuminated by weak light from two windows near the ceiling. Steel sheets had been placed over the windows to protect against shelling, but enough space had been left to allow some light to trickle through. There were around a hundred people there. A smell of oil and urine hung over the room. People whispered. A baby cried. The occupants of the shelter watched the new arrivals carefully. A woman walked towards them.

Edisa Pejanović was tall and grey-haired and in her late thirties, elegantly dressed in winter travelling clothes that were dirty but well cut – and she had a distinguished face, with intelligent eyes and narrow lips that might have been severe if they hadn't been turned up in a faint, welcoming smile. She spoke quietly but confidently to Zlatko, who turned and said to Anna and Terry, 'This is Miro's mother.'

Mrs Pejanović extended her hand to Terry and said in English, 'My great pleasure, Doctor. Please come to meet my son.'

She led them along a complicated trail among cases and boxes and frightened people to the back of the room where Miro lay in a cot. He looked up at them.

Terry placed a hand on the little boy's forehead and said, '*Zdravo*, Miro.'

23

When Miro saw the visitors he smiled. At first he thought that the man wearing a helmet that was too big for him was the doctor. The man looked down at Miro and made a funny face. Then one of the women looked down at him and Miro knew she was the doctor even before his mother told him so. She looked at him the way doctors did.

She said *Zdravo*, which he hadn't expected because he'd been told she wouldn't know how to say anything in their language. His arm was sore, where the tube was attached, and he was trying not to be sick. His mother said in English, 'This is Dr Barnes.'

And Miro replied in English, as they had practised: 'Good morning, Dr Barnes.'

'Good morning, Miro,' she said, just like his mother said she would.

Then she said something else in English and he didn't understand, so he let his mother answer for him. She knew how to speak English and French and Russian.

'How are you this morning, Miro?' Terry asked. The little boy gave her a blank look. He was pale and dehydrated.

'He has been practising how to greet you,' Mrs Pejanović explained, 'but he knows just a few words in English.' She was self-possessed, Terry thought, very calm.

Mrs Pejanović was pleased that Terry had arrived with helpers. It suggested a certain competence. The presence of Zlatko and Anna boosted her confidence.

'Would you like coffee, or perhaps tea? Or some juice?' Mrs Pejanović asked in her textbook English.

Terry couldn't imagine putting anyone in that place to the trouble of serving drinks.

'We are guests,' Zlatko said, in a low voice so that Mrs Pejanović couldn't hear. 'It is polite to accept.'

Soon afterwards, an old woman brought a tray with very small coffee cups and a brass pot, as well as a plate of dry cakes, and they sat around Miro's cot and drank.

Miro's mother recited symptoms, medication, crises and provisional treatments. She knew what Terry wanted to know. Terry understood the eternal watch this woman kept, monitoring every tiny deviation from the norm of her son's condition, which was critical. His temperature was dangerously high. He certainly couldn't be moved today.

'When's your birthday?' Terry asked Miro brightly, as the sound of her voice was drowned out by the noise of an explosion in the street above. Her hand shot up to her mouth and she spilled coffee. She looked at the others, startled, but they were calm, even Miro.

The basement trembled; dust and fine pieces of debris showered down from the ceiling onto the people camped below.

'Tank shells,' Mrs Pejanović said. She touched Terry's arm for a moment and smiled sympathetically.

Anna stood up and began taking photographs. She had her back to the cot as the camera clicked and whirred. She moved through the shelter, stopping to talk to an old couple sitting on suitcases against a damp concrete wall. Anna crouched down to chat and Terry saw that she had a notebook balanced on her knee.

Mrs Pejanović had translated Terry's question about his birthday to Miro. He blinked up at the doctor and told her when his birthday was and Mrs Pejanović translated into English. Close up, Terry could see the effects of malnutrition on Mrs Pejanović's skin. Her eyes were watery and the veins on the backs of her hands stood out. Her hands trembled slightly, but she was focused and calm. She must have been very strong to sustain her child in these hellish conditions until now.

The drip bag above the cot was almost empty. Terry asked Mrs Pejanović for a replacement. A new bag was taken from a cardboard box beneath the cot. 'You came just in time,' Mrs Pejanović said when she saw Terry looking at the nearly empty box.

Terry replaced the empty bag on the hook over the cot. She looked down at Miro and smiled and said, '*Dobro*.' He rewarded her with a very friendly smile. She felt better.

'How can he be carried?' she asked Mrs Pejanović.

'In the cot.' Her tone surprised Terry, because Mrs Pejanović for the first time betrayed a sense of doubt. Terry wondered if the other woman had expected her to arrive with a medical unit, a stretcher, an ambulance. She guessed that Mrs Pejanović had gone over in her head a thousand times the practicalities of carrying her son from here.

There were more explosions above and they could hear the rat-tat-tat of small-arms fire. It was risky running unencumbered; even riskier carrying a little boy. 'It's quite sturdy,' Mrs Pejanović added, recovering some of her earlier assurance. 'He had to be lifted over garden walls when we came.'

'He can't be moved today,' Terry said, preparing an injection. She placed the syringe in a valve on the back of Miro's left hand. 'He's going to be very sleepy for a while and he'll need plenty of liquid. Do you have water? Juice?'

Mrs Pejanović nodded.

'We'll be able to move him in the morning.' As Terry said this she was confident that Miro's condition wouldn't prevent them from getting him out the next day. The real question was whether or not they would be able to enter and leave the settlement.

Zlatko may have read her thoughts. 'We'll speak to the commander,' he said.

She turned and looked at Mrs Pejanović. She wanted to reassure her. She wanted to tell her that she'd get her son out of this terrible place, that tomorrow evening Miro would be in London receiving the treatment he needed. But she knew that this would be foolish. She took Mrs Pejanović by the hand and said, 'I will be here in the morning.'

Mrs Pejanović nodded. Terry looked down at Miro and smiled and said, 'See you soon!' He smiled, but his mother didn't translate, and when Terry looked at her again there was something like distrust in Mrs Pejanović's eyes.

Zlatko led Terry back through the shelter towards the stairs and Anna folded her notebook, hurrying after them.

'We'll speak to the commander now,' Terry told Zlatko.

He noted the change in her manner. She was finding her feet.

They were allowed through the steel door at the top of the stairs. Zlatko led them to the end of the corridor and stepped out into the street. Immediately, he stepped back in again. There was a volley of small-arms fire. He could hear the tails of bullets. Buzzing insects.

'Are *we* shooting or are *they* shooting?' Terry asked.

'*We* are, I think!' He was shaken. 'Let's get a little more organised,' he said. He tied his scarf in a knot, buttoned his coat and fastened the strap of his oversized helmet. Terry pulled on her gloves, thick suede mittens with white fur at the wrists. Anna stepped to the other side of the doorway and photographed them.

They looked briefly at the camera. Terry's expression was concerned, but she was composed. Anna framed them from the waist up. Zlatko wore a look of bafflement, as though he had just realised the oddness of where they were and what they were doing.

The camera whirred and then they heard the sound of boots coming towards them on the snow. Their escort dived into the doorway and crashed against the wall. Anna photographed him sitting on the ground. Unlike the others, he looked as though he'd been born to go into battle.

When they had all become accustomed to the presence of the soldier, he began speaking to Zlatko, who translated with his old poise: 'He apologises. He was visiting his mother in a shelter nearby. He was delayed by the intensity of the shooting.'

The soldier looked at Terry and Anna with a self-deprecating expression. He said something else to Zlatko.

'Are we ready to go now?' Zlatko asked Terry and Anna.

They nodded.

When they were out in the street there was an explosion a little bit further ahead: after the noise of the blast they heard the shattering of glass and falling masonry. There was debris everywhere; an overturned, fire-blackened car blocked one doorway.

They made it to the arcade, where the soldier glanced at the two women and spoke to Zlatko again.

'He says don't stay so close to one another,' Zlatko translated. 'It's better that we are spread out a little. Being close together is dangerous.'

The soldier ran out of the arcade and along beside the building exposed to the large open concourse on his right. Anna followed. Then Terry. Then Zlatko.

Terry watched Anna and tried to keep her distance. She was conscious of fear – not to have been afraid would have been idiotic. But as well as fear there was a kind of resolution: she knew what she must do now. She no longer wondered why she was here. Her task was clear: she had to get Miro and his mother out of that hellish place and on a plane to London. There was little scope for indignation over the difficulties involved. Nor was there much scope for introspection. As she scrambled after Anna through the surrounding ugliness and over the uneven snow, Terry felt as though she had eased a little of the burden that she customarily carried with her. She saw Anna make the cover of the tunnel that led to the garage and as she followed her into the building she felt calm.

As soon as Zlatko had joined them, the escort began speaking.

'He says he's glad we made it back safely,' Zlatko translated. 'He says he hopes he'll be here to help us with Miro in the morning.'

'Tell him we are grateful,' Terry said. 'Tell him we hope his mother is OK.'

Zlatko translated and the soldier nodded and saluted before walking away.

* * *

Zlatko led them to a room next to the garage, where Jusuf had resumed his meeting with the other officers. The arrival of three outsiders offered a brief distraction from debating dismal options.

When Anna began to take photographs, Zdravko protested and Zlatko told her to stop.

'This is Dr Barnes from London,' Zlatko explained, speaking across the table to Jusuf. 'She has permission to be here. She is supervising the evacuation of Miro Pejanović. We plan to evacuate Miro tomorrow morning.'

There were no indications of rank in the room other than the authority that each man carried in his bearing. Zlatko had guessed correctly that Jusuf was in charge.

'You should move him tonight,' Jusuf said.

Zlatko translated and Terry said, 'He can't be moved till his condition is stable. We have to wait until morning.'

Terry didn't want to discuss this in a room full of preoccupied strangers. They were talking about a life-or-death course of action. But she remembered what Jurić had said: there are thousands of Miros.

'Take him as soon as you can,' Jusuf said. 'Tomorrow. Early.'

Jusuf remembered carrying Miro Pejanović across gardens laid out like an obstacle course to get him to the shelter. That was when they thought they could hold Otes. He didn't like the way Terry stood there now, as if she owned Miro's tragedy. Then he thought about Milena; he thought about how she would treat a stranger. 'We will help you if we can, but we have others to evacuate,' he said gently. 'Don't delay. Be here early tomorrow.' He nodded to Zlatko, who ushered Anna and Terry out of the room. 'Thank you for coming,' Jusuf added in English as he and the others watched them leave.

24

Danby disliked the way Major Rocard was looking at him. The major was studying the discoloured buttons on the front of Danby's tunic, making no effort to disguise the distaste with which he viewed sloppiness in a fellow officer. Rocard's demeanour exuded an intentional and practised insolence. Danby resolved not to rise to the bait.

It had been clear to Danby from the beginning that this encounter was to have the character of a confrontation rather than a consultation. He hadn't had many dealings with Rocard and those had been civil enough – but he was in no doubt that this was a man who would put his own interests above anyone else's.

Rocard raised his eyes from the buttons and allowed an expression of rather strained patience to settle on his face. He shrugged and said, 'Yes?'

Rocard had been designated Danby's point of contact with the unit that had been on the Airport Road – none of the troops was authorised to speak about what happened. Everything was to come through Rocard, who would decide how much or how little Danby was told.

'We have to move fast,' Danby said. 'We have to get what we know into the public domain and we have to provide more details on the inquiry.'

They sat on either side of a cheap wooden desk in a large room on the second floor of the PTT. The windows were sandbagged. On the walls were maps depicting in detail the daily movements of frontline positions around the city.

'There's an investigation under way, that's all you have to say?' Rocard said.

'With respect, Major, *I* will decide what I have to say.'

Another infinitesimal shrug.

'A man died, a man who was under our protection,' Danby continued, speaking into the space left by Rocard's non-response. Immediately, he sensed that the indignation in his voice would only weaken his position in the face of Rocard's indifference.

'The man was a casualty of war,' Rocard said, his voice flat. 'He was under UN protection but that's not a guarantee and no one should think it is. We aren't nursemaids.'

'There is legitimate concern that we are not being fully transparent,' Danby carried on doggedly.

'Transparent!' Rocard's anger surprised them both. 'The officer on the ground tried to remonstrate, at risk to himself! How many reporters are doing that, Major? How many? Why should *we* have to account for what we are doing? We do more than we are tasked to do! And now you are inviting us to offer explanations.'

Danby noted the conflation of soldiers on the ground and officers at headquarters. The issue was not, in any case, about risk but about responsibility.

'The man was under our protection,' he repeated.

If the UN authorities in New York had any lingering concern about the death of the minister while travelling under the UN flag, they made no effort to show it. But Danby was concerned – he felt *implicated*. The UN attitude to the assassination had become a kind of collective sneer. Officials were able to separate themselves from responsibility as if stepping out of soiled shoes.

Danby wanted to know who opened the door, who ordered it open, who sent the British away and why.

'It's not something we can help you with,' Rocard concluded, bringing his voice back to the neutral tone of a bored bureaucrat, and at the same time making it clear that 'we' and 'you' were distinct.

'I'll get what I'm after,' Danby said. He stood up. 'If I have to go all the way to New York,' he added. *You contemptibly smug little shit.*

'You must do what you feel you must do,' Rocard replied.

Danby slowed his pace as he climbed down the stairs. He let the noise of the building work on his senses like a massage. There were voices, mostly French but with other languages mixed in, some English, some Norwegian. There were a couple of New Zealanders on one of the landings. They saluted. He walked on down.

The building smelled of paraffin. The tiles on the ground floor were muddy. They were cleaned four times a day, a punishment duty, but they were always muddy. The building was overcrowded. Several rooms were used as temporary sleeping quarters, there was a hospital in the basement, there were offices and conference rooms on the first and second floors; there was a well-stocked canteen, a shop and a recreation area. In among the paraffin was an aroma of sweat and stale tobacco. The lighting everywhere was harsh.

'Jim!'

At that moment, Danby felt more camaraderie with journalists than he did with people on his own team.

'Anna, what's up?'

She was standing beside a French captain, who didn't look pleased when Danby joined them.

'I was in the government liaison office,' Anna said, 'and this man asked me to leave. He says we're not allowed to speak to government officials here unless we have UN permission. That can't be true.'

'New standing orders,' the captain explained defensively.

It *was* true, and on these premises it was legal. 'I guess we have to comply,' Danby said.

The captain glared at Anna and then saluted Danby and withdrew.

'Seems the media aren't entirely welcome,' Danby continued. 'I'm not entirely welcome myself. What was it you wanted to speak to the government man about?'

'What do you think?' she said. 'You got anything new?'

'I'm doing what I can.'

* * *

The UN's main humanitarian office was located along a long dark corridor that led from the reception area where Anna and Danby stood.

Inside the office Terry had taken up a position in front of a steel desk behind which a young woman sat smoking.

Terry had come in and confidently informed Selma, the young woman, that she was taking Miro and his mother to London and wanted them on an aid plane.

'You need documents for the boy and his mother,' Selma said. Terry's letter from the UNHCR Geneva office wasn't enough.

''They can't get on a plane unless they have a document from this office, and they can't have a document unless I see their passports.' Selma's voice was flat – its very flatness discouraging further discussion.

Selma was indignant when outsiders acted as though they had special rights. Rights for people whose countries were not at war. Rights for people who hadn't been shelled, or half starved to death. Terry's stylish waterproof jacket irritated her.

'It's already been approved by Geneva,' Terry insisted.

Selma drew on her cigarette and exhaled. Then she said, 'I'm explaining the procedure. If you don't follow the procedure, you won't get the boy on a plane. It's as simple as that. Stop back here when you come from Otes tomorrow morning, before you go to the airport.'

Terry turned when Anna came into the room. Selma looked down at a pile of forms and began to mark them in pencil. Terry thought of the Argentinian soldier, the first person she'd dealt with when she arrived.

War, she grasped, can bring out the pedantry in people.

When Anna and Terry returned to the reception area, Danby was still there. Anna did the introductions.

'Dr Barnes has come to take a little boy from Otes. He needs treatment in the UK,' Anna explained, 'but they won't let the boy and his mother on a plane unless they have a stamped pass from this office.'

'When are you taking him out?' Danby asked Terry.

'In the morning. Getting him out of Otes will be the trickiest part.'

'You've been there?'

'Today.'

'The fighting's bad?'

'I don't know what's bad, but it looked awful to me.'

'It's *very* bad,' Anna said. 'The government isn't going to hold on.'

'If I can help in any way,' Danby told Terry, 'let me know.'

He didn't feel just at that moment that he could be of very much help to anyone.

Terry and Anna walked out through the sandbagged entrance of the PTT.

'Are you coming to the song contest?' Terry asked. The question sounded strange and frivolous to her, as though the song contest were the next attraction in a holiday weekend.

'I was supposed to,' Anna said, 'but there's been a change of plan. Brad and I are going to Pale.'

'Now, *that's* interesting!' Zlatko remarked. 'You must tell me when you get back what our country cousins are saying!'

Anna grinned. 'I will.'

Terry reached out and patted Anna on the arm. It was as though she watched her hand move of its own volition in this unaccustomed gesture. She felt the hard fabric of Anna's winter jacket and then the shape of her upper arm. 'Please be careful,' she said.

She could not have put into words the impact of the other woman's reaction: Anna's face became suddenly tender. She clasped Terry's elbow and said, 'I will,' and then added gently, 'You too.'

25

Miroslav's world was defined by stories – stories that were end-lessly embellished, challenged, shared and added to. Milena heard competing accounts of the time Miroslav nearly lost his fingers to a wood-saw. Aged four (three according to one account), he was playing in the yard. His father had left him unattended for a few seconds (half an hour in another version). Miroslav sat down next to the wood-saw and flicked the switch. He gazed into the spinning blade, moved his face close up to it and reached out to touch the edge. His mother saw him from an upstairs room and screamed. His father raced from the shed on the other side of the yard, the distance too far to prevent Miro-slav from doing what he was going to do. The little boy pointed to the wood-saw and shouted, 'Look!' He touched the blade.

It was Sabina, Miroslav's older sister, who intervened. She was still a child then, but she knew that if she pulled the cable from the wall socket the saw would stop spinning. She reached up to the socket below the kitchen window and pulled the cable out.

The saw stopped just in time. Miroslav received a scratch that drew blood and he began to cry, but it was just a scratch.

Milena heard this story from Sabina, from Miroslav's father and from Miroslav's mother. Miroslav's mother, proud of her son's gift for fixing things, wondered what his life would have been like if those few seconds when he touched the blade had been different. Sabina chuckled over her impact on her brother's destiny. 'If it wasn't for me, he wouldn't have been at that university and then he wouldn't have met you!' she told Milena. Miroslav's father screwed up his face – deep lines beneath bushy white eyebrows – and shook his head. 'A few seconds,' he said. 'A lapse! And the world changes!'

Two of Miroslav's three brothers were married; both of his sisters were married. There were eight nieces and nephews – their stories joined them in every permutation of intimacy and distance. By the time Miroslav and Milena were married (the fifth couple on a weekday morning at the town hall) almost a year after they first met in Sarajevo, Milena had made her own place in Miroslav's family. It was different from the way things had been with Željko and Jasna. Milena and Jasna and Željko (when he was home from Germany) didn't need stories. There were just three of them.

Life in Miroslav's family was like a pressure cooker. They all argued, sometimes boisterously, sometimes bitterly. The sons and daughters lived near their parents' home outside Foča. A brother and a sister, and their respective families, occupied a higgledy-piggledy extension to the main house, built room by room as marriages took place and offspring arrived.

Miroslav and Milena might have added more rooms and lived there, but since Miroslav had got a job at the factory in town they chose to live nearby. His father lent him money to buy part of a plot that was owned by the municipality. A brother of Mirko Milutinović – who had brought Milena's piano from Sarajevo to Foča – was on the municipal council. He was persuaded to table a motion with the planning committee proposing that the land be put up for sale. The motion was accepted and bids were solicited, so discreetly that no one outside Miroslav's family knew the land was being sold. Mirko Milutinović's brother accepted a nice commission for his hard work on Miroslav's behalf.

They built their house in the course of a single summer. Miroslav's older brothers, Boro and Saša, came in cars and trucks with bricks, tiles, beams, cement, windows, doors and pipes.

Miroslav worked hard in that first summer with his brothers, mixing concrete, laying bricks, plastering ceilings and walls. Milena used to go and inspect the day's progress on her way to work in the evenings.

Jasmina came one evening – Jasmina whose chance acquisition of tickets had led to that life-changing visit to Sarajevo for the Olympics. By now, Jasmina was seeing a councillor called Ratko Babić (who was too young and inexperienced to be allowed onto anything as lucrative as the planning committee). Ratko looked good, for a politician. He didn't wear the baggy, shiny, boxy suits that the old councillors favoured; he didn't wear shirts with collars that were too small and always undone. He dressed smartly. Milena could see why Jasmina liked him.

They walked from the town centre to the house. It was still hot though dusk was approaching. Miroslav's skin was caked in dust. He was happy. Milena could hardly describe the effect her husband's happiness had upon her. He was building their future. He was lifting and laying for both of them, for their children when the time came. His work expressed his love for her.

His jeans were grey with dirt and dust. His faded yellow T-shirt was torn at the front. He was lifting bricks from a huge pile that had been dumped near the house, all the while with a cigarette in his mouth. Milena and Jasmina watched first of all from the other side of the road. Miroslav hadn't seen them. He was preoccupied with piling the bricks neatly in a wheelbarrow, half smiling; smoke drifted up from his cigarette.

They walked across the road. Jasmina stopped to light a cigarette, and Milena went on into what would be her house. She could smell dust and cigarette smoke. Miroslav looked up and smiled, white teeth showing against a backdrop of grimy skin.

'You're filthy,' she said. She kissed him, tasting dust.

'I am,' he said.

He showed her again where everything was going to be. They were building the stairs. Miroslav's brothers, Boro and Saša, stood at the top of the broad concrete chute where they would put the steps. They were extending steel rods down to the floor below.

'Hey,' Boro said, looking over the edge of the chute and nodding to Milena. She waited and a moment later Saša's face appeared. 'Hey,' he said.

Boro and Saša were older than Miroslav; the two sisters came in between. The older brothers were like variations on a theme. They both had thick moustaches, drooping faces and thick black hair. They drank a lot and smoked a lot and spoke, compared to the rest of their family, relatively little. Milena liked them and they liked Milena.

Jasmina walked round the outside of the house, admiring the solid walls and imagining what the garden would look like when it stopped serving as a space for concrete mixing. Milena stood with Miroslav in the centre of their world. She knew where everything would go and how it would look – the curtains she would hang, the carpets she would choose, the furniture and the colours of the walls. This was what she wanted: this house and the life that she and Miroslav would live in it.

Miroslav was content. He had no dangerous dreams. He didn't want to leave Foča to make his fortune. He had his fortune already. He was lucky and complete.

Work on the house never stopped the whole summer long. Boro supervised the plumbing and wiring. He spent days lugubriously digging ditches and lowering pipes into them. Saša got the materials – he never said where he'd acquired the wooden beams for the windows on the first floor, or whether they had actually been paid for, but they looked suspiciously like telegraph poles. He brought some men at the beginning to help lay the foundations and put up pillars and heavy load-bearing joists.

On a few weekends, Miroslav's younger brother, Slavo, came to help. He was a schoolteacher – thin and bespectacled. His brothers teased him because he was physically weak and knew nothing about mixing concrete or achieving the right consistency of plaster. All things considered, they assured him, he was practically useless in the building trade.

Of all of the family, only Slavo disliked Milena, or so she believed from the beginning.

Like Miroslav, Slavo had studied in Sarajevo, but unlike Miroslav, he had wanted to stay there. He tried hard to secure a teaching post but failed. In those early days he didn't know which people at the Education Ministry to speak to, so he was obliged to return to Foča to teach literature at the local high school.

Milena thought that Slavo looked down on her. He looked down on everyone, but she believed he looked down on her particularly. He looked down on her because her mother and father had abandoned her. He looked down on her because she had made a place for herself in Miroslav's family.

In the summer they used to go to Miroslav's parents' house. Sometimes there were fifteen or twenty people sitting around the long table that stood out on the broad terrace in front of the house. In the wintertime the table got soaked in the rain. It had once been painted white but most of the paint had long since been scoured from its surface by the elements. When they sat at the table in the summer it was covered entirely with a white embroidered table-cloth. There were two chestnut trees at the front of the house and the table was set beneath the smaller of these. From the terrace you could see right along the valley to Foča.

Boro played the guitar well, and Slavo sang equally well. Slavo had an exceptional memory. He knew all the verses of folk songs. He could sing about battles long ago, recounting who had fought whom, who had distinguished themselves and who had run away.

Milena watched him then, when Slavo sat on summer evenings beneath the chestnut tree and looked off into the distance through his schoolmaster's spectacles as he sang about ancient heroics. Those were moments when Slavo took his place in the heart of his family, and Milena watched from the edge.

When the house was finished, Jasna and Željko visited from Germany. Milena heard the car drawing up outside and went to the door. Miroslav had not come home from work yet.

Željko smiled his naughty smile while Jasna fished in her bag for a cigarette. Jasna had put on weight since she moved to Germany. She looked older; her face was pale and slightly puffy around the eyes. Milena looked over Željko's shoulder and then she let out a little cry.

'Your dowry,' he said. He meant it as a joke, but it came out serious. She could not speak.

Her piano was on the roof of Željko's car.

When Miroslav came home, he and Željko brought it inside.

This joke, about the piano being Milena's dowry, was the only occasion when Željko ever acknowledged that he and Jasna had taken the place of Milena's mother and father.

The piano was placed, naturally, in the sitting room. It completed the far wall. There was a poster above it, *Sunflowers* by Vincent Van Gogh. In the mornings the room was filled with light, and the piano and the painting together made up a little tableau that pleased Milena.

She played on special occasions. Boro sometimes brought his guitar if there was a family gathering at Milena and Miroslav's. He tried a couple of times to tune the guitar to the piano but failed. He was very deferential towards Milena. She was a real musician, could play in any style, and had the gift of choosing melodies to suit the company. She didn't show off. When she played at family gatherings, they all sang along. Except Slavo. She knew that he would not sing in her house. He would not even sing his ancient folk songs though Boro was there with the guitar to accompany him. And while Boro had tried hard to get his guitar in tune with the piano, Slavo insisted that singing to a piano accompaniment was beyond his modest talent.

About a year after Milena and Miroslav were married, Slavo embarked on a romance. The girl was a friend of Milena's friend Mira. Her name was Elvira. She was plain and opinionated, but she was in love with Slavo and she saw the good that was in him. However, she struggled to show him a way of engaging with others that wasn't infected with bitterness. She and Slavo made an odd couple – plain and serious but, for the few months of their romance, they tried hard to be like other people.

Elvira, though, was a realist. She saw in the end that Slavo was going to grumble his way all through life and in due course she broke off the relationship. Milena felt a little bit sorry for them both. Once, Elvira came to visit with Mira. They sat in the kitchen and drank coffee. Elvira spoke about Slavo with a mixture of sympathy and exasperation and it occurred to Milena that this girl, with her flat face and small pale eyes and unmanageable hair, had once thought that Slavo represented her best chance of happiness.

Shortly after Elvira left him, Slavo tasted success for the first time in his life. The man responsible was Jasmina's fiancé, the councillor, Ratko Babić. Ratko and Slavo crossed paths not in Foča but in Sarajevo. Ratko was a little younger than Slavo. When they were introduced, Slavo behaved with his customary wariness and disdain. Ratko would have thought no more about it, but Slavo was from Foča and Ratko was inclined to cultivate him. Ratko's party was new and needed recruits. By itself, that would not have been enough to get Ratko past Slavo's boorishness. Something profound, however, happened that afternoon, when Slavo and Ratko and some others met in a large light apartment opposite Zetra Stadium in Sarajevo and spoke about politics. Slavo got onto the subject of government jobs and the iniquitous way in which they were doled out. He sketched a conspiracy with fluency and persuasive detail. He spoke passionately, but – more important in Ratko's view – *plausibly*.

Slavo, Ratko perceived, had the ability to articulate resentment. He arranged to meet him several times, and with a little flattery got him to join the party.

Slavo took to politics, heart and soul, carried aloft by a movement that claimed to represent a whole people. He became a figure in Foča. It took a year or two, but by the time he had become well known, his fame did not seem improbable. He was, after all, more than a little eccentric, and eccentricity is often an early sign of greatness.

This was Miroslav's brother.

* * *

One day Jasmina came to see Milena. A dangerous rumour was going around.

Milena's face turned crimson as Jasmina spoke. When she replied, her voice was high and uncertain.

'It's a lie!'

'I know,' Jasmina said, reaching out to take Milena's hand. Ratko, Jasmina's fiancé – they were married three months later – had heard that Fudo Omeragić, the barman in the café where Milena worked, had had an affair with one of the female staff. The rumour was that Miroslav had met Fudo in the street and threatened him. That quarrel could have been about money, but the rumour put two and two together and the gossip became that Milena was having an affair with Fudo.

'It's not true,' Milena said. 'Miroslav hasn't quarrelled with Fudo.'

But Miroslav *had* quarrelled with Fudo. Milena simply hadn't heard about it yet. She heard about it that evening, when her husband came home, late and drunk.

She asked him what was wrong. Her voice was as it had been when she spoke to Jasmina, high and uncertain. She tried to be calm.

He took a step towards her, and she realised that by not stepping backward she was risking violence. He seemed to consider what to do. She wanted to reach out and touch him. He moved his head one way and then the other, looking from the window at the back of the kitchen to the doorway onto the dining room. Then he hit the wall beside him with such force that she thought he might actually break the masonry. She jumped.

'What's wrong?' she asked again, this time her voice closer to a scream.

'You're not working in that bar any more.'

He went up the stairs. Milena sat on the sofa and lit a cigarette. She wasn't breathing properly.

He didn't speak to her for days. He slept in the spare room. Then his sister, Sabina, came when Miroslav was at work. She had persuaded her brother that there could be nothing in the rumour.

'He's a fool, darling,' Sabina told Milena, hugging her, enveloping her with large fat arms. 'They're *all* fools, but you know that already.'

When Miroslav came home, Milena waited in the kitchen.

'Tell me you didn't do it,' he said.

'I did nothing.'

He appeared to be mollified. 'I was angry because I love you.'

'Then you should trust me.'

He looked at her sharply when she said that, as though she'd spoken out of turn.

Later, when Milena went to visit Jasmina she asked her where Ratko had heard the rumour.

'From Slavo,' Jasmina said.

Milena never visited Jasmina again.

But Slavo visited Milena and Miroslav. He became more sociable as his political influence grew. Milena never confronted him. She never asked him why he had spread lies about her. She did not have the strength to go to war with Slavo. She was struggling to recreate the oneness she and Miroslav had lost and did not want to fight his brother.

At family gatherings, no one tired of listening to Slavo. We don't get the best jobs, he said, or the best houses or the best bits of land. They are cheating us. Milena knew that Slavo didn't include her in that 'we'.

When they were small, Miroslav looked after Slavo, protected him from the rest of the family. Now Slavo took on a grotesque – in Milena's view – role as Miroslav's protector. *He is the one who helped you least when you built your house*, she thought. *Now he is the one who is telling you what to think.*

But Slavo did things for them too. When the municipality began to look into land allocation and the question of Miroslav and Milena's property arose, Slavo and Ratko together made sure that Mirko Milutinović's brother's commission for making the land available and ensuring that no other bidders knew it was for sale never came to light. The transaction was investigated along with several others and following two long meetings, at the end of the second of which more money changed hands, the land allocation and Miroslav's father's purchase were upheld. Everyone breathed a sigh of relief, including Milena. With that and other such cases, Slavo demonstrated that he could serve his clients.

Milena accepted his patronage, as the others did. If she found fault with his politics she could not have told him why. Milena didn't know about politics.

She missed the bar. She never stopped resenting her husband's insistence that she give up that work. He said he didn't mind if she went back to the dress shop, as if that were a generous concession on his part, an indulgence. She didn't want to do that. Anyway, she consoled herself with the belief that she had reached the age where homemaking would be more satisfying. Just as Miroslav expressed his love for her when he built this house, she expressed her love for him by making their home beautiful.

It was a cheerful place. In spring and autumn the trees in the garden rustled and sprinkled shadows into the sitting room. The walls were painted yellow and white downstairs, and blue and green upstairs. All of the windows were blue. Sabina pretended she had to wear sunglasses when she came to visit.

Sabina was Milena's favourite in the family. They used to sit in the afternoons, drinking wine and smoking. They talked about sex and shopping. Sabina had a hoarse voice and she was always laughing. She was very vulgar, very forthright. She swore all the time. Milena trusted her. They would sit in the kitchen and look straight ahead at one of Milena's yellow walls and talk for hours. Sabina had two sons who were old enough when the war started to join the paramilitaries in Foča.

Sabina, like the rest of the family, didn't disagree with Slavo's politics. It made a certain kind of sense: whatever Miroslav said about engines, his family deferred to him, because he was the mechanic; whatever Slavo said about politics, his family deferred to him, because he was the politician. That was how they looked at things.

Milena dreamed of her children. She felt sometimes as though she were holding her little boy and her little girl in her arms. She stroked their hair; she whispered to them. The house was built for them. It was bright and safe. Miroslav would stand by his children. That was one of the reasons she had chosen him. Milena's purpose in life was going to be to look after her children and make sure that nothing bad ever happened to them.

But Milena and Miroslav didn't have children.

After a year, people began to tease. Why weren't they expecting? After two years, no more teasing. It started to dawn on Milena that she might never be a mother.

Miroslav was not a bad man. After the quarrel over the rumour of an affair, he tried to fix things between himself and his wife. They made a decent life in Foča; they had family and friends. Miroslav did well at the factory; being Slavo's brother helped.

When their world changed, when Slavo's men began to burn the town, when they destroyed the mosque and chased the Muslim families from their homes, even the strongest discovered what their weaknesses were, and Milena and Miroslav were not the strongest.

26

Brad slowed the Land Rover so they could get a better look at the road. His foot hovered above the accelerator. He was ready to move out quickly at the first sound of shooting. The vehicle was responsive though ponderous because of the heavy bullet-proof windows and the reinforced steel cabin.

They peered through the front window for any evidence of the previous day's murder. They were just about at the spot where the killing had taken place. It was very quiet. There was no barricade, no sign of the vehicles that had been there the day before, no heavy tracks in the snow. The UN investigation was clearly not yet underway – no blue helmets with tape measures and chalk.

The road was bleak beneath a white sky, snipers and irregulars under cover on either side.

They drove towards the airport in silence.

At the first UN checkpoint a Legionnaire emerged from his little sandbag house. Brad gave Anna his pass and Anna opened the window and handed her own and Brad's ID cards to the soldier. He looked at the cards and then looked through the window.

'Closing the stable door after the horse has bolted,' Brad said. The soldier stared at him, and Brad added, smiling as he spoke, 'A bit late to get so goddamn careful.'

The soldier smiled back and said in a Texan drawl, 'You guys think we're assholes.' He paused to watch Brad's surprise. 'You're not sitting out here every day taking shit.'

'Hey, no offence,' Brad said.

'Yeah right.' The soldier handed the cards back. He signalled to the APC blocking the airport access road and it began to rumble out of the way.

'I'll be more careful in future!' Brad muttered, moving into first gear.

'Wait for the APC on the other side to signal before you cross the runway,' the Argentinian at Movement Control told them.

'What's the signal?'

He shrugged. 'Maybe he'll flash his lights. Maybe he'll wave you across. Just watch, and don't move until he gives the signal.'

They drove out of the loading area and onto the slip road that ran the length of the runway. Winter paleness spread across the airstrip. A C-140 bounced onto the tarmac. For a few seconds it ran beside them and then it decelerated, like a child's clockwork plane coming to a halt on a thick carpet, and turned abruptly.

A quarter of a mile from the terminal, they drove onto a road perpendicular to the runway. An APC sat on the opposite side. Brad flashed the Land Rover's headlights. They watched the APC. There was no response. Anna pointed into the distance.

Approaching, half a mile away and one hundred feet above ground, another transport was about to land.

'They'll let us pass before that,' Brad said. 'Surely?'

'Surely not.'

'That'll take a minute before it gets here.'

'That's how airports run,' Anna said. 'Maximum safety.'

'Not *this* airport.'

As Brad spoke, the APC flashed its headlights.

'He means us to cross.'

'But there's a plane coming in,' Anna said. 'He's signalling us to wait!'

Brad gunned the engine and drove onto the runway. Anna swore. The plane came at them.

When they cleared the runway, Anna swore again. The plane roared towards the spot where they had crossed. Brad was pleased with himself. 'You're right,' he said. 'They meant us to wait.' The APC was still flashing its lights and they could see through the tiny windscreen the soldier inside gesticulating towards them angrily. They drove round the APC and along the other side of the runway.

A second APC blocked the road into Lukavica. The Land Rover stopped. A soldier came out of the sandbag hut beside the APC and ran towards them crouching. Anna opened her window.

The soldier wore the expression of a man who expected to be shot. He wanted to get back to his sandbag hut quickly. 'You can't go ahead,' he shouted up at them in French. He pulled the collar of his tunic tighter. 'There is fighting on the road. They've been shooting all morning.'

'What about the other way?' Brad asked. He spoke calmly. He was inside the Land Rover, protected from the bullets that the soldier feared were about to rain down on them.

The Frenchman shrugged. He turned to go back.

'Is the barbed wire across it?'

'Maybe.'

Brad thanked him and then said to Anna, as the soldier raced towards the sandbags, 'He has no idea what's happening beyond his guard post.'

'What's the other way?' Anna asked.

Brad began to turn the Land Rover.

'There's a track further up, but sometimes it has barbed wire across it. Sometimes not.'

Brad liked the way the Land Rover handled. It bounced over the snow. They turned and faced the direction they had come. There was another APC directly opposite, twenty yards away, where they had turned off the slip road and onto the runway. They both looked north along the runway: no planes coming in. Brad revved the engine and they roared back onto the tarmac. The APC began flashing its lights.

'What are they going to do, shoot us?' Brad said. 'I'm beginning to understand why everyone ignores them.'

When they had got across they turned to their right and drove another two hundred yards to the end of the runway. To their left there were apartment blocks, almost all of them burnt out. These formed the first line of defence on the city perimeter. Ahead and to the Land Rover's right the woods were infested.

The airstrip was no-man's land and both sides fired on vehicles crossing it – small arms, mortar, tank rounds. The Land Rover moved at twenty-five miles an hour. To go faster would have been to draw attention. Anyway, Brad didn't want to overshoot the track. To go more slowly would have been to tempt fate. So they rolled along at a steady pace in the clear light, the words 'PRESS' written in large black letters on the side of the vehicle offering a prospect but not a guarantee of protection.

'I'd rather be covering a knitwear conference in Phoenix, or a boat show in Maine,' Brad said.

'No you wouldn't.'

He glanced at her.

'Probably not.'

They reached the track. On either side was a circular pile of razor wire but the way ahead was unobstructed.

The Land Rover trundled off the flat surface of the airstrip road and onto the unpaved track. They began to bounce, rising and dipping at acute angles. Someone had fixed a scarecrow by the side of the track with a noose around its neck.

The potholes were deep, and some were filled with snow and ice, which made it difficult to judge exactly *how* deep. They moved at a crawl, the Land Rover lurching one way and then righting itself. They passed through an orchard and the track's surface improved. There was no sign of life on either side. Only when they reached the first houses did they come upon troops.

A bearded giant holding a machine gun lifted his cap and waved to them good-humouredly.

They were across.

Brad swung the Land Rover onto the main road into Lukavica. A snaking UN convoy of fifteen trucks passed them in the opposite direction, coming from Pale.

Soldiers walked on either side of the road, carrying weapons and supplies.

* * *

At the Lukavica barracks Brad and Anna found Myrna, who smiled brightly when they entered her office.

Myrna fixed media interviews with Rebel commanders and politicians, told reporters about press conferences, arranged safe passage.

'You are the first today,' she said, adding characteristically, 'and very welcome. How are you both?'

They said they were well.

Myrna wore a tight sweater and a long fitted skirt.

'Coffee?'

They said that would be lovely.

Myrna left to see about the coffee and when she came back she lit a cigarette. The room was already dense with cigarette smoke and the detritus from a wood-burning stove in the corner, which produced a steady effusion of embers and ash. Anna's eyes began to water.

'You want to know about the events on the Airport Road yesterday, but I can't help you,' Myrna said. She shrugged. 'I wish I could.'

They sat on plastic chairs breathing in smoke. Brad lit a cigarette.

'I understand an investigation is being launched,' Myrna continued. 'You'll have to go to Pale to find out about that.'

'The soldiers came from Lukavica,' Brad said.

'What soldiers?'

'The ones who shot the minister.'

'We don't know who shot him. It could have been his own people, or even the UN. That's why an investigation is underway.'

'But your soldiers who were on the Airport Road came from Lukavica,' Brad persisted.

'Did they? I guess you'll have to check that with Pale.'

A soldier entered with a brass tray on which sat three cups of coffee. He distributed the cups politely and asked if he could bring them anything else. Myrna stubbed out her cigarette and lit another.

Myrna had rouge on her cheeks to cover the paleness of winter and a poor diet; she had bags under her eyes and she wore too much mascara. Her large brown eyes darted restlessly from Brad to Anna and all points in between. She had a well-proportioned nose, a ruby-red mouth, nicotine-stained teeth and a dimpled chin.

'We had hoped we might be able to talk to someone here,' Brad said. He was starting to dislike Myrna.

'You have to go to Pale.' She spoke through cigarette smoke and floating particles of wood ash.

Anna opened the door a little in order to breathe the outside air; Myrna and Brad inhaled and exhaled more cigarette smoke.

'You need a document,' Myrna added. 'I will provide you with this document. We want to help you. We know it is important that you get the facts.'

Twenty minutes later, after supplying Myrna with details of their press accreditation, and the registration, make and colour of their vehicle, they pulled out of the barracks and headed for Pale, the Rebel headquarters to the east of Sarajevo.

'This is such a waste of time,' Brad said. 'They could have found someone to speak to us at Lukavica. She's been told to send us up to Pale because they want to mess us about. They haven't decided what they're going to do. If they had a line they'd have had someone to speak to us down there; she would have had a press release to give us.' He remembered how he had lost his temper at that morning's confrontation with the General and he resolved to stay calm, but then, unable to keep an angry inflection out of his voice, he added, 'I hate the way they lead everyone a merry dance!'

There were mortar emplacements dug into the hillside next to the road several miles out of Lukavica. The besieging troops were safe in the pine forests. It was easy to pick out the streets and buildings down below. Gunners stood outside their huts and smoked, loafing like hunters, their eyes fixed on the Land Rover as it passed. They noted the press markings. Some glared, others grinned.

The journey took less than an hour, and after the first twenty minutes, when they were close to the frontline, the road moved deeper into Rebel territory. There was little traffic, but the cars that passed – ancient family saloons and battered pick-up trucks – were not military. As they approached Pale, the elevation became less steep, the trees receded and the road emerged onto a fertile plateau, snowbound but visibly less rugged than the country they had passed through on their way up from the city.

The press office was on the outskirts of town, located on the top floor of an Alpine chalet. Anna and Brad climbed the narrow stairs, carpeted and smelling of pine. The office was cramped. Two girls sat in one room typing and smoking. Another room housed a small telephone exchange. They found Dejan in a third room.

Dejan was one of those individuals who fizz with ideas. He was absorbed by the war. He struggled with it; he was an authority on it; he had a hand in it. No one maintained a finer balance between analysis and commitment. Many politicians, on both sides, were all commitment; many of the UN people were all analysis. In the end, the foreigners were inclined to grow cynical, and the politicians were inclined to turn their commitment into something dark. But Dejan gave the impression that he was doing what he was doing because history had presented him with a challenge that he was prepared to meet.

Before the war he'd been an English teacher.

He stood up and leaned over his desk and shook hands with Brad, who introduced Anna.

Dejan commiserated with Anna on coming to the country in the present circumstances and wished that she'd been able to visit in happier times. He spoke with sympathy and intelligence – his English was as correct as his manners.

Dejan had a thick beard and old-fashioned 1970s-style glasses with big lenses and wide plastic rims. He was about fifty, beginning to go bald.

They sat down to coffee in the smoke-filled room.

'Can't help you at all,' Dejan said. 'Myrna sent me a message to say you were coming and I tried to find out what I could, but all I can say is that we are investigating the incident, and we'll certainly try to get to the bottom of what happened.' He drew on his cigarette.

This little speech, with its all-I-can-says and its get-to-the-bottoms, was clearly rehearsed.

'Who's taking part in the murder inquiry?' Brad asked.

'I can't tell you that yet.' He glanced from Brad to Anna and back again.

'Will the killer be handed over to the UN?' Brad asked, getting impatient.

Dejan exhaled thick smoke through his nose and said, 'I honestly can't tell you anything. We don't even know for sure that one of our people did it. It might have been his own side, or even the UN.'

They noted the similarity to what Myrna had said, about the minister being shot by his own people.

'It was one of *your* people,' Brad said, 'and he murdered the minister in front of UN soldiers and about sixty of his own side!'

The anger that welled up, the same anger that had overflowed at the press conference, was like a physical illness, an unstoppable reaction to callousness. But Brad guessed that what had triggered this anger was the newsdesk's decision to hold his story the night before while the rest of the world's media filed ahead of him. He had been reporting massacres for months and, long before, he had travelled to faraway places to write about injustice and cruelty, yet only now did he find himself in the grip of rage. It was as though he suddenly confronted reality and found it to be utterly intolerable. And in the midst of this rage he looked recklessly at his own role in the gruesome freak show of conflict and he could not absolve himself of blame for what had happened at the barricade by the lagoon in Sri Lanka.

These thoughts overwhelmed him as he sat across the table from a reasonable and hospitable middle-aged English teacher who was glib about murder.

'You know and we know and everyone else knows that one of your soldiers shot an unarmed man while he was sitting inside a UN APC!' Brad said, his voice rising through the sentence in a sharp stepped crescendo until it attained on the last syllable the quality of a bona fide shout.

Dejan's sense of self-preservation turned out to be as well honed as that of the French soldier at the airport who had danced nervously beside the Land Rover before retreating at top speed to his sandbags. He hunkered down. 'Is there anything else I can help you with?'

Brad got to his feet. 'You can't help us!' He looked at Dejan as though he was about to punch him, poking his finger at him and shouting, 'You'll be in the dock one day! You'll be in the dock with the rest of them!'

Brad walked to the door. The two girls in the adjoining office watched with disapproval. Anna got up quickly and followed Brad down the stairs.

Outside, they climbed back into the Land Rover and Brad executed a quick three-point turn.

They drove in silence through the outskirts of the village and into the pine forest.

'What the fuck!' he said finally, by way of breaking the silence. 'I don't expect them to throw up their hands and apologise but they shouldn't be so fucking smug!'

They followed the winding road down to the bottom of the valley.

'People who fight wars and people who cover them should face up to responsibilities,' Brad said as they passed the fortified dugouts above the city. He said this with such bitterness that Anna thought he was going to hammer his fist on the dashboard or on the window beside him.

'Shit happens,' she said. She was beginning to sense that his unexpected and unhelpful outburst in Dejan's office was about more than just the shortcomings of media spin.

'You have to take responsibility for some things,' Brad said. 'The UN aren't taking responsibility; the Rebels aren't taking responsibility – but someone's responsible!'

'The guy who fired the gun,' Anna said.

'But why was the door open?'

It was open, Anna thought, because the French troops tried to reason with the Rebels.

And she too thought about Sri Lanka.

On the outskirts of Lukavica they left the main road and drove through the orchard and past the hanged scarecrow. They waited until a plane had landed and then Brad revved the engine and drove onto the runway again.

27

'We have to be there by half past two,' Nina said. 'What time is it now?'

Nina wanted to walk faster. She didn't think Milena understood that they couldn't be late. Milena was smoking a cigarette and walking rather slowly.

'It's twenty past,' Milena said. 'We have plenty of time.'

'I don't want to be late.'

'We'll be on time, Nina.'

'Shall we go faster?'

The girl began to walk in front of Milena and pull her along by the hand. If you did this with Mrs Hatibović or Mrs Nurudinović they wouldn't speed up, but if you did it with Stanislav he would start to walk more quickly. It depended on the person. Nina wasn't sure what Milena would do, whether she would tell Nina not to be silly or whether she would start to walk more quickly. Mrs Hatibović and Mrs Nurudinović would say: do you think you're a donkey and I'm a cart? They would carry on walking at their own pace. Stanislav would say OK, OK, and if he was smoking he'd blow out smoke and screw up his face because he was annoyed, but he would speed up.

Nina pulled Milena and she just laughed, which Nina liked, and let Nina pull her faster.

The concert venue stood on a hilltop. The walls of the building were of blackened concrete; the windows were sandbagged. It was a grey day, with an overcast sky, and Milena felt sorry for Nina because she was so excited as they approached the ugly building.

A stream of people headed for the entrance, lots of children, lots of mothers and fathers. Milena held Nina's hand and they made their way across a car park where there were burnt-out cars and shell craters.

Mrs Mulić, Nina's teacher, had explained to the children that this year's concert was very important and that they all had to be on time because one day when they were older they would look back on this event and they would be proud that they'd been a part of it. She said they would remember this day for the rest of their lives.

When Milena and Nina entered the big hall Nina thought they were in the wrong place. The floor was dirty, and where there were no sandbags at the windows and no glass you could see straight through to the outside. She had thought it was going to be a proper concert hall. She looked for Mrs Mulić.

'Are you sure this is the place?' she asked Milena.

'Yes, of course.'

Then, out of the blue, with sudden and eccentric curiosity, Nina asked, 'Do you have a husband?' It had occurred to her that Milena might have a little girl of her own, but she thought she should ask first about a husband. If Milena didn't have a husband then Nina knew there was surely no point in asking about children.

Milena didn't say yes or no. She just smiled, in the way grown-ups smile when you've said something funny though you don't know why it's funny. She had a nice smile. She squeezed Nina's hand and said, 'Let's find your teacher!'

The stage was a rough wooden platform. Musicians tuned their instruments beside the platform. Instead of an orchestra there was a small band. They had electronic equipment, and some technicians were running around shouting to one another, fiddling with wires and complaining about the inadequacy of the generator at the back of the building, which had been brought into service especially for the concert.

Around 200 people had already gathered, shuffling aimlessly near the stage, mothers and fathers and soldiers. The adults stood in groups smoking – a pall of smoke had already formed above the crowd – and children ran about shrieking.

Mrs Mulić stood near the stage with a small group of con-testants. When she saw Mrs Mulić, Nina knew they were in the right place. She was still surprised because it wasn't a proper theatre and there were hardly any seats. She knew that eve-rything was different because of the war so she guessed they had to have the concert there because the proper theatres were closed, or maybe they were busy. Mrs Mulić was wearing her black dress. She only wore her black dress for special occasions, like prize-givings. Nina stepped forward and said hello to Mrs Mulić, then pointed up at Milena and said, 'This is Milena. She brought me today.'

Mrs Mulić extended her hand and smiled at Milena in a kindly way.

'Thank you for coming,' she said. And then, because she was agitated and because Milena simply smiled and didn't say anything, Mrs Mulić added quickly, 'This is the first time they've all been together. It's such a pity the hall isn't more suitable.'

Actually, the hall would make your heart break, Mrs Mulić thought. It was dirty and cold and full of cigarette smoke and she had to gather the children around her in front of everyone. There wasn't a place for them to sit down. On their way here any one of them could have been shot, and now that they were about to begin it was in the back of Mrs Mulić's mind that a shell through the roof might kill them all.

Mrs Mulić had been among the most enthusiastic when it was first proposed that they hold the festival regardless of the circumstances. She understood that it was important. *They* were singing; the *other* side were shelling. Now, she had concluded that it was foolish. She was sorry all of these children were standing around her. She carried beneath her quick schoolmistress's smile a heavy burden of anxiety.

'Nina's been so excited, and she's been practising for weeks,' Milena said.

Mrs Mulić noted the accent. 'Are you a relation?'

'A neighbour.'

Milena wore too much make-up, Mrs Mulić noticed.

'Stanislav is going to get here as soon as he can,' Milena told Nina. 'I'm glad we found the place. I wasn't sure of the way.'

'You said you knew!'

'I thought I did. I just wasn't completely sure. Anyway, we got here, didn't we?'

There were five boys around Mrs Mulić and seven girls including Nina. They were aged between six and twelve.

'I'll be watching you and so will Stanislav, so don't be nervous,' Milena said, and then she left Nina and the others and moved to the back of the hall.

Milena fished in her bag for cigarettes. The concert was scheduled to last more than two hours, and she expected to stand the whole time. Then she would be on her feet for another four hours at work, and before that she had to walk all the way to the city centre. At least, though, she had enough cigarettes.

She took a cigarette from the packet, without taking the packet out of the bag, so people couldn't see she was smoking a luxury brand. People noticed everything, and if you weren't from the city they became curious. How come she has Marlboro? That was the first thing. Then they would move on to asking where she came from and why she was here and Milena hated that.

She watched Mrs Mulić shepherding her charges towards the stairs that led up to the stage. People looked up to Mrs Mulić. Teachers taught you how to read and write, which was a great gift even though most people didn't really think about it. Teachers knew the family background of their pupils and they could help them through difficult times. If Milena had had brains, she thought, she would have loved to have been a teacher.

Her brother-in-law's problem, Milena knew, was that he failed as a teacher. So he did other things instead. And then the war changed everything.

Teachers changed too. There were refugee teachers and teachers who were politicians. Ordinary teachers, who weren't refugees or politicians, didn't have schools to teach in. Now the children's song festival, which teachers across the land had promoted and prepared for as long as Milena could remember, wasn't an extravaganza any more. It was an uncertain affair in an ugly hall.

Milena used to watch this event on TV every year, and so did everyone she knew. Children from Foča made it to the finals one year, and they cheered them on, shouting encouragement at the TV – Miroslav, Milena, Sabina, Fudo Omeragić and his wife, and some others who dropped by Milena and Miroslav's place. They drank beer and ate snacks and smoked. Then they went out on the town. Saturday nights used to go on until the middle of Sunday morning. There was always something on.

The song festival was a fixed marker in the calendar, one of the signposts in early winter ahead of the two Christmases. Milena loved the way children were introduced, from all over the country, the way they did it at Eurovision. Even when children didn't sing well, you willed them on to do their best.

But now the people in the hall were pale, their clothes drab. There was no one there, child or adult, who wasn't hungry.

She wondered why they bothered with the television camera. Two technicians were arguing about how to get it started, and the director was arguing with the two technicians about where it should be placed. Hardly anywhere had electricity any more, so who was going to watch the concert on TV?

The twelve finalists climbed onto the stage and Milena saw Nina straightening her dress and looking out across the audience. She waved to Nina, who saw her and smiled.

The compere got the ball rolling on the stroke of three o'clock. She introduced the musicians and the twelve performers and encouraged the audience to join in singing the opening medley of songs. The gloom dispersed and the event began to feel like a real concert. When the first child stepped forward to sing, the audience were in the mood to clap and cheer.

Milena thought about the cushions on the sofa in the sitting room of their house in Foča. Years ago, when they watched this festival, Miroslav and Fudo would sit on the sofa drinking beer and making jokes and Fudo's wife, Amela, and Milena would sit on armchairs, waiting for others to come to make up the party before they all went out.

The cushions were yellow. Miroslav bought them. They were the final touch, when they'd finished the house, after building, drilling, hammering, plastering, painting and furnishing. He came home one evening from work. He'd seen these four yellow cushions in the fabric shop. He thought they'd go with the carpet and the walls and he was nervous because he thought she might not like them.

He was a good man.

Milena lit another cigarette. Two in a row, an indulgence she couldn't afford. She had to ration her tobacco, but how to ration her thoughts? How to ration the way she thought about Miroslav and what had happened to them?

There wasn't a day that they didn't try. Even when the ease between them disappeared. They still tried. To give up would have been to lose a universe; it would have been to abandon what they had made.

This was the loss with which Milena lived now.

She remembered a July day when they went to Krvavac to swim. Amela was visiting her sister in Germany. Fudo and Adil Agic from Miroslav's factory joined them late in the afternoon. Milena had brought beer and sandwiches. The three men went down to the water's edge and left Milena sitting on her own on the rug which she had spread on the ground. She listened to their voices. Miroslav's hoarse laugh. She knew that one of them was telling a dirty joke. The air was warm and fresh, and she could hear children further away, giggling and shouting as they dived into the river.

She had everything she needed then to make something in life. They expected children; they expected to go on that journey, to love haphazardly, resourcefully, the way that families do, to shape new destinies. She had everything she needed.

A little girl was singing. She wore white tights and a tartan skirt and a red sweater and her blonde hair was plaited. She held the microphone in both hands.

Milena wanted to cry. She looked at the little girl, listening to the song, and drew on her cigarette.

Miroslav worked in the new wing of the factory, the part that opened just when he finished his studies. It was the only place Miroslav had ever worked. Most of the boys who'd been in their class at school ended up at the factory. The money was good. Milena and Miroslav were saving to buy a car.

The sick feeling came back into her stomach. She sometimes tried to remember all the ordinary things Miroslav did. He liked when friends came round, on a Saturday afternoon or a Sunday morning, and they went off to help a neighbour repair a car or mend a roof. He loved helping. He was the sort of man who was always available to make up the team when the time came to lift a roof beam into place or push the sides of a new garage up onto its concrete floor. And afterwards he would accept a beer or a small glass of *loza* and drink and talk with the others. He was a good neighbour.

But he was a follower.

Milena thought of Jusuf's resolute expression, those sad eyes – not the eyes of a follower.

Miroslav followed when the time came to choose sides, when the town divided. The time when Fudo Omeragić was marched down the street and Milena watched from the window.

That was when they chose some friends and discarded others. Adil Agović, who used to drive Miroslav to work in a big battered white Mercedes (which had unaccountable Austrian papers), was no longer a friend, nor was Enes Salihović, whose roof Miroslav once helped to repair, nor was Zeinil Sarac, whose wife used to bring cakes when she'd been baking, nor was Muhamed Hatibović, who owned the fabric shop.

Everybody chose sides.

It was a macabre dance to which they knew the steps. They'd never *learned* the steps, but they knew them, and they danced accordingly.

But when the criminals came from nowhere and took over the town, why did ordinary people not see that that was wrong? What are they doing? What are they fucking doing? Miroslav, they are burning the mosque! Are they fucking *insane*?

The crowd moved slowly along the middle of the street, in the middle of the town. Fudo gesticulated, tried to argue. His big moustache drooped; his eyes opened wide and his cheeks were drawn. He was taller than the others, but there were many more of them. This was Fudo who was once capable of bringing rowdy patrons to heel.

The men at the front pushed him. Milena strained to see what was happening. There were about a dozen of them. On the other side of the river, she saw soldiers sitting on the benches smoking.

Miroslav was near the front of the crowd. Milena saw him clearly. He was encouraging the others, shouting nonsense. His face was filled with rage.

Milena did not run out into the street to help Fudo. Like so many other decent citizens, Milena froze. The mob continued on its murderous way, Miroslav at the head.

Milena knew that Miroslav was not a bad man.

But Slavo made his brother wicked. It was from this wickedness that Milena fled.

Abruptly, she came out of her reverie, and heard the compere congratulate the first contestant.

The little girl walked away from the microphone with funny steps, as if she were walking on a wet pavement avoiding puddles. Everyone laughed and she got another round of applause. The judges were at the front, four of them sitting on a bench. The next contestant was introduced. He was nine years old. He wore a pale blue bow-tie and red dungarees. He had red hair that had been flattened with some kind of oil, but a ridge of hair stuck up stubbornly at the back. He strode to the microphone and introduced himself very earnestly. Then he looked to the musicians and waited for his cue. The music began, gurgling out of the keyboard and guitars. The drummer, a fat man with a kindly face and a balding head, kept up a lively back beat. The bandleader nodded to the little boy and the song began.

* * *

Sanela and Jamila came in after the first number. Jamila joined friends at the front and Sanela found a place on the stairs at the back where she could see everything. She kept an eye on the entrance: Zlatko was to arrive from Otes before the end of the concert.

The band played sympathetically, willing the young singers to do their best. The contestants were keyed up. The festival was important because all the people there in that bleak hall full of tobacco smoke were showing that despite the explosions and the bitter cold and the snipers and the shortage of everything, they were not defeated.

Sanela never thought she'd worry this way. It was the way her parents used to worry when she was a teenager. Zlatko had common sense. She knew he wouldn't do anything stupid. But you didn't have to do anything stupid to get killed. She longed to know that he was safe.

The second song wasn't as good as the first, but everyone clapped as if it was. The earnest little red-haired boy stood back from the microphone and gave a deep bow. The compere came on again, clapping and smiling. She kept things moving along. The third singer was a twelve-year-old girl who launched into a popular ballad by Kemal Monteno. Everyone knew the words and sang the chorus. It was a song about the city, optimistic and lyrical, about living not dying.

Sanela remembered her first disco. She was fourteen. The disco was held at her school, a monumental building on the banks of the Miljacka. She was so excited. Her father took her there in the car. It was seven in the evening and the disco finished at nine. Another girl's father came to take them home. Sanela's mother came into her bedroom before she left, she told Sanela to wear less make-up. At the disco Sanela danced with a boy she liked. He wanted to kiss her but she didn't let him.

When you kill people you kill every single moment they would have had. You kill what might have been. Her great-uncle Izet was killed by the Germans in 1943. *He might have lived long enough to meet me*, Sanela thought. *He might have lived long enough to watch television, hear an electric guitar, drive a car, see men landing on the moon.*

In 1912, when his family trekked from Turkey to the west, Izet was carried on a litter across fields filled with sunflowers; they made camp at night beneath stars and a sickle moon.

The start of Izet's short life was tumultuous: that journey between empires. One hot afternoon he crawled away from his litter while the others slept. He crawled into a field of sunflowers and sat on the earth and looked up at a huge flower, its ochre underside turned almost brown by shadow, set against a cobalt sky. The flower was so large that Izet could place its circumference before his line of vision and obscure the sun.

He was staring at this beautiful flower when a girl crawled towards him and sat on the other side of the stem. She looked up and watched what Izet watched. They sat like that for minutes, silently. The girl wore a white shift. Her feet were bare. On her head was a red cap with glass embroidered into a single braid around the edge. She had big eyes. Her mouth was firmly closed.

When they heard voices they stood up and ran back the way they had come. Two sets of families looked for them. Each found their own.

Sanela had no way of knowing that such a thing happened to her uncle Izet, who died long before she was born. But she knew, of course. Two children met one day on that ancient road, one heading west, the other heading east. They met in a field of sunflowers, on an afternoon in 1912, and their eyes stayed in one another's memories. Their sunflower stayed with them, ochre against the sky's vast blue, and a long stem reaching heavenward between them. That image could not be erased.

Monteno's song filled the hall. Everyone sang. It was a dirty place, full of smoke, with sandbags at the windows and mud on the floor. But a place of such ineffable beauty now among these righteous people. Sanela started to cry.

*   *   *

Sanela felt a hand rest gently on her wrist.

'Are you OK?' Milena proffered a paper handkerchief.

She was surprised to see Milena, and surprised to see something as rare and valuable as a paper handkerchief. She was embarrassed: she was crying in public. She took Milena's handkerchief and dabbed her eyes, making little black mascara lines on the white tissue. She glanced around. If anyone else had noticed that she was crying they gave no sign of it. The people nearby were smoking, looking ahead at the stage, patiently participating in the concert.

'It was just the song,' Sanela whispered. She dried her eyes and said thank you.

'I know what you mean,' Milena said.

Sanela wanted to cry again. Milena *did* know what she meant.

Then, as Sanela slipped the damp handkerchief into her pocket, Milena tapped her wrist discreetly and held out a cigarette. She had opened a packet inside her bag, keeping the label hidden. Sanela took the cigarette and raised it to her lips. It was a Marlboro. Milena flicked a pink disposable lighter and Sanela drew on the flame.

Milena did the same and then glanced at Sanela.

'I'm fine now,' Sanela said. She felt sheepish.

Milena paused for a moment, looking at Sanela as if to check that she really was fine. She nodded and puffed on her cigarette. 'I'm glad I ran into you,' she said. 'I've been thinking about Brad –' There was a burst of applause as the song came to an end and Milena had to raise her voice so as to be heard. 'I really like him and everything, but I don't want to meet him tomorrow. Can you tell him that?'

Milena was so close that Sanela could feel her warm breath in the cold air.

Sanela and Milena were no more than acquaintances. They had chatted a few times at the bar, and Sanela had translated for Brad when he did the first interview. She had thought his approach clumsy and she wasn't sure tomorrow's interview would be any better. Briefly, she wondered if Milena had been warned off by someone. It was possible. She could imagine some of Jusuf's associates telling his girlfriend to steer clear of reporters.

'How come?'

Milena pursed her lips in a prim, old-fashioned way to indicate that the matter was delicate; she drew on her cigarette and exhaled. She seemed to be considering how to respond. 'I liked visiting you at the theatre,' she said. 'I know you were angry with Brad's questions, but he was just doing his job. I don't know about those things anyway.' Sanela nodded. She was relieved they had got Brad's misjudged interrogation out of the way. 'It's just that, well –' she smoked and looked towards the stage. 'Some things should be private.'

There was another burst of applause as the next contestant took to the stage.

'I'll tell him,' Sanela said, speaking into Milena's ear. She noticed a strand of grey on the side of her head and it occurred to her for the first time that Milena must be about a decade older than her. Until then she'd thought about them being in much the same age group. She saw that the skin under her eyes was puffy beneath a layer of make-up.

Sanela wondered if she'd agreed too readily. With everything that was going on she didn't think Brad would mind very much if they didn't do the interview, but that wasn't the most important thing.

'You know, he wanted to speak to you because you have been through things that other people haven't,' she said.

Milena looked at her with an expression of surprise and then she shook her head gently, touched Sanela's arm and said, 'Sweetheart, we've all been through so many things.'

28

Smoke coiled around the walls and windows and floated up to the concave ceiling. It impregnated raincoats, sweaters, fur hats, woollen trousers, and gloves and scarves. It swirled around the stage, over the heads of the contestants, and settled in a sinuous cloud over the band.

The compere was introducing the eighth number when Zlatko and Terry arrived. Terry tightened the collar of her jacket against the interior cold and peered through the grey miasma. Smoke began to permeate her consciousness.

She wanted a cigarette.

Zlatko shepherded her through the people at the back of the hall; a passage was made for them. Terry felt incongruous and alien. There were women there dressed as she was – but she looked *different*. People stared at her. They were curious, mostly, but some were resentful, she was sure. Alone in this hall, she could cross the siege line. The rest were prisoners in their own city.

When they reached the very middle of the crowd Terry saw Doctor Jurić talking to a group of soldiers. Zlatko tapped him on the shoulder and pointed to Terry. She felt like a package safely delivered.

Jurić looked more relaxed than he'd been the previous day. 'I'm very glad you could join us!' he said. 'Let me introduce you to one of our senior officers.' He indicated a large fat man in military uniform who stood close by.

The fat man, universally known as 'the Bull', on account of his girth and his supposed indifference to anything that got in his way, extended a chubby hand. Terry shook it and was rewarded with a beefy, slightly lecherous smile. He was just the sort of pot-bellied middle-aged man you routinely see in coronary care, Terry concluded. He was smoking, of course. He had dark, stubbly jowls and bloodshot eyes.

Jurić said something to the Bull, who growled a question in response.

'How did you find Otes? Was it bad?' Jurić translated.

'Very bad, I think.'

The Bull nodded. He took a drag on his cigarette and spoke again to Jurić.

'He'll make sure you receive whatever help you need in evacuating Miro,' Jurić told Terry.

Zlatko began recounting what they had seen. He had assumed his city persona again. His coat was unbuttoned; his scarf was wreathed round his neck loosely. The Bull asked questions and then began to lose interest, gazing at the floor and at the stage, but another officer quizzed Zlatko in detail.

Jurić listened, glancing at Terry from time to time. Then he broke away from the others and surprised Terry by taking her arm. 'I'm glad we met here,' he said, almost in an undertone. 'You will have a chance to see some children who are healthy and happy. Afterwards, we'll go on to dinner. There are people I'd like you to meet.'

Terry opened her mouth to reply but wasn't sure what to say. Jurić's breezy tone seemed at odds with reality; they were in a bombed-out husk of a building surrounded by shivering people and the doctor was inviting her to a dinner party.

He gave her an appraising look. 'We are here,' he said, 'because it's a convenient place to meet, and because I wanted to speak to some others who are also here' – he gestured towards the Bull and then generally around the room. 'But mostly we're here because I *have* to be here, and these people' – he gestured again, holding both hands palms outward and swivelling his body like a property agent, she thought, showing prospective buyers the fitted kitchen – '*have* to be here. We have to do ordinary things. We have to do what we are accustomed to doing, and we are accustomed to holding our song contest at this time of year. By being ordinary we resist! By singing we resist!'

He stopped, suddenly embarrassed.

'Dinner,' he added, less melodramatically. 'Dinner is just dinner.'

Terry became aware of a familiar perfume. She couldn't think why it was familiar at first, but then she heard Sanela's voice.

'Good afternoon, Doctor.'

She turned and looked into Sanela's solemn eyes. The girl drew on her cigarette and blew smoke out of the side of her mouth. 'How was Otes?'

'Well, we found little Miro,' Terry said.

Sanela nodded, in her serious way. 'Good,' she said.

Then Zlatko broke away from the soldiers, put his arms round Sanela and kissed her. Terry was startled. She had met Sanela and Zlatko separately. It was a shock to discover that they were a couple. Then she began to wonder why she was shocked, why she never could fathom the ways of the human heart. She wondered if it was her own coldness that had driven her husband into another woman's arms. Terry didn't set out to be cold towards others. She was simply reticent; she had always been so. She didn't know how to make small talk. She didn't tell jokes; more often than not she didn't understand other people's jokes. Standing in this smoke-filled hall surrounded by an extraordinary assortment of people, she was tongue-tied and awkward. She wished fervently that she could respond to these people in the way she wanted to.

Terry's normal approach was to be more efficient than anyone else. That was how she made a contribution to the greater good. She didn't think about it like that, not consciously, but now she began to discern a pattern. She let other people show emotion, while she reined in her feelings. Terry kept her deepest fears, her deepest aspirations, her deepest disappointments out of sight. Her typical response to a challenging situation was to break it into its component parts and see how the parts could be rearranged in a more satisfactory way. And now she was in a place where hospitals had dirty floors and her priorities were not everybody else's priorities. In her own hospital Terry made things happen and she made sure they were the *right* things – but here she couldn't do that. She couldn't exercise authority, couldn't rein in the unruly chaos of violence and disorder and replace it with something more satisfactory. And the people around her couldn't do that either – but, unlike her, they seemed to have a capacity to adapt. Everything they did was makeshift and provisional, yet the great gaps that opened up between the ideal and the actual didn't always reveal things that were ugly and obscene. Sometimes kindness was uncovered, and solidarity, and empathy, and a skewed view of the universe that offered glimpses of unimagined beauty. Terry thought of these things and caught her breath.

'Now, Terry,' Zlatko said, looking conspiratorial, 'I have to go and speak to my Cabinet contact!' He tapped his nose with his index finger in a can't-say-more gesture. 'I'll see you later, though,' he said, 'at Doctor Jurić's.'

Terry wanted to thank Zlatko for his courage and helpfulness, but she was still struggling to find the words by the time he had kissed Sanela and walked away.

'Now, Doctor,' Jurić began, 'let's find you a comfortable place to sit.'

A little boy had just finished singing and, taking advantage of the applause, Sanela and Jurić led Terry back through the crowd and along the side of the hall, squeezing past people, all the way to the front. Jurić spoke to a man sitting on one of the benches there, who stood up at once and indicated to Terry that his place was available. She wished they had let her stand at the back, but the man clambered over his neighbours and came towards her, smiling and pointing to his place and saying something which she didn't understand, clearly pleased to give up his space for her.

Terry stepped clumsily over legs and shopping bags. 'Can I get you something to drink?' Sanela whispered to her unexpectedly as the compere introduced the next singer. 'A whisky, a cup of coffee?'

'Honestly, I'm fine.'

The man who had given her his seat said something to Sanela. She whispered, 'Please have something, Terry. It is our custom. You are our guest.'

She asked for coffee. The man nodded, satisfied, and went to a table beside the stage where Terry caught a glimpse of some thermos flasks. He came back quickly with a plastic cup which was passed along to her.

'Enjoy the festival,' Jurić whispered. He was standing beside Sanela at the end of the bench. 'We're glad you're here!'

A woman sitting behind Terry told Jurić to shush. He put a finger to his lips and raised his palm to show that he would be quiet and then made an ostentatious display of looking attentively towards the stage.

The judges sat just in front of Terry, making notes and conferring earnestly.

The compere called out Nina's name.

Nina left the line of contestants and moved to the front of the stage. She stood at the microphone and paused, as she had been told to do, until she was calm. In a steady voice she said she was going to sing a song called 'Golden Lilies', 'which is about our country, where lilies will always bloom'.

There was a huge burst of applause and cheering, which surprised Nina. She waited for the clapping to stop, and looked into the audience trying to see Milena and Stanislav. Then the band struck up and Nina sang.

The first bars were clear and strong. The little girl had a sweet voice and after a few notes the audience settled. Nina was old enough to sing proficiently. At the same time, she was young enough for the audience to respond indulgently to the gestures and pose that she had conscientiously practised. She raised her arms, she threw her head back, she swayed from side to side – and she sang from the bottom of her heart.

Terry gazed at the others in the hall. There was a universal paleness; lined, weary faces watched the stage, women in winter coats, men in anoraks and leather jackets and military uniforms. In a corner of the crowd she noticed a boy, late teens or early twenties. He had the saddest face she had ever seen. He had a very slight squint, which made him appear even sadder. His head was cocked to one side and he leaned forward a little, looking up at the stage.

Terry was moved by the little girl's song and as she listened she watched the sad boy watching the stage and she wanted more than anything else in the world that these people would be comforted, that all their courage and decency and goodness would not be squandered or forgotten.

29

Anna returned from Otes with material for a feature story. The old couple she had interviewed in the shelter had told her about a journey over mountains and across frontlines, at first with a cart full of belongings and then, after the cart was stolen, with their suitcases – two pensioners walking on a snowbound country road at night, in fear of their lives. They'd come to Otes because their daughter had a room there, but they were told that she'd gone out one day to try and find bread and hadn't returned. Now they sat in their winter coats surrounded by concrete and fear.

Zlatko had found his first-hand view of the battle less useful. He sympathised with the old couple in the shelter; he sympathised with *all* the people who'd been hurt by the war, but he was more inclined to try and work out *why* things happened than to dwell on the tragic consequences of events. His kind of news wasn't found in villages where there were shells exploding but in corridors like the one he walked along now.

It was a well-proportioned Habsburg corridor bathed in orange light from tall windows. Thick walls, high ceilings, double doors, parquet floors, burgundy and gold colours. Zlatko loved this shabby old municipal building.

He was on his way to visit a minister who had distinguished himself as one of the more effective organisers in a generally disorganised group of people. This man had developed his casual but disciplined style of management during two decades as a successful and no doubt strategically unscrupulous businessman. In present circumstances, he was generally assumed to be combining politics with profit. He wasn't going to be poorer as a result of the conflict. Overall, Zlatko believed, the person he was going to see probably did more good than evil.

Zlatko would refer to his contact as 'one of my sources' or 'a reliable member of the government' or 'a well-placed official'. In person, he was Omar, his nickname in Zlatko's circle because he looked like Omar Sharif.

Omar was generous. He supplied Zlatko with stories that quickly made their way into print, in a city where accurate information was hard currency.

Zlatko walked along to see Omar, admiring the warm light of the corridor, a tonic for the spirits on a winter day. There were bits of tarpaulin over some of the windows and the masonry around the ceiling had been shattered in places by shell impacts on the outside walls. But none of that could take away the elegance of the corridor.

Omar's secretary, Alma, kissed Zlatko on both cheeks and asked, 'What's happening?' Zlatko had known Alma since university.

'I'm sorry about your father,' he said. Her apartment had been shelled, her father killed.

She pursed her lips; her eyebrows rose above wide blue eyes and her head moved gently to one side.

'No one else was at home, which was a blessing,' she said.

She must have explained this a hundred times, each time reliving the event.

'It was a month ago, during one of the ceasefires.' She smiled oddly and said in an unconvincingly wry tone, 'Some ceasefire!'

Her father wouldn't have been in the apartment if he hadn't forgotten his wallet. He was at the end of the street when he realised he'd come out of the house without it and needed to go back. While he was in the house the shell hit the building and he was killed.

He had pretended for a long time that the war wasn't happening. It was exactly like him to go back to the house for his wallet even though there was nothing to buy and he had practically no cash. But his wallet reminded him that there was a time when driving licences and family snapshots and telephone numbers meant something. He went back for it and he died.

'My mama's shattered,' she said. 'But we're managing.'

'Where are you living now?'

'We're staying at a neighbour's house. There was nothing to move. We lost everything. But mama and me, we're alive.'

'I'm sorry,' he said again.

She gave him a shy sad smile. Then she knocked on the door of Omar's office and looked in. She announced Zlatko's arrival, stepped back and said, 'Go in, Zlatko.'

Omar was of medium height, stocky. His eyes were very bright and his moustache was neatly trimmed. He looked up from his desk and signalled to Zlatko to sit on the sofa.

'Have to finish this,' he said. He was writing on a notepad, the white paper bright in the glare of an old-fashioned brass desk lamp.

Zlatko looked around Omar's dark wood-panelled office. It was large and lavishly furnished. There were polished coffee tables and big pot plants. Oil paintings on the walls. There were no windows. Omar had always worked in offices without windows. In present circumstances this was a good thing. People died because shells came through windows. However, Omar worked in an office like this because it suited his way of doing business. He spent hours on the telephone and poring over letters, documents and agreements in the bright glare of his desk lamp, unconscious of day or night.

On a small lacquered table next to his desk was a pistol in a leather holster.

Omar stood up and walked round the table. Alma brought coffee.

'What's happening?' Omar asked when Alma had left.

'I hoped *you* would tell *me*.'

Omar sat in a leather armchair near the desk, next to his gun.

'Has the Cabinet decided what to do?'

'About what in particular?'

'The minister's murder?'

'We've called for the General's resignation.'

'Has the UN responded?'

'Not as far as I know.'

They sipped coffee. Then Omar said, to Zlatko's considerable surprise, 'You were in Otes this morning!'

He said it as if he were pleased he knew, as if he thought Zlatko would be impressed. It was part of his pretending that Zlatko was still the little boy he'd known years ago.

'You have me followed!'

'I know things! People tell me things! You were there with the British doctor.'

'That's right.'

'Now, tell me. How is it in Otes? Do we have any possibility of holding on?'

Zlatko told Omar what they had seen, which, he knew, wasn't much. What they had heard was probably more illuminating – the level of shelling and small-arms fire was greater than anything in the city. Omar asked sensible questions, not all of which Zlatko was able to answer as completely as he would have liked.

He had given Omar enough to expect something in return so he said, 'Is the Government going to pull out of the peace talks because of the assassination?'

'Don't know about that.'

'What was the minister doing at the airport?'

'Went to meet a foreign delegation.'

'Why didn't they come into the city?'

'Wasn't safe.'

'What are we doing about an investigation?'

'The State Prosecutor is liaising with the UN. We've launched a criminal inquiry.'

'The UN will cooperate?'

'The General says our people will have every assistance.'

'I was at the General's press conference,' Zlatko said. 'He'll protect his soldiers, come what may.'

Omar shrugged. 'It will have to be investigated.'

'But the UN was responsible!' Zlatko said. 'They have moral obligations.'

Omar sat back in his big leather armchair and when he spoke he gave the impression that he really did think Zlatko was still a child, that he was being extraordinarily naive. 'Does that matter?' he asked. 'Does it serve any purpose? We've sent our people to investigate and the General says he'll cooperate, but we know he won't – we'd be idiots to think any differently. Nothing much is served by indignation.' He took another sip of coffee and looked at Zlatko for quite a long time, and then he said, 'You can help me ... when I say *me*, I mean *us* ... the Government ... your own people ... whatever.'

'How's that?'

'There is a witness. He's in Ilidža, but he won't be there long. He has a guilty conscience. Either that or we are blackmailing him. Whatever.'

'A witness?'

'He saw what happened on the Airport Road. He has friends on this side. I believe he's in the cigarette business. He wants to talk. You're good with the journalists at the Holiday Inn ... choose one of the ones that's winning prizes; they'll jump at a story like that.'

As he walked Zlatko to the door, Omar explained how a journalist would be able to contact his source in Ilidža.

Outside, Zlatko chatted with Alma briefly before leaving.

30

Nina came second. She was elated. She had sung as well as she could and she thought the boy who came first deserved to win. By the end of the concert the hall was almost full and the atmosphere was electric.

When the compere announced Nina's name the little girl was amazed. She stood very still. Everyone looked at her, and though she wanted to step forward she couldn't be truly sure that she had heard the announcement correctly. Was she really a prize-winner? The boys on either side pushed her forward and she saw Mrs Mulić looking up at her and pointing to the front of the stage. Everyone was clapping.

She received a bag filled with sweets. It said UNICEF on the side and Nina knew that UNICEF sweets were really good. She bowed to the audience. Everybody clapped again. Nina saw Stanislav and she waved (a short wave because she wasn't sure if waving was allowed) and he waved back. She was very happy.

When they left the hall Nina walked hand in hand with Stanislav and Milena as far as the main road, where Milena left them to go to work.

'Mrs Hatibović will tell all the neighbours,' Nina said to Stanislav as they entered their apartment block. Mrs Hatibović knew everything; she would spread it about that Nina had come second and that she'd been given a bag of UNICEF sweets.

Mrs Hatibović was sitting with Mrs Nurudinović in Mrs Nurudinović's apartment when Nina and Stanislav arrived. Nina showed them her prize.

'She was the best,' Stanislav said. 'She should have been first.'

Nina was pleased. Even Mrs Mulić looked happy at the very end, when she was saying goodbye. She said it was a concert they would all remember for the rest of their lives.

'I can't wait to see it on television,' Mrs Hatibović said. 'You'll be a star!'

'Just as soon as we get the electricity back,' Mrs Nurudinović remarked pragmatically.

Mrs Hatibović was, like Mrs Nurudinović, a widow. She didn't have children. Her husband had died very young, soon after they were married. He was a scaffolder; he fell off a building. Then it was just Mrs Hatibović. Forty years on her own now. But she always had good friends. She liked spending time with Mrs Nurudinović, who didn't feel sorry for herself like some people in their situation did.

Before the war, Mrs Hatibović had shrewdly concluded that things would quickly get very bad if it came to fighting, and she had stocked up. She had a reserve – tins, beans, dried food – but she had never imagined this was going to have to see her through such a long time. Her reserve was dwindling.

Nina wore a yellow scarf. She was still sitting in her winter coat. 'That scarf suits you,' Mrs Hatibović said. 'It makes you look posh.'

Nina wondered why Mrs Hatibović frowned sometimes when she said nice things. Sometimes Mrs Hatibović said things that sounded angry, then she smiled and everyone laughed.

She was looking at Nina through her thick spectacles. Mrs Hatibović was smaller than Mrs Nurudinović and thinner. Her face was very lined. She lit a cigarette. So did Mrs Nurudinović.

Just after they lit their cigarettes there was a crash, very loud and very near. The plastic sheeting on the outside window rattled. There was a whoosh. Nina knew there would be another explosion. She felt Stanislav's hand on her shoulder. He was pushing her towards Mrs Hatibović, who made a space for Nina at the table next to Mrs Nurudinović. Mrs Hatibović put her arm round Nina. She knew the two old women were scared. Stanislav sat facing them. He looked towards the window. They waited for the next explosion.

It came after ten seconds. Then they heard more impacts further away and Nina thought they would never stop.

'Screw them,' Mrs Hatibović said. She sometimes said things like that. She used swear words. Sometimes she swore and then she smiled and everyone laughed.

Mrs Hatibović had a strange smell, like perfume but with something chemical in it like disinfectant. It was quite a nice smell. Nina smelled it now, because Mrs Hatibović was holding her very close and very tight.

'Screw them,' Mrs Hatibović said again. Nina looked up to see if she was giving one of her odd smiles, but she wasn't. Then Mrs Hatibović added, 'I hope their mothers find them in a pie!'

Nina wanted to laugh, but she was too scared. She saw Stanislav smile.

'They're targeting the TV Centre,' he said.

'Well, I hope they miss,' Mrs Nurudinović remarked, 'because I want to see Nina singing in the concert.'

They were speaking in normal voices so Nina guessed that they must think the worst was over. It was so much easier to be in a bombardment when you were with other people, she thought. Stanislav hardly ever let her go out on her own. He said the worst thing in the world would be to be caught outside all by yourself in the middle of shelling.

Then, just when they had started to think it was over, there was a huge explosion. The noise was enormous, and the building shook. Nina started to cry and Mrs Hatibović patted her on the head. Nina didn't want to look at Mrs Hatibović because she didn't want her to see that she was crying. She thought Mrs Hatibović might be crying too. She thought the building was going to fall down.

They heard people shouting on the stairs. Stanislav went out to see what was happening. He went down in the dark. He could smell smoke, and also the smell that plaster makes when pulverised into dust and turned into a freezing cloud, a sort of chalky smell.

He could hear people shouting that the sixth floor had been hit. He went on down. Their apartment was on the fourth floor. When he got to the hall on the sixth floor there were already a dozen people there. There was another explosion very near, in the car park outside. Stanislav ducked with the others. A woman was crying, standing at the open door of an apartment. Stanislav went towards her and put his arm around her. Then a man came out of the apartment. Someone shone a torch and Stanislav saw the man's face in the edge of the torch beam. His eyes were wide open. 'They were in the kitchen!' the man said. 'Sitting in the fucking kitchen! And they're OK!'

The woman was shaking. Stanislav saw that there was a little girl in the hall standing in the corner by the open apartment door. The woman stepped away from him and took the girl in her arms. Then some neighbours started to lead the woman and her daughter away.

'Fucking hell! They're OK!' the man with the wide-open eyes told Stanislav. 'Big hole in the wall, and they're OK!'

Stanislav went down to the fourth floor. The apartment there hadn't been damaged. When he got back upstairs he told the others what had happened on the sixth floor. Mrs Hatibović knew the names of the woman and the little girl. 'The father's a policeman,' she said.

The evening carried on as normal after this. There was macaroni and tinned fish for dinner. They had eaten the same for the last three meals. They drank diluted orange juice, and as a treat in honour of Nina coming second in the national children's song contest, they shared a chocolate bar saved from a French aid package.

'Maybe the building will collapse,' Mrs Hatibović said. She peered round the table through her thick glasses.

'They're solid structures,' said Mrs Nurudinović, whose husband had been a builder.

'They should have put heating in the bomb shelter,' Mrs Hatibović said.

'No one ever thought we'd actually have to use the bomb shelter,' Mrs Nurudinović replied.

'Well, we should have thought of it. We should have been prepared for the worst.'

'Who wants to live preparing for the worst!' Mrs Nurudinović said. 'We were happy when we prepared for the best!'

'And look where it got us.'

'We'll see these buggers out. That's for sure!' Mrs Nurudinović said.

Nina was surprised, because she'd never heard Mrs Nurudinović swear before. She didn't think Mrs Nurudinović ever swore.

Then Mrs Nurudinović said, 'Justice is slow, but it will come.'

Mrs Hatibović put her hand gently on Mrs Nurudinović's shoulder. 'We're looking forward to seeing you on the television,' she told Nina.

31

When darkness fell, the attackers fired flares over Otes. Great shards of orange light illuminated the fields that separated the settlement from the western suburbs. A haystack in a field a hundred yards from the government command centre was set on fire by incendiary bullets and burned till after midnight, shedding an eerie flicker over nearby houses that had been destroyed by shelling. The winding, potholed road across the fields and the old industrial estate was now the only link between government troops in Otes and the Western Corpus headquarters near the PTT building. A hail of fire came down on vehicles using the road.

As the light from one flare dulled, before another was fired a battered Toyota made a dash for the city. Jusuf drove, a wounded soldier lying across the back seat. The Toyota made it as far as the haystack before snipers opened fire. Jusuf guessed that the attackers were properly organised now. There was no automatic fire; they weren't shooting at random. A bullet whistled behind the car and then, after a second or two, there was another close to the windscreen. Jusuf slowed the Toyota to take the first sharp turn as a star shell exploded above him. The soldier in the back groaned as the car accelerated abruptly coming out of the corner. The tyres growled in the frozen snow.

They've missed their chance, Jusuf thought. He guessed the marksmen were tired. Or maybe they were celebrating victory prematurely, too drunk to hit a slow-moving target at a hundred yards.

After the turn he was more confident that they wouldn't be picked off. He took the cigarette between the middle and index fingers of his right hand and steered the car with his left. Then he reached behind and offered the cigarette to the soldier, but the man was in too much pain to lift his hand and take it.

'You'll be in hospital in twenty minutes,' Jusuf said. The soldier groaned again. Both his legs were broken. Twenty minutes was a long time. Two bullets hit the snow in front of the Toyota. They buzzed. Jusuf had felt confident moments before but now he was less sure. Maybe they're not celebrating prematurely and maybe they're not tired. Maybe they just waited for us to reach this stretch.

A government car that had been used to carry troops in and out of the settlement lay abandoned nearby. Jusuf had seen it in Otes in the afternoon so it had been hit in the last few hours. Another star shell turned the land around them a garish shade of yellow. They drove beyond the cover of some bushes past the main factory complex. Jusuf accelerated but then had to slow down again at another sharp turn. He put the cigarette between his lips and took the steering wheel with both hands. He wasn't going faster than twenty-five miles an hour.

The Toyota hit a pothole and the soldier yelled. Jusuf knew they were approaching their own line. The last stretch of the road was the most uneven. He tried to avoid the next few potholes, but it wasn't easy in the darkness. He saw the barrier ahead. It was raised, as it should have been. He rolled the window down and looked into the guard post as he drove past. A soldier was crouched behind sandbags, his rifle trained on the Toyota.

'We're nearly there,' Jusuf told the wounded man in the back.

The Television Centre was taking a pounding. Jusuf stopped the car outside the Corpus headquarters and ran into the building. Troops lounged in the lobby. He picked out a man he recognised and told him to take the wounded soldier in the Toyota to the State Hospital.

He started to move along the main ground-floor corridor. 'It will need two of you to carry him from the car,' he said over his shoulder. '*Don't* lift him by the ankles.'

At the end of the corridor was an office similar to the command centre in Otes, bigger but with the same elements. There was a large table covered in maps and ashtrays overflowing with cigarette ends. There were weapons on narrow tables along one wall. Around the central table sat a dozen men.

Jusuf entered and closed the door behind him. The Bull sat at the head of the table, at the far end away from the door. He carried on speaking as Jusuf came in and took a seat opposite. The Bull was explaining why more troops wouldn't be dispatched to reinforce Otes.

'It can't be defended,' he said. He shrugged. 'Even with an attack elsewhere.'

There might have been a small chance of holding the village if there was a push further along the city perimeter.

'You guys have to face facts,' he concluded.

The Bull didn't know much about military strategy but they listened to him with care. Jusuf believed him when he said that no more troops would be sent; he was well-connected – if he said there would be no more troops then there would be no more troops. If he had decided that Otes was to be abandoned then it would be abandoned.

The men disliked being told what to do by a politician in khaki. But in the end they would toe the line. The Bull was sure about that. He wanted the Otes business finished quickly. He was tired and he had a headache.

'Can we hold the road for another day?' he asked Jusuf.

'I doubt it.'

'How many civilians are still there?'

'Fifteen hundred.'

'We'll evacuate them as soon as it's light. You had better come up with a plan.'

The Bull and his aide left. Jusuf stayed and they began to plot the evacuation.

At seven o'clock the meeting broke up. Alija was waiting for Jusuf in the corridor outside. When he saw Alija, Jusuf felt his spirits rise. In his bearing, his assumptions, his fastidious manner, Alija was like a creature from another world. He was efficient. He was educated and, as far as Jusuf knew, he wasn't corrupt.

Jusuf was exhausted and wanted to sleep, but in twelve hours they were going to move hundreds of people over hard terrain. The night would be devoted to desperate preparations.

Jusuf led the other man into a nearby office. He found a sheet of paper and sat down, pen in hand.

He wrote: *We are living in times that God did not intend for us. There will be better days. We shall prevail. We shall be together.*

Alija found an envelope in a cupboard on the other side of the room and handed it to Jusuf, who wrote Milena's name on the front and put the note inside.

'Take this to the bar,' he said. 'I'm going back to Otes.'

* * *

Alija walked out into the frozen night. Otes was lost. He'd known it would end like this. It had been clear to everyone, he thought, except those who were fighting the battle.

Alija had been right about many of the things that had happened since the start of the war. He had foreseen the horror. Yet, despite a capacity for realism that sometimes bordered on the cynical, he had not foreseen the extent to which sudden access to power and importance can corrode judgment and morality. Men who had been modest figures were transformed into capricious princelings by the fighting. So many politicians became drunk with the unfamiliar excitement of a country in freefall. They loved to talk about constitutions and referendums and all that razzamatazz. They loved the attention, the conferences, the special flights, the police cars with sirens blaring making a path for them in city traffic, because now they were men of power.

And so many people discovered dangerous pleasures. National pride brings wonderful comfort to a stunted imagination. It is thrilling to see your people on the march, to learn that you have been oppressed, to be convinced that you must rise up!

Chauvinism is seductive.

It is degrading too. It leads to dirty frozen hospitals.

The night had become clear and Alija could see stars. For a moment he was lifted out of his thoughts by a view of glittering light across the heavens.

But Otes was lost, and that put the whole western part of the city at risk – his city and his world. He could not contemplate the infinite in tranquillity.

He drove on through snow-bound streets without headlights. He didn't drive fast, and he tried to drive carefully. It took him twenty minutes to reach the bar where Milena worked.

'She hasn't come in yet and I don't suppose she'll be coming now,' one of the waitresses told him. 'Must've got stuck in the bombardment. Probably stayed at home.'

Alija decided to call at Milena's apartment in the morning. It was too late to return to Alipašino Polje now.

Instead, he went to his friend Dr Jurić's dinner party.

32

Soon after Wikram was killed, Brad had left Sri Lanka. He didn't want to take a newsroom job and a dispute arose over where he would be posted next. The dispute became acrimonious and ended in the paper letting him go. He set himself up as a free-lance – with the usual protestations of satisfaction at having been liberated to follow stories that really interested him. At first it was relatively easy to get work; in the media goldfish bowl he had a modest but marketable reputation. But he'd lost the knack of selling his own narrative of events. Once, his judgment had shaped his employers' judgment, but now editors called him back on stories, asked him why the competition had a different angle, why his own pieces were late or out of kilter. And all Brad could do was rage.

Which was why, long after that violent evening in Sri Lanka, his latest job looked like it was slipping away. The message he received just before the night-time bombardment presaged the end. He read the words silently several times. Then he shouted at the computer.

'Sonofabitch!'

He read again, and remarked indignantly, 'Moron!'

Your early file was confused and unusable, the news editor had written. *We need clear, factual reporting, without fireworks.*

'Without fireworks!' he hissed, looking at the computer. He drank more beer. 'How do you report an assassination without fireworks?'

He picked up the TV remote control and flicked through the channels. The hotel generator was working again – who knew for how long – and the satellite cable had been fixed. He stopped at CNN. A woman in Atlanta predicted snow in parts of Europe. She smiled indulgently and spoke about skiing.

Brad looked at the message again. He hadn't come to terms with it yet. *Anna's piece was very much better than your own,* it concluded. *Suggest you liaise with her more closely. Present performance not up to scratch.*

He was still absorbing the import of these words when Anna came into the room.

When she had arrived in the city Brad had wanted to know everything about Anna, but there wasn't a great deal to know. She had worked briefly in Guatamala and Nicaragua, writing stories about low-level insurgency. She spoke a little French and Spanish and she'd spent six months on the newsdesk, which meant she knew everyone in the organisation very much better than Brad did. What he didn't ask and never found out was if she understood the predicament that he was in.

Brad would have been surprised by the answer if he'd asked the question, because Anna *did* understand his predicament. If he'd been more gracious she would have tried hard to make it clear to him – and to the newsdesk – that he was in charge and that she had no intention of stepping on his toes, never mind stealing his job.

Anna could see what the newsdesk couldn't – that Brad hadn't surrendered to his demons. But he hadn't given her a chance to do much more than scurry around trying to stay out of his way.

'I'm going back to Otes tomorrow,' she said. Her voice was even.

He gave her an obtuse look. She might have described it as a childish look except that his features were so strikingly worn and weary that they chased away comparisons with a little boy. 'I need the Land Rover,' he said.

'For what?'

He would think of something.

'You can come if you want,' she said, 'but I'm taking the hard-top. Dr Barnes is bringing the little boy out first thing.'

Brad shrugged. Sanela had sent a message saying that the next day's interview – the one he'd planned to do with Milena – had been cancelled. 'OK, we'll both go.'

The implications of the newsdesk's admonition – liaise more closely with Anna – were profound. He guessed that if he tried to assert his authority he would discover that there was no longer any authority to assert, and he guessed too that whatever he reported tomorrow, a story about evacuating the British doctor would trump it.

'Is anyone else going?'

'Don't think so,' she said. 'Can I take one of these?' She stood over the crate of Carlsberg.

They hadn't really socialised since Anna's arrival in the city. Briefly he considered the fact that with his beer stash dwindling he was going to have to make another trip across the frontline to get supplies, but then he nodded. 'Sure. Go ahead.'

He had never actually seen her drink alcohol. Her abstemiousness matched the view he had formed – that she was too earnest.

She bent down and extracted a can from beneath the cling-film. The beer was at room temperature, which meant that it was nicely chilled.

Along with everyone else, Brad had noticed that Anna was pretty, but he hadn't thought until that moment, watching her open a can of beer, that she was vulnerable too. He hadn't until then thought of her as being anything other than hard-nosed and ambitious. She was, in fact, very young to be doing this kind of work.

Then he remembered the message he'd just received and he wasn't inclined to indulge Anna. She was on good enough terms with the newsdesk to conspire with the people who wanted him out. Yet the rage was dying. They were having a drink together and there was no point in renewing their quarrel.

When Anna eventually spoke she returned to the main issue of the day.

'The door should never have been opened,' she said. 'They fucked up!'

It was, he knew, more complicated than that. 'It's only a fuck-up when things go wrong.'

He turned the hard chair round, the one they used at the computer. Anna walked over from the window and sat on the bed.

'They tried to talk their way through,' he said. 'They thought they could do that.'

'But they have standing orders; they're not supposed to open their APCs for inspection.'

'You don't always think things through!' he said, his voice too loud.

Throughout the day, he had spoken with more force than he'd intended.

The curious mellowness that had briefly descended on them wasn't quite shattered by his impatient tone, but it was shaken a little.

'You *can't* calculate,' he continued. 'Not in *those* circumstances. You just do what you think is going to work. You can't do more than that. And if it doesn't work you don't get a second chance.'

She remembered his odd remark about responsibility, after he'd stormed out of Dejan's office. She understood that there was more going on in Brad's head than a preoccupation with what had happened on the Airport Road.

Brad lit a cigarette and exhaled. 'They opened the door,' he said. 'They didn't panic; they did the opposite: they thought they could negotiate. They weren't overwhelmed by their circumstances, by being surrounded and outgunned. They were over-confident.' He sipped his beer, and she noticed that he had brought the can so abruptly to his mouth that some of the contents rolled down his chin. He wasn't looking directly at her but into the middle distance. 'I thought I could fix it,' he said. 'I thought I could reason with the soldiers at the barrier!'

He knew he'd said something wrong, but he didn't know what.

Anna spoke in a soft steady voice. 'You said "*I*". You said "*I* thought".'

'Yeah?'

'Are we talking about the French soldiers or something else?'

'You have to *be* there,' he said. He practically whispered, yet even to whisper these words seemed to require an immense effort.

He felt an almost unbearable weariness. He had never spoken about what happened when Wikram told him to drive around the barricade. And now he was too exhausted to sustain the evasion. He was too tired to keep at bay the scene when they returned to the government side of the lagoon. The soldiers hadn't been able to block the road completely. Brad saw the guns but he was convinced they could talk their way through.

'You have to *be* there,' he said. 'If you haven't been there you don't know.' He was still looking into the middle distance and he didn't understand why he was talking about this; all he knew was that he *must* confront it. 'Do you think anybody wanted it to turn out the way it did?' He could have been talking about the road from the lagoon or the road from the airport.

Anna was very still.

Then Brad said, 'I thought we could get past them!' He felt the sudden pain of a dressing ripped from a wound, and then in the aftermath there was a kind of relief, a kind of tranquillity. 'I thought we would go on to Talawila, have dinner and a beer,' he said softly. There was a moment of absolute silence and then Brad concluded, tying up the memory with a kind of implacable inevitability, 'I got hit when I got out of the car. When I realised what was happening Wikram was lying on the other side of the road. They had shot him in the back of the head.'

He looked down and drew on his cigarette and sipped his beer and he thought of all the stars in the universe moving through space and how he would have to stop each one of them and make it go back in order to change the course of time and return to that barricade and make a different choice, drive round like Wikram said, drive round and hurry away.

Brad didn't see Anna standing up. The first he knew that she had moved was when he felt her hand on his shoulder.

* * *

Soon afterwards, they went down to the restaurant on the first floor. The only seats available were at a table with Michael Baring.

'If that sonofabitch patronises me, I'll wallop him,' Brad whispered.

'Mind if we join you?' Anna asked Baring.

As they sat down, Zlatko came in. A fine layer of snow lay in a ridge across the hair above his forehead, where the hood of his duffel coat had left his head exposed. There was more snow on his sleeves at the elbows. He brushed this away as he scanned the room.

When he spotted them, Zlatko walked over quickly and said to Brad, 'Can I talk to you?'

'Yeah, sit down.'

'I can't stay. Can we go outside?'

In the hall it was pitch dark. Brad lit his torch and shone it against the wall so that it reflected dimly on both of them.

'What's up?'

'Can you be at the Strand in Ilidža tomorrow morning at half past eleven?'

'Why?'

'There's a guy who'll talk to you.'

Ilidža, a settlement near the airstrip, was on the other side of the siege line. 'Brad, he knows who killed the minister. He was *there*.'

Brad inhaled the freezing dark and let Zlatko explain.

33

The apartment was warm, which pleased Alija very much. Warmth was a luxury he hated to be without. He moved about the city from public building to public building, visiting offices where there was usually a supply of heat. Comfortable temperatures go with power: in snowbound cities it is warm where decisions are made.

Jurić's flat was heated by a large stove in the sitting room.

The doctor introduced him to a dark-haired woman dressed in blue jeans and a mauve cashmere sweater with a silk scarf around her neck. She shook hands and greeted Alija politely in English. She was trying hard to appear confident, but there was uncertainty in her manner.

'This is Dr Barnes from London,' Jurić said. He watched Alija shyly take the doctor's hand and introduce himself in English.

Alija allowed a characteristic expression of meekness to cover his face. Jurić recognised this as a mask: Alija's unassuming persona, his self-effacing attention to other people's needs, was his way of mastering circumstances. He measured people shrewdly and got a sense of how they were likely to behave.

Alija looked at Terry and said in English to Jurić, 'I hope you are looking after Dr Barnes.'

Terry answered quickly. 'Dr Jurić has been very helpful.'

'Dr Barnes has come to accompany a little boy back to Britain for medical treatment,' Jurić explained. Then he remarked, without any irony, 'We are grateful.'

Sometimes she thought they were making fun of her. They were all so polite. She thought of the soldier in Otes who apologised for holding them up when they were ready to leave the shelter, like a taxi driver arriving late to collect a fare.

'We appreciate the help we have received from other countries,' Alija said, rather stiffly. 'It is something that sustains us.'

He spoke, Terry noticed, with the sort of clipped accent that is acquired through diligent study, rather than an accent like Jurić's, which was easy and confident and obviously the product of lots of practice.

'Where is the little boy?' Alija asked.

'In Otes,' Terry said. 'We're going back for him tomorrow.'

'You've been there already?'

'Today,' Terry said.

'Zlatko drove,' Jurić explained.

Zlatko was sitting with Sanela in a far corner of the room. He had arrived just ahead of Alija, after speaking to Brad at the Holiday Inn. Alija smiled at them. 'You're going back to Otes tomorrow?' he asked Zlatko.

'If I'm not too hungover.'

'Go early!'

Sanela heard the same words and understood them better than her lover. Perhaps somewhere in his easy-going optimism Zlatko also heard the warning in Alija's advice to go early, but he took no heed.

'Come and sit down and have a drink!' Zlatko told Alija.

Sanela watched Alija approach. She disliked the way he turned up everywhere. And now he was at this party, telling Zlatko to go early to Otes.

Sanela wished Alija hadn't come to Jurić's. She wished Dr Barnes hadn't come either. There was an unsteadiness about Dr Barnes.

'Have you any juice?' Alija asked Jurić.

'No juice, Alija, only Scotch! You'll have to break the habit of a lifetime!'

'I'd rather not, thanks,' Alija replied in an easy-going tone that suggested he was accustomed to being teased by Jurić.

'Juice is a problem,' the doctor said, 'particularly in these times of scarcity. Why can't you drink whisky like everyone else?'

Alija smiled patiently and sat on the edge of the sofa next to Terry.

Terry sipped whisky and smoked and wondered what any of her heart-specialist colleagues in London would think.

Just a few hours had passed since she had thought she was about to die in the white waste between the arcade and the garage. After the song contest, Sanela and Terry stopped at the Holiday Inn on their way to Jurić's place. In her room Terry remembered her passport. That she could have forgotten about it until then was inexplicable and unforgivably stupid. She was acting differently from normal. Her thoughts had started to form new patterns. Her way of feeling had changed. In her everyday world she would not have overlooked her library card, never mind her passport.

Alija waited for Jurić to return from the kitchen with a soft drink. There was a bottle of Scotch on the coffee table in front of the sofa, and canapés – cheese and meat paste and biscuits. These had been laid out on three plates. Alija reached over and picked up a biscuit and put it in his mouth. It was stale and the meat paste was ice-cold. Jurić handed him a glass. He drank the juice, washing away the taste of the canapé.

'So,' Jurić said in English. 'What news?'

Alija shrugged.

Jurić said to Terry, 'He gives away no secrets, but he knows everything!'

'That isn't true, of course,' Alija remarked, in the sort of untroubled voice that distinguishes someone who knows everything. 'Tell me,' he asked Terry, 'in Otes who did you speak to, in our army?'

'To your friend – Jusuf,' Zlatko replied on Terry's behalf. 'He said it could be done, in the morning.'

Alija nodded again and then he said, 'I wish you luck.'

'Are you in the army?' Terry asked Alija.

He threw up his hands to indicate that nothing could be further from the truth. 'I've never fired a gun!' he said. 'I run errands.'

'He keeps secrets,' Jurić said. Then, after a moment's silence, 'Alija is an adviser in one of our ministries, but what he really does is run the government!'

'Alija!' Zlatko said. 'We need you to sing for us!'

'Time you earned that orange juice,' Edis the theatre director added. He was sitting with Jamila on a large armchair.

'How's the play?' Alija asked.

'It's not a play, it's a musical,' Edis corrected. 'It's going very well. I wish it wasn't.'

'Edis thinks we should be doing something more serious than putting on musicals,' Jamila explained.

'I thought it was your production.'

'It is. I have created a Frankenstein!'

'It's good for morale,' Alija said and at once he was sorry. The musical *was* good for morale, but he understood Edis' frustration. He knew the theatre could do more than raise spirits.

'Edis has written a new play,' Jamila said.

'About the war?' Jurić asked.

'Not *this* war. It's set in the eighteenth century.'

'Alija, give us a song!' Zlatko interrupted. He was quite drunk.

'It's a party,' Jurić agreed. 'In honour of Dr Barnes! Sing her one of our songs!'

Jurić stepped out of the room and returned with a guitar. He handed it to Alija, who put his orange juice on the table and began to pluck the strings and tune the instrument.

The room was lit unsteadily by two candles on the small table beside Sanela and Zlatko and two more candles on the coffee table. The latest blackout had lasted three weeks.

Terry stood and walked to the other end of the sofa, where there was a space to sit. This gave Alija more room. Sanela spread the covers on the sofa before Terry sat down.

Alija's face looked softer by candlelight, less spectral. His beard was very thick. He was about the same age as Jurić and Edis, mid thirties, and the guitar in front of him hid his thinness.

Alija strummed the guitar and began to sing. His voice was harsh, in keeping with the style of the music. He played short sharp chords and sang initially in a strange staccato, then he developed the melody so that it was softer and easier to follow.

'This is an old, old song,' Sanela whispered to Terry. 'It's about love, of course. The singer yearns for his girl, but she has been promised to another.' She stopped and then added, 'I suppose that isn't a very original story!'

The listeners nodded appreciatively when Alija executed long chains of descending and ascending notes in which the resolution chord was constantly deferred as the singer followed more and more complex progressions. It was mournful and beautiful.

The song ended and Alija began another. After the opening bars, he and the rest of the company looked to Jamila and she joined in, closing her eyes as she sang. She had a husky voice, a deep contralto. This song was mournful too, austere and exquisite. Edis looked down at the coffee table, smoke spiralling into the darkness from his cigarette.

Terry watched Jurić, sprawled in an armchair. He seemed completely relaxed. She thought about his hospital, where they lacked the most basic medicines, where the wounded queued in dirty corridors.

Jamila wore mascara and red lipstick. She wore one earring, in her left ear; it was silver, three small chains with hearts suspended at the end. Edis had short grey hair, thick eyebrows and three days' beard. His face was lined. He chain smoked.

They all lived on humanitarian aid, queuing in the snow and sleet to collect water from broken pipes. They spent nights in freezing, unlit rooms. They were familiar with the calibre of heavy weapons, expert at telling how far away a shell had landed by the sound of the explosion. Every day, twenty or thirty of their fellow citizens were murdered. Every single courtesy these people showed, every gesture of fellowship, every act of kindness required courage. Their decency demanded optimism and reserves of hope.

Jamila finished singing and they clapped and cheered. She smiled and the mood lifted. Jurić filled glasses and complained because he had to go to the kitchen to fetch more orange juice for Alija.

'Will you sing for us, Doctor?' Jurić asked.

Terry began to shake her head, fearing that Jurić would insist, but instead he said, 'We'll sing one of your songs, and you join in. Yes?'

She nodded gratefully, wondering what one of *her* songs might be.

Alija played a few familiar notes and began to sing 'Yesterday'.

At least Terry knew the words.

Zlatko lifted his glass and looked at it in the candlelight. When Sanela moved, the left side of her body rearranged itself against the right side of Zlatko's body. He loved the touch of her. He loved the way Sanela dressed; he loved the way she read the newspaper, with a studious expression that made her look severe; he loved the way she dissected ideas, her own and other people's. It was all abstract to her. Zlatko loved the way Sanela was glad to see him even when she was in a bad mood. He loved the way she was good tempered even when she was bad tempered. She would announce that she planned to be unreasonable and warn him that if he wanted to speak reasonably he should speak to someone else. Sanela was a woman Zlatko could not have created whole from his imagination. She was of herself; she was independent and particular.

Sanela began to sing when Alija played 'Yellow Submarine', this also in honour of Dr Barnes. Towards the end of the song they realised that the chorus, in which everyone, including Terry, joined in, was being accompanied by a loud but irregular beat. It wasn't part of the music. It was someone hammering on the front door. The song trailed away and Jurić went out to see who was there. A current of cold air flowed into the living room from the hall when he returned with the new arrival, a small neat man wearing a rumpled suit and a checked shirt with an acrylic tie that had a huge knot. His name was Mehmed and he knew everyone in the room except Terry. He greeted the company shyly and followed Jurić to where Terry was sitting.

'Mehmed particularly wanted to meet you,' Jurić explained.

Terry stood up to shake hands.

'His family is in the east,' Jurić added. 'We believe that people outside Bosnia may not understand how difficult the humanitarian situation is there.'

'I hope you are going to sing for us, Mehmed!' Zlatko called from the armchair opposite.

Mehmed looked horrified and raised both hands, palms facing outward, and said, 'I can't. I can't.'

'It's true,' Edis remarked. 'He can't!'

Sanela went back to sit beside Zlatko and Mehmed sat down beside Terry. Alija began to sing about an ancient love affair.

'I learned that you would be here,' Mehmed told Terry in heavily accented English. He nodded towards Jurić, who had gone off to fetch a juice. 'I work at the hospital.'

He took a document ten or fifteen pages long from the inside pocket of his jacket. Jurić handed him a glass of orange juice.

'This is information which I would like you to pass on if possible,' Mehmed said. He gave Terry a shy smile. 'I know it's an imposition, but I would be grateful for anything that you or your colleagues in London can do.'

She opened the document.

'I know,' Mehmed said quickly. 'This is very bad.'

There was a picture of a child with a crushed head.

'It is important we show people what is happening to civilians. I'm sorry if this disturbs you. The reality is more disturbing than photographs.'

The text began with a list of towns – Srebrenica, Žepa, Goražde and others. Beside each town were numbers of people who had died since the beginning of the war from disease, hunger, cold, gunfire, shelling. The numbers were broken down to show the high proportion of dead children.

'These settlements are cut off,' Mehmed explained. 'They can't be supplied. The Rebels stop aid convoys crossing the lines. Conditions are bad. The statistics speak for themselves.

In Žepa we know for sure they are carrying out amputations without anaesthetic. They have no surgical instruments. No antibiotics. Perhaps you could have these documents photo-copied; spread them among people you know. Perhaps you know some politicians?'

Terry studied the document. Edis watched Mehmed watch-ing Terry. He felt sorry for Mehmed, whom he knew to be a good man. He had a brother in Srebrenica and he had been part of a group that had gone to plead with the General to do some-thing about the civilians trapped in the eastern enclaves. Now he was giving his painstakingly put-together document to a doctor from London whom Edis was pretty sure couldn't do much to help. He was sorry that Mehmed was investing so much hope in this encounter with Terry.

Edis began to think about his play, set on a night when the city was sacked by Eugene of Savoy. He had several scenes in which citizens met together fearfully in rooms like this, and they addressed the problem of violence. They addressed the problem of violence even as violence surrounded them and threatened them.

And there was a character like Alija, for whom explanation helped. Understanding why Eugene's troops were burning the city didn't compensate for the burning but it made it less fright-ening. Then there was the Mehmed character. For him there could never be an adequate explanation. His response to the violence was emotional. He represented the indignation of the ages – dead children, burned bodies, raped women, massacred civilians: he was uncomprehending, aghast.

In Edis' play there was no dialogue between these two. There could not be: their views were incompatible.

Inevitably, there were in the drama two doomed lovers – a Catholic girl taken with her family from the city under the prince's protection, and the Catholic girl's Muslim boy.

Edis sighed. Every piece of drama came back to Shakespeare and he'd spent so much time making his play something other than Montagues and Capulets. But it always came back to this. It was in every fibre of his artistic being.

He looked at Zlatko and Sanela sitting across the candlelit coffee table. Some things simply happen, he thought, like snow in winter. It isn't necessary to turn everything into art. He had no desire to put Zlatko and Sanela in his play. They were real life. They were not doomed.

Edis was thinking this just at the moment when the music stopped and the building shook. They all sat forward.

Jurić had been standing next to the window. The crack of the detonation was close enough to startle him. He jumped forward and spilled some of his whisky.

The room went quiet.

Then the silence was shattered by a second explosion and a third.

'The hall,' Jurić ordered.

They moved quickly to the hall, where there was just enough room for everyone to sit on the floor. It was cold. Jurić hurried back into the sitting room and brought blankets from a cupboard. He was stepping back into the hall when there was an explosion that was close enough to send shrapnel and small bits of masonry through the tarpaulin windows of the kitchen.

Terry felt an arm on her shoulder. It was Zlatko. 'We're safe here, Doctor,' he said. 'Thick Habsburg walls!' He slapped the plaster behind him and leaned his head against it, and she wondered whether he was being ironic.

Jurić began to hand his guests their winter coats and they struggled into them and then huddled under the blankets. The bombardment continued. Sometimes there was a lull and they would relax and talk about moving back into the sitting room, but then the explosions began again. 'They're targeting the presidency,' Jurić told Terry. 'It's in the next block.'

'Looks like we're here for the night,' Zlatko said.

Jurić nodded. 'It is too dangerous to return to the hotel,' he told Terry. 'Zlatko will take you back in the morning to pick up your things.'

The others greeted the prospect of a night on Jurić's floor without complaint. They had been in this situation many times. The explosions continued for hours, great screaming tremors in the night.

Terry lay awake in the darkness and listened to the shells. From time to time the others joked, whispering in their own language, chuckling softly, tossing and turning and giggling like children.

Terry woke at four. Sanela lay close, her head resting on Zlatko's arm.

A sliver of moonlight streamed through a crack where the sitting-room door had been left ajar. Jurić was asleep, lying flat on his back beneath the blankets. Alija lay beside him, and closer to the door Mehmed and Edis and Jamila.

They slept in the frail light of a winter moon. Terry closed her eyes. Before she dozed she felt a curious peace, as safe as anyone could feel on such a night, sleeping with heroes.

34

Milena walked uneasily down the deep gash in the hillside where the road wound serpent-like in the broad space between the apartment blocks. For weeks she had walked to the bar from Alipašino Polje wearing leather boots with thick rubber soles. When she brought them from Foča she had thought them ugly. But that was an ugly day. She chose her things quickly. She wasn't thinking about style.

In Sarajevo the boots had proved their worth, as Milena trudged back and forth over the snow from Alipašino to the city centre and back again.

But on this night she wasn't wearing her boots with the thick rubber soles. She wore a pair of close-fitting stylish boots. Her best, in honour of Nina's appearance at the song contest. It was her custom to change into these boots when she got to the bar, but she hadn't wanted to wear the ugly out-door boots when she took Nina to the concert. She thought they made her look like a peasant from the countryside, and she didn't want to embarrass Nina.

The soles were thin, and Milena's feet were cold. She couldn't get a proper grip on the snow as she walked and slid down the serpent path towards the TV station, hurrying past the burnt-out trams till she reached the back road.

A heavy fog closed in on the darkness. She could see just a few yards ahead. Once, on the main road, as she crossed the tram tracks, stepping over twisted power lines that had been brought down in a bombardment and never repaired, she thought she saw a man lying on the ground nearby. She stopped, scared, and looked more closely, but it was a shell hole filled with black water, scarring the snow.

The tram station was surrounded by high railings. Peering ahead she made out the sharp steel points piercing the darkness and the fog like a ghostly stockade.

Milena kept music in her head, playing again and again, rewinding. She clutched at the bars of Kemal Monteno's song. It was simple and true and good. It was a kind of shield for her, protecting her as she stumbled through the dark. She hummed the chorus, so softly that only she could hear.

She moved on past the railings, peering straight ahead. If anyone approached she wanted to see them first. She didn't want to be surprised. She was ready to run back across the road.

Her coat felt heavy, and she was very tired. Ahead was a one-hour journey by foot across snow in unsuitable boots, in foggy darkness. After that, hours of work in a noisy smoke-filled bar. And her lover was in the west, where the sound of explosions could still be heard. And her people were far away from her. The people who became her family long ago. Željko and Jasna were in Dusseldorf. She had tried to contact them after the siege began, sending a letter out with an old woman, a friend of Mrs

Nurudinović, who had left with her invalid husband on a Red Cross convoy. But she had no way of knowing if Željko and Jasna had received her letter.

She told them what had happened and why she had left Foča. She'd had to write quickly, sitting with Mrs Nurudinović, who had just heard that the woman and her husband were going on the convoy. Milena had only a few minutes to scribble a note to Željko and Jasna. She told them she was OK. She had work, a place to stay. She told them not to worry. She didn't tell them what was in her heart. She didn't tell them that it was breaking.

She did not say thank you to Željko and Jasna for everything that they had done. Afterwards, this weighed upon her. Yet it was not something that she could put into words. Even if they were in the same room, it would have been hard for Milena to talk like that to Željko and Jasna.

From the very beginning they didn't talk about things, at least not about *those* things. They didn't talk about Milena's mother and father. They just never spoke about it. The three of them lived for years and years doing the things that families do. Željko and Jasna loved Milena with the tenderness and care of a mother and father, and Milena loved them as if she were their own child. And all those years they never spoke about it. How could she have put anything down in a letter? These were things about which she could not speak. Her hastily written note said she was OK, and was signed with an affectionate kiss. It was the best she could do. Now it weighed upon her and she wished she had said more.

She was very tired. Her feet began to feel numb. She remembered Nina's hand in hers when they walked to the hall. Milena wore black leather gloves and Nina wore blue and white woollen mittens.

She had to walk more slowly because of the fog. It took her an unusually long time to pass the TV building and the tram depot and make her way to the back road.

She tried not to think about work, standing and smiling interminably and calculating change and combining orders and staying on the right side of the new barman, whose qualifications for the job appeared to rest on the fact that he was a cousin of the owner.

Not like Fudo, who had a gift. Fudo who filled the tiny riverside bar in Foča with his genial presence. He was the most uncomplicated man Milena had ever known. At least, he seemed so to her. They used to have jokes that ran between them for days and left the others excluded – odd things that Fudo and Milena found funny. She treasured their friendship. It was a priceless part of the life she made in Foča. The day that Miroslav accused her of infidelity drove a hole through that life. And the day he went with the others to get Fudo – that day she could barely think about. The day she watched from the window.

Fudo was so much taller than the others, and yet he had been afraid. Those men used to sit in his bar. They respected him. Everything that had once bound them to one another and to Foča lay in ruins when Fudo Omeragić was set upon by former friends.

Miroslav was the leader of that pack.

Miroslav who had been her faithful lover.

Milena sought to understand Miroslav's betrayal. When she made space between them – a space measured in time and distance and barbed wire and bereavement – she looked again at their lives and tried to understand the force that shattered the house, and the life, that they had built.

She set Miroslav's sense of wounded honour against the wounded honour that began the war. The seed of suspicion grows in the psyche of individuals and of nations in the same way, the seed of resentment, the seed of hostility and fear. Once the sickness has taken root it is hard to cure. Milena could not bring herself to confront openly her husband's guilt, but she blamed those who sowed the seeds, those who played upon resentment and turned his weakness to wickedness. When the great plague came, Miroslav might have turned on Fudo, but Milena understood that he turned on Fudo more easily because of what was whispered years before about Milena. That little vial of poison spawned a monstrous crime.

She clung to memories of Miroslav. She was walking now towards the place where they had met. A little further on, on the right side of the street, was the apartment where Mira's aunt and uncle used to live. She'd heard that they had gone to Zagreb before the start of the war. Mira was somewhere in Croatia.

Ah, that morning. It had been as cold as it was now. When they arrived by bus from Foča, three girls from the countryside, visiting the city on their greatest ever adventure. And Miroslav was there, waiting for them, waiting for her. They were fated to be together. That she knew. And they had had happy years, when they built their lives together and loved one another.

She walked along a narrow stretch of road with trees on either side. Behind the trees to her right was a long line of low grey buildings that looked almost like cottages. Perhaps they had been there since before the First World War, she thought, when this road was a country lane. She was on the oldest road into the city. She was walking through an area that was once covered by fields of wild sunflowers. Nearby was a railway goods yard. She knew it was there but she couldn't see it because of the fog. The trees were black and leafless.

Milena thought about summer, imagined the trees thick with leaves, speckled brightly with rays of flooding sunlight. She thought of bird song, considered the way Miroslav, by the water's edge at Krvavac, once lifted her up from where she sat on a rug beneath a tree and kissed her, passionately, one August afternoon. They were alone, but she could hear the sound of children playing nearby.

He made his life with her. He made his wedding vows and kept them – until the day he dishonoured himself at the head of a mob, the day he turned into a murderer. And so she left him, and escaped to the city.

She heard small-arms fire from Pero Koserić Square, and ahead, between the bakery and Mira's aunt and uncle's old flat, there were two mortar explosions.

She kept on walking. She felt foolish wearing these boots. Probably no one had noticed them when she and Nina had been at the concert. But she would have hated to have embarrassed the little girl.

And the child had sung so beautifully. Milena could have accompanied her on the piano. She imagined Nina in the city-centre apartment with the grand piano and the books and the long sofa. She saw her standing in front of the picture of the old market, where the wizened men in puttees walked towards the artist. Nina standing straight, with a blue dress on, a white lace border round the neck and cuffs, singing earnestly.

Milena knew how to accompany a song in a way that carried the singer's voice, elevated it, danced with it. She imagined the notes melding with Nina's voice and making something infinitely beautiful and pure in that beautiful room, something Nina would remember when she was old like Mrs Nurudinović and Mrs Hatibović.

Some kinds of beauty are immutable. They cannot be destroyed by cruelty or stupidity or violence, or even death. They inhabit the soul. They are the breath of God.

Milena felt a river of weariness run through her. She didn't have the heart to walk further, all the way to the centre of town.

She wanted her father. She wanted to see him, walking towards her on this city street.

When Milena was a child she dreamed of her father. She could not speak about him, because her mother never spoke about him and Milena knew her father had been wicked to leave. Her mother had to fend for the two of them all alone.

But she dreamed of him. Milena dreamed of sitting on her father's knee and whispering to him. She dreamed of leaning up so close she could feel the coolness of his skin, and almost touch the bristles on his cheek and she whispered to him.

'Daddy.'

She would have given everything she ever owned to hug her father. She knew that he must have been lonely when he went away. He went off on his own to the city, leaving everything behind. He must have thought about Milena sometimes.

She wanted her father to walk towards her on this tree-lined street. He might have walked through this place once. He *must* have walked here once. It was the oldest road into the city, the path that was taken by every boy and girl and man and woman who fled here, or who came to seek their fortune, or who came to build an ordinary life. Her father must have walked along this street beneath these trees when he ran away from Foča. He must have walked here, with his heart beating, a poor man from the countryside all on his own. The way he spoke would have given him away, where he was from.

Milena had stopped thinking about the noise all around her. She was no longer scared, but she was immensely tired. She didn't keep to the inside of the pavement or hug the barrier at the intersection before the bakery.

She wanted her father. Once, when she was about fourteen, Milena was betrayed by a boyfriend, Srečko. She learned about this not by being told but by being confronted with the evidence – Srečko walking hand in hand with another girl, on the road from the school to the city centre. Milena began to cry, quite suddenly and uncontrollably. And because she was embarrassed by her tears she walked quickly into a side street, hoping that no one would recognise her. She walked to the end of the street and tried to get her feelings under control. At the end of the street was an orchard that stretched to the edge of the river. Milena walked along the river bank out of the town and when she was tired and the path petered out, she sat on a rock and looked into the river. She imagined that if she jumped in at this point, where it was deep and slow moving, she could lie face down and the water would roll over her gently and she would go slowly down to the muddy river bed and open her eyes to look at the plants there, the plankton and weed, and she would grasp the soft earth in her fingers and lay her face on shells and stones. She would stay in the clear water and look at the fishes swimming from Foča all the way through rapids and waterfalls to the sea.

When she travelled to the sea with her mother, when she was very small, Milena nursed a secret wish that her father would be waiting for them at the coast. At the bus station, when her mother went to make a telephone call, Milena willed herself to believe that her father was going to come and collect them. It would be a surprise that they had prepared together, a surprise for Milena, and then the three of them would go to the sea together.

Every visitor who ever came to Željko and Jasna's house and heard Milena play the German piano told her she had a gift. The music teacher at school told her she had a gift – so it must have been true, because the music teacher didn't normally lavish praise on her pupils, and Milena, an otherwise unremarkable student who was inclined to be part of an unruly crowd, was not a likely recipient of the music teacher's approval.

Playing the piano was what she was known for. That and the fact that her mother and father ran away.

Milena spent her life not turning her gift for music into a way of living with loss. She did not use music to reflect the bleak reality inside her heart. She learned how to undermine the strength of any tune, with subtle changes of chord and clever phrasing, to keep the listener off balance and surprised. She learned the tricks of the piano player's trade. She never played the music in her soul. To do that would have been to recognise the meanness of fate.

She did her bar work like that, never going below the surface pleasantness. It made her good at what she did. She knew endless ways to ease a conversation into the comfortable byways of acquaintance and sometimes friendship. Over the years she had perfected her craft, until she could navigate a company with the greatest of skill. She was a master of her craft. Even when shells exploded outside she didn't forget to count the change, and say please and thank you.

She feared that that was how she conducted her affair with Jusuf. Perhaps it was ruthlessly superficial. Perhaps she had devoted her huge energy over all those years, her vast reserve of hope and love, to the business of being with others without ever showing what was deep inside her. Her father left before she was born, and then her mother ran away, and let Milena come home from school one day to find strangers.

Or perhaps she was cheerful and hopeful and fun to be with because she resolved *never* to be mean. Perhaps she lived her life in anticipation of healing that wound. She could have left Foča when she finished school. But if she'd gone away, perhaps they would not have been able to find her, her mother and father, when they came back to be with her.

Or perhaps she should have come here sooner. Perhaps she should have come to look for them.

Because all those years her father did not know and her mother did not know what a beautiful woman she had become. She did what they were unable to do. She made her way in the world; she paid her debts and fended for herself, and if she had had children she would have loved them so.

The touch of her hand would have been upon her daughter's hair. She would have sung to her.

The shells came in thick and fast now, and there were thunderflashes and fires; there was a sound as that of the sky torn.

Milena could feel the touch of her mother's fingertips. She saw her mother's face and knew that she was tired, infinitely tired from a lifetime of disappointment, and she reached up and touched her mother and held her close. If they had been like others and they had had time to play together and go to the sea and sit and look at the waves, she could not have loved her mother more. Because her love was infinite.

She came to this place to meet her mother and her father. She was drawn here, as they were drawn here. Like them, she spoke with a country accent that marked her out. But this place was where her husband first looked at her, where her father fled, where her mother joined him.

She saw her father walking on the road. He was a short man. He had a thick moustache, and not the kind of sharp suit she had imagined, but a country suit, of wool, and a white shirt with no collar. He had thick hair, and in his eyes an expression of such remorse that she ran to him and flung her arms around him and whispered. 'It's OK, Daddy.'

And she walked with them beneath the trees, along that endless road towards the sea.

35

Danby read the printout again and frowned. Sergeant Matthews stepped back a pace, watching his chief in the light of a night lamp by the side of the camp bed.

Danby sat on the edge of the bed in shorts and singlet. He waited for a few moments more and then he said, 'No reply.'

When Matthews had gone, Danby lay back and stared into the darkness.

The message from New York said that the minister's assassination was to be investigated by a specially appointed commission. UN staff in the city were to avoid public comment pending the results of the inquiry. UN officers couldn't investigate themselves, so the inquiry already announced by the General was to be suspended (in reality it had never begun). The names of three distinguished diplomats were written on the printout. These three would head the formal UN investigation. Their names and biographies were the only pieces of information that were to be passed on to the media.

No date was set for the arrival of the commission. The nature and scope and duration of its investigation weren't specified.

Danby could imagine the next day's briefing. The media wouldn't buy a distinguished commission. They would see it for what it was. They would see it the way Danby saw it.

He was angry because *he* was the one designated to market this farce. The point of Danby's work a lot of the time was to place a positive spin on negative developments. Part of his brain was doing that already: the commission demonstrated that the UN was serious about putting its own house in order. The calibre of the diplomats who'd been appointed showed that the inquiry would be high-powered and thorough. It was appropriate that UN staff make no further comment about the assassination since this might be regarded as an attempt to influence the outcome of the inquiry.

But Danby knew that this wasn't right.

He believed in separating right from wrong and now he was to be the front man for something less than honest: this didn't sit well.

He thought about the mission, mired in chaos. Despite it all, they had kept hundreds of thousands of people alive, fed them, brought them medicine, brought them the hope of a negotiated end to the fighting. There were massacres that hadn't been stopped, but there were massacres that *didn't* happen and they didn't happen because UN troops showed up.

Danby dozed fitfully, weighing up usefulness and virtue and honesty and cowardice. In the morning he was still angry, and he became more irritable still at breakfast, sitting with Major Thomson at the large oval-shaped table in the Delegates' Club dining room.

'Rocard had a word with me last night,' Thomson said.

Thomson could see that Danby was in low spirits and he wondered if the pressure was getting too much for the Irishman. It was often the ones who seemed most in command who cracked when the going got tough.

'Yes?'

'He was concerned.'

Thomson was hungry and he'd just been presented with ham and eggs and fried bread. He hoped Danby wouldn't be difficult.

'He told me you had been to see him,' Thomson went on.

'I wanted information.'

'That's just it,' Thomson said, placing a piece of moderately soft egg on top of a slice of ham and skewering this on the end of his fork. 'All of that is to be left to the new commission.'

'You know about the commission?'

'Yes, of course I know about the commission!' Thomson allowed an edge of irritation into his voice. 'I'm public affairs too, in case you'd forgotten!'

Danby gave a thin smile and said, 'Then you may be able to tell me when this commission is going to arrive?'

'Not until after the airlift resumes.'

'Resumes?' Danby put his cup down and it clattered on the saucer.

'There are problems in Geneva,' Thomson said between chewing ham and egg. 'Some concerns regarding security. Flights will stop today until we can extract guarantees from the factions that aid planes won't be targeted.'

Danby stood up. 'I wasn't told about this!'

'I'm telling you now,' Thomson said. He tried not to sound triumphant.

'There are no more flights?'

'We have to bring in some essential stuff this morning ... nothing after that.'

Danby began to walk away. Thomson stood up and said, 'This isn't for public consumption. We don't want a stampede to the airport. Nothing's to get out to the media.'

Danby hurried upstairs to the Situation Room. Matthews was standing by the window smoking. He put his cigarette into an empty cigarette packet and crushed it in one hand, closing the window with the other. He hadn't expected Danby to come up from breakfast so soon.

'Let me see the overnight traffic from New York and Geneva,' Danby snapped.

Matthews was nervous. 'Anything in particular, sir?'

'Just show me the printouts.'

'Sir, not all the messages are in the regular file.' Matthews walked to a table in the corner of the room. He came back with a sheet of paper.

'This came in ... for limited circulation until this morning. Doesn't say what time this morning.' Danby took the message and read it. Only three officers were authorised to do so. Thomson was one of them; Danby was not. The airlift was to be suspended indefinitely at noon.

Danby left the Situation Room and walked down to the first-floor lobby. He couldn't immediately think of anything that he could say or do that would make him less angry. Then he turned and climbed back up the stairs. There was one constructive thing he *could* do.

'I want you to go to the Holiday Inn,' he told Matthews. 'There's a British doctor there. Her name is Barnes, or Burns, something like that. I don't know what room. She's evacuating a little boy to London. They have to get to the airport by twelve, but she won't know that so you need to get the message to her. If they delay she won't get the boy out.'

The soldier nodded. Danby spoke quietly. 'And Matthews, no need to tell anyone where you're going.'

'I'll be off then, sir.'

'If she's not there, there's a journalist who might be able to get a message to her.' He gave him Anna's details. 'They were together yesterday. If you have to speak to the journalist, make it crystal clear the information is unattributable.'

36

Alija was irritated because he had to make an extra trip. It would take twenty minutes to go to Alipašino Polje, and another twenty minutes to climb up to the sixteenth floor and climb back down again. Milena might want to send a reply to Jusuf – another ten minutes – and then ten minutes more to drive back to headquarters. He was going to waste an hour. He had to be back at the State Hospital by eight. Jurić had promised him syringes and bandages for Otes. Thinking about syringes made him angry. There was almost nothing left to put in them – no antibiotics, no painkillers.

He hit a tailback on the road near the bakery. A Ukrainian APC at the head of a UN convoy was stuck on a corner. The huge tyres were churning up snow. A grey Fiat 500 had tried to drive round the APC and had slipped into a ditch. Two Ukrainian soldiers were helping the people from the Fiat lift it back onto the road.

They were close to a sniper area. People hurried past. A Ukrainian officer stood behind the APC smoking a cigarette. There were eight lorries in the convoy, with a second APC in the rear. The officer was trying, lazily, to get the vehicles in the convoy to reverse. He lifted his cigarette hand and flicked it, as if waving away a beggar in the street. He wanted them to make room so that the lead APC could take another shot at the corner.

It took them five minutes to extricate the Fiat from the ditch. Alija hit the steering wheel with his hands several times to relieve his impatience. There wasn't another route to Alipašino.

The Ukrainians and the Fiat people argued and swore. At last, when the car was clear, the APC began to reverse. It got round the corner after two more unsuccessful attempts.

For forty years the Ukrainians had threatened to roll across north Germany with the rest of the Warsaw Pact. Now they couldn't roll from one part of the city to another without getting stuck. The Ukrainian UN troops hadn't been paid for months. They were notorious black marketeers. Alija, like everyone else, got his petrol from the Ukrainians. They bought cars and stereos, and their APCs were always running out of fuel.

The convoy began to lumber past and the cars ahead of Alija started to move. There was a huge line of people outside the bakery waiting for bread, and it had begun to snow again. The sky was low and grey and the temperature was well below freezing.

After the bakery the traffic eased. Alija reached Alipašino around seven. Milena's apartment block was built on a steep hill, exposed on all sides to shellfire. Two teenagers stood in the entrance. 'Where are you going?' one of them asked. He was about eighteen. He had a beard that hadn't grown properly and he wore a jacket that was too thin to protect him from the cold. The other boy clapped gloved hands against his thighs trying to warm up. All the apartment blocks had guard committees. Alija couldn't imagine these two youngsters offering much resistance if the Rebels entered the city, but he knew he would start to believe the war was lost if kids like this were too scared or too indifferent to stand in the cold and go through the motions of defending their homes. He showed them his military ID and they stood aside. The younger one tried a salute.

The temperature in the tiled lobby was lower than the temperature outside. It was like stepping into a deep freeze. Alija walked past the defunct lift to the dark and dirty stairway. On the sixth floor there were workmen. He stopped to catch his breath and ask what was going on.

One of the men looked up, shrugged. 'Direct hit last night.'

'Anyone hurt?'

The man shook his head.

Alija was perspiring by the time he reached the sixteenth floor. It was dangerous to break into a sweat in these temperatures.

There was no reply when he knocked on her door. He couldn't hear any sound from inside. The door of the apartment opposite opened and an old woman looked out. She stood with her hand on the door ready to close it quickly.

'She hasn't come home,' Mrs Hatibović said. 'Who are you?'

She peered at Alija through thick glasses.

These buildings weren't designed to freeze, he thought. They weren't designed to be dark. Now pensioners live amid concrete ice blocks – soft tissue and old bones in darkness and cold. Our ideas of ease and security are no more than memories. He knew if he stepped towards her she would close the door.

'I'm a friend of Milena,' he said. 'I have a letter for her.'

She relaxed but kept her hand on the door. 'She's usually home about now, but she didn't come back last night,' she said. 'I can give her your letter.'

He wasn't sure. He was wasting time. He stood in the dark waiting to decide, and his instinct told him not to hand over the envelope.

'Please tell her I was here,' he muttered. 'My name's Alija. I have a letter from Jusuf.'

Mrs Hatibović nodded. 'She usually tells us when she isn't going to be home,' she said.

'I'm sure she's fine.'

Outside, the two teenage sentries and some other boys were standing next to his car. They moved out of the way when he appeared.

She usually tells us when she isn't going to be home, the old woman said.

At the bakery people were still queuing in the snow. One shell would wreak havoc there.

There were a hundred people in the city more important to Alija than Milena Ristić. But she hadn't turned up for work. She hadn't gone back to her own apartment. She might have stayed with friends. But Alija knew she hadn't.

He drove into the forecourt of the State Hospital. It was quiet in the lobby but the corridor next to the downstairs operating theatre was full of people. He found Jurić.

'You should have stayed for breakfast,' Jurić said. 'We had chocolate!' He'd already been working for an hour. 'That man your boss brought from Otes last night is comfortable. We took lots of shrapnel out of him. Maybe it can be recycled.'

In Jurić's office there were two cardboard boxes. 'Syringes and bandages,' Jurić said, indicating the smaller box. 'Bandages,' he pointed to the larger one. 'And that's all we have. Wish we could give you more, but we can't.'

As Jurić was leaving, Alija said, 'Can I see your casualty list for last night?'

'First floor,' Jurić said. 'Ask the sister in casualty.'

Alija found the sister in the hall. She was talking very quietly and firmly to a woman who was crying. The woman's daughter was dead. The sister was gentle and steady.

A middle-aged man stood nearby. He was unshaven and badly dressed and he had a tattoo on the back of his left hand.

'Ivo will take you home,' the sister told the woman.

Ivo stepped forward. He patted the bereaved mother's shoulder. 'I'll get you back and we'll find some neighbours to take care of things. Come on, pet.' He took her hand and helped her to her feet.

Alija asked for the casualty list. The sister went into the theatre next to the corridor and came back with a clipboard. Alija examined the names. Milena's wasn't among them.

He was already nearly an hour behind schedule, but in the car he decided to make a detour.

The Koševo Hospital was larger than the State Hospital. Like the State Hospital, bits of the Koševo had been blown away. It was wrecked. He showed his card to the policeman on duty at the casualty entrance. The man directed him to an office on the first floor where he found a nurse and asked to see their register of casualties treated in the last twenty-four hours.

The nurse wasn't impressed by Alija's ID. 'You'll have to see the director,' she said.

'Where can I find him?'

She sighed in a bad-tempered way and then said, 'Wait here, I'll get him.'

The doctor was in his fifties, with a balding head and thick grey beard. He was very short. He walked towards Alija with quick, important steps and looked up at him with beady eyes.

'Yes?'

'I'd like to see last night's casualty record.'

'The nurse could have shown you that!' the doctor barked. He walked over to a table on the other side of the room and picked up a ledger. Alija followed the little man and looked down at a list of names written in longhand. Beside each name was an admission time and a record of treatment.

'What name are you looking for?'

Alija saw it halfway down the right-hand page. He pointed to it.

The doctor drew his finger across the ledger. 'Admitted at eight last night, shrapnel, no surgery.' He didn't read the last part, bringing his finger to a halt at the word *deceased*.

He looked at Alija expressionlessly. 'Was she a friend?'

'A friend of a friend,' Alija said.

He walked out of the office and into a long corridor that smelled of disinfectant and frost. The stairs to the ground floor were very broad and it was difficult to see because the stairway was dark. The policeman at the door nodded. Alija stepped outside. He felt his shoes grind fresh, crisp snow.

In those moments, walking down the broad stairs and out into the freezing gloom, Alija began for the first time to think kindly of Milena Ristić.

37

'You gave her my note?' Jusuf asked.

Alija looked as though he was about to say something difficult.

This morning was already difficult. More than a thousand villagers were on the move, with an inadequate escort over open country. Half of them hadn't got across the river yet.

Before Alija could reply, they were interrupted. When anyone entered or left the command centre there was an upsurge of small-arms fire. The attackers now had a direct sight line from two blocks away.

Zlatko and Terry came in.

'I'll handle it,' Alija told Jusuf.

He patted Zlatko on the arm and said, quietly and earnestly, 'We haven't any more time! Let's do this now!'

Terry was reassured by Alija's calm, methodical manner. He nodded to her, rather formally, and walked to the door.

'I need you two!' he called through the doorway. Moments later two soldiers hurried in, neither of them the one who had escorted Terry, Zlatko and Anna the day before.

The soldiers were in their early twenties. They wore combat jackets, blue jeans and trainers. One had a helmet. They both carried rifles.

'This is Dr Barnes,' Alija said in his strange emotionless voice as a mortar shell exploded outside in the street. Terry looked at Jusuf, who was standing at the other side of the room examining a map laid out on the table. He started speaking into a walkie-talkie. 'She's going to take Miro Pejanović to London,' Alija went on, over the noise of wood breaking and masonry falling. 'Go with her to the shelter and bring Miro back here.'

The soldier with the helmet poked his head out of the door. He was thin, gangling, with a pointed, unshaven face and bags under his eyes. When he moved, he moved quickly, leaping into the open.

He reached the other side of the street. They could hear the sound of his trainers scuffing across the frozen snow in the silence that followed the mortar explosion. Then there was a burst of gunfire. Further along the street bits of building material were coming unstuck, making cracking sounds as they sheared off and fell to the ground. In the distance there was a constant small-arms tattoo. The soldier waved frantically, signalling to the others to come out.

Terry experienced a sudden fear that was like the last over-whelming sensation of panic she remembered from diving into a swimming pool as a child. She knew that she must act without hesitation. To hesitate would be to allow panic to take over.

Another sensation was working in her brain. She was uneasy because of the attitude of the soldiers. The day before, the garage next to the command centre was full of men shouting and swearing and waiting for orders. Now it was nearly empty, and those soldiers who remained were silent. She could see that the two men Alija had ordered to escort them were scared.

Zlatko was different too. He was surprised by the state of the village. He was surprised that the government troops and the civilians had moved out so quickly. The village was ghostly.

Terry began to run. She expected another burst of fire but there wasn't any. She heard her own steps on the ice. She heard Zlatko and the other soldier running behind her and didn't look round. The soldier in front got up and began to run along the side of the building. She followed.

She looked down at the ground as she ran. The snow was harder than the day before. It was easier to see where to run but the surface was slippery. She jumped awkwardly over a long coiled piece of rusting steel and lost her balance on the other side. She slapped her left hand against the wall of the building and steadied herself. The soldier was moving fast and Terry ran hard to keep up.

Terry remembered intensive gunfire from when they had run towards the arcade the day before. Now it was quiet. There was no one in sight. She kept her eyes fixed on the soldier in front. He made it into the arcade and she thought he would stop there and allow the rest to catch up but he didn't. He kept running. She lost sight of him when he moved out of the other side. For a few seconds she was alone. Those behind hadn't caught up.

There were sharp shards of thick plate glass in the shopfronts. A door lay flat on the ground at one of the entrances, blasted off its hinges. She saw a calendar advertising oranges.

Cold air rushed towards her and she was out of the arcade again and running after the lead soldier twenty yards ahead. There was an evil silence.

The soldier waited at the entrance to the shelter as the other two caught up. Zlatko led the rest of the group along the corridor and down the stairs.

When Mrs Pejanović saw them she gave a small cry and put a hand to her mouth.

She had given up expecting them to come.

She didn't want Miro to see that she was scared, but he could tell that she was and she knew he was going to start crying.

She and Miro had been alone for hours. Mrs Pejanović had reached the conclusion that she'd been wrong to put her faith in the British doctor. She knew, though, that they couldn't have taken Miro over the river into the city. He was too weak. The last men to leave had helped her to move the cot across the shelter next to the stairs. She thought they were going to force her to bring Miro and leave with them. They said it was madness to stay.

Beside Mrs Pejanović was a large plastic suitcase tied with string. Terry saw the suitcase; she saw how different Mrs Pejanović was now, standing with her little boy and her luggage tied with string. She was a clever woman, and in other circumstances she would have exuded authority. Terry had been struck by her self-confidence. But now Mrs Pejanović was trembling. The change was startling. The last vestiges of Mrs Pejanović's world had collapsed; the only residue of life in the cellar was a miasma of fear, of desperation. Terry touched the woman's arm as she walked past. Silently and certainly she imparted a fragment of new hope.

Terry understood why she was there. She felt as though a great weight had been lifted from her. She was where she was supposed to be and she was doing what she was supposed to do.

She looked down at Miro and smiled. '*Dobro!*' She reached into the cot and the little boy held her hand very tightly. He was crying.

He was dressed for the journey, a T-shirt, a shirt, a sweater and cotton tracksuit trousers. Terry examined him and took his temperature. She moved with methodical speed.

'We've got to go now,' Zlatko told her. They heard shouting in the street above them.

'They're coming!' Mrs Pejanović said.

Terry opened her bag and extracted a syringe.

Zlatko walked towards the stairs and then back again, three or four paces. He opened his mouth to speak, but said nothing.

Terry filled the syringe from a small vial and bent over Miro. The others watched. She administered the injection, slowly and carefully, whispering very gently, '*Dobro, dobro.*'

Then she stood back and told the others, 'OK, let's go.'

The soldiers lifted the cot.

Mrs Pejanović struggled with the suitcase, but it was clearly much too heavy for her so Zlatko took it.

When he lifted it, the material on either side of the handle stretched and he thought it would come off. He raised the case onto his knee and then heaved it onto his shoulder. That way he carried it up the stairs.

There was a smell in the shelter, something rotten. Zlatko looked down at the ground, through the steel railings on the stairs. He saw roaches scuttling among refuse and along the walls.

Upstairs he kept the suitcase on his shoulder and walked out into the open. Terry walked beside him with Mrs Pejanović and the two soldiers moving ahead of them carrying Miro in his cot.

The soldiers began to run; Zlatko followed, the suitcase balanced on his shoulder. There was a patch of ground where the snow had been cleared away and the surface was less slippery. He kept to that part of the pavement as he ran.

The way the soldiers were holding the cot made it sway violently. Terry watched the drip, thinking the tube might become detached. She and Mrs Pejanović hurried after the soldiers into the arcade.

They turned and watched Zlatko as he put the suitcase on the ground and tried to drag it by the handle.

'Come on!' one of the soldiers shouted at him. 'Don't stop!'

There was a crash. A tank round exploded between Zlatko and the arcade. He staggered back and nearly fell over the case. He looked down at the ground and stood still for a moment. The soldier who had shouted at him ran out and grabbed the case and they came back together. Inside the arcade, Zlatko leaned against the wall and breathed deeply.

The soldier with the helmet took charge. He lifted the case and told Zlatko to take the other end of the cot. Mrs Pejanović helped lift one side of the cot and Terry walked on the other side, holding the drip in place. Like that they moved out of the arcade. They moved more efficiently, but they had gone only a few yards when there was another explosion. They retreated to the cover of the arcade doorway.

Zlatko peeped out. 'I think they can see us,' he said.

The attackers were in the apartments forty yards to their left. There was no cover between the arcade and the command centre. The soldier with the helmet lifted the suitcase in both hands and ran out into the street. He didn't keep to the side of the building but ran, zigzagging, down the middle of the street and then into the doorway of the command centre. There was another explosion before he made it to the door. He disappeared behind black smoke.

'Take Miro out of the cot,' Terry said.

She detached the drip from the cot frame and Mrs Pejanović lifted her son out. As she did this she fumbled with the tube leading from the drip and Miro began to cry.

Terry was at that moment quite sure about what she must do.

She hadn't come to this place to bring medicine. She hadn't come to ease Miro's entry into Britain. She had come to carry him across this street. His mother couldn't do it. She would have crawled through fire for him, but now Mrs Pejanović wasn't capable.

Terry took Miro, pressed the tube against his side and held onto the plastic hook of the drip bag. Mrs Pejanović was too confused to protest. Zlatko took Mrs Pejanović's arm, and the soldier lifted up the cot and they ran from the shelter of the arcade out into the middle of the street.

Miro put his arms around Terry. His fingers were hot. She felt each of his fingertips on the back of her neck. His body was warm and he was very light. She knew it was dangerous to bring him out in this cold. She looked down and saw his thick black hair. There was snow all across the street and on the abandoned car halfway between the arcade and the command centre. The windows of the apartments were smashed. Bits of glass sprouted from dark squares making strange patterns, reflecting snow, reflecting the running figures.

And it was as though time slowed. Terry felt the boy's arms around her and it was as though the two of them were floating together out across a glittering stream, as though in these few frantic moments they were contemplating the essence of what it is to live. There is, she thought, no other purpose in life than to love. Who are the brave but those who struggle to love even when they don't know how, those who are clumsy and awkward and uncertain, those who misread relationships? All she knew now was that she wouldn't give up. She hadn't given up and she wouldn't give up. There is no purpose but to love, to show kindness. She understood better now. She had tried and she had failed, but she hadn't given up and she wasn't ever going to.

She ran closer to the building on the command-centre side of the street. She thought the ground would be more even there.

She could hear nothing. She looked down at Miro, held him tight. The ground beneath her became uneven and she realised that she'd strayed off the concrete and onto a grass verge thick with snow. There were pieces of steel pushing up and a metal bracket protruding from the side of the building. She grabbed hold of the bracket to steady herself, and felt a sharp pain as the metal cut into her hand like a knife. She saw the path again and in two steps she had moved from the rough ground onto the smooth. From there she ran with greater confidence.

38

Brad woke, his head drenched in a dull pain. Someone was banging on the door. He rolled out of bed and stood up unsteadily.

Outside his room, Anna cursed softly under her breath. Either he was too hungover to wake up and open the door, or he had left for Otes without her. She started to think he might have gone without her.

If she couldn't get into his room she couldn't transmit what Sergeant Matthews had just told her about the airlift being shut down, and if Brad had taken the Land Rover she would be stuck in the city, unable to get into Otes and cover Terry's evacuation of the little boy and his mother.

At last, he opened the door. It was freezing but he was only wearing shorts and a T-shirt. He walked back inside and she followed. He searched in his bag and found some Alka-Seltzer, then he went into the bathroom and closed the door.

He heard her switch on the computer terminal and start typing. The Alka-Seltzer began to fizz, drowning out the faint tap of Anna's fingers on the keyboard. The transmission light was blinking when he came back into the room.

'What did you send?' As he asked her this he felt slightly dizzy and sat down on the edge of the bed.

'You look terrible,' she said, with more sympathy than disapproval.

He located his shirt beneath one of the bed covers and put it on. Then he stood up and put on his trousers and socks and shoes.

She waited for him to ask her again, but he didn't. He found his sweater, then his flak jacket and coat. 'Let's go,' he said.

'You're not fit to drive.'

'I've got the keys!'

Fifteen minutes later they were driving across thick frozen snow past the factory complex. When the small-arms fire started it came from close on their right, across an expanse of undulating snow punctuated by black clumps where steel and wood broke through. Brad was hungry and he would have given anything for a glass of cold fizzy water.

Anna trusted the Land Rover's armour plating but she was afraid Brad would drive them into a ditch.

Tank rounds began exploding. There were only one or two seconds between rounds, and the explosions were close to the road.

'Fuck,' Brad said.

He began to steer more actively, as if that would somehow reduce their chances of being hit. He was going at twenty miles an hour. He desperately wanted to go faster, but the road was winding and the potholes were vicious.

They drove through the tank fire for less than sixty seconds, but it seemed to both of them as though they were suspended there, dangling right before the frontline. On the final entry into Otes there was a barrage of rifle shots. Bullets whizzed in front of the windscreen. They heard repeated cracks, like gravel or pebbles thrown violently at the rear section of the vehicle. Bullets at the end of their trajectory hit the van's steel side. Then two bullets smashed into the window beside Brad with full force. A small area of armoured glass in the corner cracked into an opaque mesh.

'Fuck,' Brad said again, accelerating on the last stretch towards the cover of the garage. They looked ahead at the small crowd of people standing inside the garage. 'Fuck,' he said, a third time. 'What's *he* doing here?'

'He got to know the doctor,' Anna said, feeling an unfamiliar solidarity with Brad.

'Better late than never,' Michael Baring greeted them cheerily as they stepped out of the Land Rover.

Brad scowled and took out his notebook. Anna began to snap pictures of Miro and Mrs Pejanović as the soldiers stood aside to give her a clearer view.

Miro's mother was trying to comfort him but she couldn't hug him properly because he was in the cot, with a tube sticking into the back of one hand. His mother whispered to him urgently. She looked at Anna as she snapped the shutter, freezing tears on Mrs Pejanović's frightened, once beautiful face.

'What happened to you?' Anna asked Terry.

Terry dabbed her hand with a handkerchief. Blood flowed between her fingers. 'A small cut,' she said.

Zlatko was inside the Toyota. 'Whaddya doing?' Brad shouted above the noise of explosions.

'I'm going to turn the car,' Zlatko said.

He reversed out of the garage. The Toyota's engine screamed and the tyres skidded on the snow. Zlatko brought the vehicle forward and swung it round ninety degrees. Then he started back towards the garage.

The sudden explosion sent a wave of shrapnel and smoke into the garage. Brad pulled his helmet over his face and turned towards the interior. He felt warm air rush at him. A soldier threw himself over Miro. Mrs Pejanović fell backwards onto the concrete floor. Anna, standing close to Terry, felt the doctor pull her inward, away from the blast.

Brad could hear the sound of shrapnel and metal landing inside the garage. He heard more explosions further away, and there was a smell of smoke and burnt metal. He looked back towards the Toyota as the smoke cleared. The car was wrecked. The tank shell had scored a direct hit.

Alija ran out of the garage and stood in the open looking into the car. Zlatko lay in the mangled front seat, his body split in two. One half was on the floor around the torn-open gearbox. The other half was wedged in a steel mesh between the dash-board and the seat.

Alija recoiled.

Mrs Pejanović crouched over Miro's cot. Her son screamed in fear, but he had not been hit. The soldier who had protected him sat on the ground. There was a large bloodstain growing on his shirt at the small of his back. He sat stunned, looking at the ground. A cut above his eye sent a steady stream of blood down over his face.

Brad looked around and said, 'Where's Michael?'

'I'm here,' Baring announced uncertainly. He stood up on the other side of an abandoned car near the front of the garage.

Brad went to where Baring was standing. Baring had gone pale. 'There's a guy waiting for me at the Strand café in Ilidža,'

Brad told him. He spoke like a tape recording, his normal tone disconnected from the mayhem surrounding him. 'He witnessed the assassination on the Airport Road and he wants to tell his story.' He described the prospective source. 'You'll recognise him. He expects a foreign journalist to come and speak to him at eleven-thirty. He won't wait.'

Baring looked at him with an unfocused expression that made Brad think he wasn't listening properly. For the first time in their brief, unhappy acquaintance it occurred to Brad that Michael Baring was his senior by at least ten years. 'I'm supposed to meet this guy,' Brad told him again. 'I can't go, so I want you to go instead. He was there when the minister was shot.'

Baring's eyes widened.

'Zlatko got this for me,' Brad explained. 'Just go to Ilidža.'

'What are *you* going to do?' Baring was still dazed, but he was coming round.

'I'm going to take this kid out of here now that Zlatko can't.'

Brad walked back to Miro's cot. 'Get him into the Land Rover,' he told Anna and Terry.

They lifted the cot into the back and Terry and Mrs Pejanović climbed inside the rear cabin beside Miro.

Anna climbed into the front.

Brad reversed the Land Rover and they moved out into the open towards the spot where Zlatko's body lay in the wreckage of the Toyota.

'The last plane leaves at twelve,' Anna said.

'Whaddya mean?'

'The airlift is being suspended.'

'How the fuck do *you* know?'

'I just heard, OK? I heard this morning.'

'That's what you were sending?'

'That's what I sent. Go faster!'

Brad swung the Land Rover onto the track out of the village. There was more small-arms fire.

He saw Zlatko. He saw him again and again, before the shell exploded, after the shell exploded, life truncated and twisted, changed by impulses, seconds-long impulses and their eternal consequences.

There was a loud crack. The window beside Anna turned into a white spider's web. Her hands flew out in front of her and she rose from the seat as if she'd been pushed out of it by an electric shock. She felt her helmet move forward on her head. She hadn't fastened it properly and it fell over her eyes. Frantically, she pushed it back and stared at the shattered window beside her. The shards were held together by the industrial alchemy that makes glass as strong as steel, yet they were held together now like pieces of thin ice on a thawing pond.

'It hasn't broken!' she said. She actually heard the startled words coming out of her mouth. It was as if her body and her brain were separate.

She thought, *There is nothing I can do to change the violence of the universe.* She had never felt so helpless. She recoiled from this and almost before she knew what she was doing she had slipped the pen from its little pocket underneath her flak jacket and she was holding it over her dog-eared notebook. She wanted to write something. She wanted to describe what was happening. She held the pen over the paper and she realised that she was crying. But she wanted to write more than she wanted to dry her eyes.

She felt Brad's hand on her elbow.

Even though he was wearing gloves and she had four layers of clothing on, bouncing along over potholes on a battlefield, she experienced a moment of comforting tenderness.

'Hey,' he said.

Perhaps he had intended to say something else, but he didn't.

After the bullet hit the window, Brad accelerated sharply. He knew they might skid, but there were more explosions coming and he believed they were now being targeted. They could see plumes of smoke ahead. More tank shells blasted into the buildings sixty yards away on their right.

In the back of the vehicle, cut off from the driving cabin, Mrs Pejanović looked down at Miro and then out through the rear windows. She did not think about death in those moments but about life.

Mrs Pejanović remembered when the symptoms of Miro's illness first became apparent. Two months after his sixth birthday he sat down on the top step of the stairway that leads up from the town to the Olympic Museum in Sarajevo. He sat like an old man and, between gasps, he said, 'Mummy, I can't breathe.'

They thought it was asthma. The first doctor thought so too and so did the second. It was only because of a chance meeting with a heart specialist who was an acquaintance of Miro's father that they discovered the real problem. And the real problem was infinitely more serious than Mrs Pejanović or her husband could have imagined. Miro had been staring into the face of death for years.

Now on this bitter day they had emerged at last from what Mrs Pejanović had begun to see as an antechamber of hell and she thought, *We are in hell. It is cold and violent and filled with hate.*

And her son's life depended on the twisting potholed road across this wasteland to the airstrip a mile away.

Terry balanced on her haunches; from time to time she placed the palm of her right hand on Miro's forehead. Her left hand hurt. She had tied the handkerchief in a tourniquet around her palm and the skin on the back of her hand had gone white. The Land Rover lurched from one side to the other, sliding on the road. Miro screamed.

He screamed because he was afraid. Fear and the frigid temperature in the back of the Land Rover could tip his cardiovascular system into a fatal crisis. Terry had imagined before she left London that she might have to insist on minimum standards of transportation when it came to removing Miro from the city and transferring him to the air ambulance. And now they were bouncing along a rutted track on a mechanised wheelbarrow.

She placed her good hand on the boy's cheek. His temperature was dangerously high. She slipped open her holdall and took a syringe from the topmost inside pocket. She worked mechanically. As she filled the syringe the Land Rover jerked suddenly upward. Terry tried to steady herself. The syringe spouted fluid.

She filled it again. The Land Rover jerked again. *This is like a slapstick scene from a comedy*, she thought, but there was nothing comic about it.

Mrs Pejanović pulled Miro's sleeve back and disconnected the drip from the valve on the back of his hand. Terry got hold of the cot and then of Miro's arm and found the aperture on the valve with the tip of the syringe. She loosened her body for seconds so that if the Land Rover jerked she would not jerk with it and stab the child.

She did all this with an image playing like a backdrop to her consciousness and it was the image of Zlatko when she had met him the day before.

She had been preoccupied by the unsatisfactory nature of her arrival and the absence of any apparent preparation for her visit. She was baffled, and into this uncertainty came a bohemian accountant with the sort of philosophical optimism that seemed to compensate for everything.

When she thought about Sanela, Terry felt a knife in her heart and caught her breath. She put the syringe back in the bag. Mrs Pejanović rolled down Miro's sleeve and whispered to him.

What words could express the immensity of what had taken place? Zlatko lay there in that terrible place.

Mrs Pejanović was crying. She glanced back at the road twisting behind them. All around was violence and noise.

39

In the garage Jusuf strode over to the spot where the soldier still sat on the concrete floor. He crouched down beside him.

'How bad is it?' There was blood all over the man's face and he was shaking.

'It isn't bad,' he said. Jusuf began to unbutton the soldier's shirt. The man winced as the wet material peeled away. There was a six-inch gash deep in his back just above the waist. Jusuf could see shards of metal inside.

'Take him in the car,' he told Alija.

Alija bent down and helped the man to stand.

Minutes before, Alija had broken the news of Milena's death to Jusuf.

'What are you going to do, commander? Are you going to withdraw?' Michael Baring looked at him expectantly, pen poised.

For a fleeting moment Jusuf felt as though he was above this scene, as though he was looking down at their sad and brutal predicament.

'We're going to withdraw,' he said in an emotionless voice. 'Go back to the city. It is madness to be here.'

Baring followed Alija's car out of the garage. The two vehicles moved slowly past the spot where Zlatko had been hit.

* * *

By nightfall Jusuf had supervised the evacuation of the last inhabitants, and the orderly withdrawal of his own men to a new line along the River Željeznica.

The Bull was keen to establish that since he had never visited Otes during the fighting he could not share responsibility for the defeat. That belonged exclusively to the commanders on the ground.

'This isn't going to reflect badly on anyone,' the Bull explained at the final conference in the map room at western army head-quarters.

The Bull didn't understand how they had managed to get the civilians across the river and he was careful not to ask, Jusuf noted. He guarded his ignorance with discretion. Jusuf watched him and was impressed. Except maybe for one of his young aides, the Bull was the only one in the room who hadn't seen the inside of the Otes command centre. He looked each one of the defeated commanders in the eye and said the defeat would not reflect badly on any of them. Jusuf knew he would get another command only with Alija's help. Alija could get round the Bull and his faction. Alija could negotiate in the ministries.

'Alipašino Polje,' he told Alija when they were in the car outside.

There were flashes over Bistrik and Grbavica. No one in the streets, snow thick on the ground. The car skidded on the steep incline opposite the Television Centre and they had to reverse and take a second run at the hill, this time on the left-hand side of the road where the snow had been churned up by an APC.

They climbed the steps to the freezing apartment block and entered the lobby. The boys who had challenged Alija in the morning were absent from their post.

When they got to the sixteenth floor Jusuf took out the key that she had given him but which he had never used. He opened the door.

Inside, they removed their shoes. There was no mat on the floor, just the hall carpet. A pair of Milena's boots sat on a piece of newspaper next to the shoe rack. Thick black boots with rubber soles for walking over snow.

In the kitchen Alija looked out of the window, drawing back cheap net curtains. Apartment buildings glittered in the moonlight.

Jusuf shone a torch in the bedroom. Milena's album of photographs lay on the night table. He sat on the bed and opened the album. She had pasted the photos neatly onto the thick pages and covered them with clear plastic. Captions were written in fine felt pen. There was a photo of Milena when she was small. She wore a red dress and white socks and black shoes and she looked at the camera with a solemn face. He leafed through the album: Milena baking with her mother, playing with friends. There were pictures of her at school, wearing the uniform that girls wore twenty years ago, looking earnest. There were pictures of her in jeans and T-shirt when she was twelve years old.

There were wedding photographs and family snaps, by the seaside, in the country at gatherings around a big table beneath a tree. Two people smiling to the camera, together on a sofa.

What did she think about when she was alone here?

Jusuf sat on the bed. He felt as though a great ocean receded into the moonlight across the frigid tops of towers. She had fled here because she was good. This little girl who looked out from photographs with a kind of indomitable joy, she had refused to be tainted by evil.

He sat enclosed by concrete and the pale moonlight holding photographs of a life. He wanted to cry out to heaven. The extent of his loss confounded him.

They heard the sound of knocking outside and Alija opened the front door. Jusuf walked into the small hall.

Mrs Hatibović was startled when she saw them. She stepped back.

'Where's Milena?'

Alija moved out onto the landing. Mrs Hatibović carried a lantern, a wax lamp inside a bottle held with a piece of wire. It spread an orange light around her and shadows on the walls. 'Milena was killed last night,' Alija said. 'Shellfire near the TV Centre.'

Mrs Hatibović put a hand to her mouth, a small, tough old woman illuminated by her lamp in the freezing hall. 'God grant her rest,' she whispered. And then, shaking her head sadly, she added, 'May he welcome her in heaven.'

Alija left Jusuf outside the apartment on Tito Street. He drove another two blocks to the Chamber Theatre, where he climbed the stairs methodically, glad that he met no one on the way. At the top landing he paused for a moment and then he knocked.

When Sanela saw him, horror settled in her eyes.

Baring was dismayed by the drive out of Otes. Everything on the road was targeted. He drove as fast as was prudent, kept his eye ahead and focused on reaching the barrier at Stup. Battlefields were among the few places on earth where Michael Baring was liberated from his own overweening self-regard.

He couldn't remember the name of the driver, the one who was killed – Sanela's boyfriend. He could see that the British doctor was shaken though. He would put that in his story about little Miro's evacuation. He'd had ten minutes to interview mother and son, and the doctor, before the others arrived.

Now he was on his way to Ilidža and he reckoned there was a possibility, albeit a slim one in view of the source, that he might get material for a third strong story. By evening he would have stashed away a good two thousand words for next day's paper. A thousand words were guaranteed to make front page.

He swung the car onto Sniper Alley and started towards the flyover. He relaxed his grip on the steering wheel, eased himself back in the driving seat and breathed deeply, starting to feel calm again. Just after he passed the newspaper building a bullet, fired from Nedjarići two hundred yards away, pierced the rear left window of the Golf and exited through the floor.

Baring cursed.

He leaned forward over the steering wheel and accelerated. The next one, he thought, may kill me and I will be left here on this godforsaken bit of road.

He zigzagged the car and made the flyover, where he swung off the road and onto the slip road that led up to the bridge. No more shots were fired. When he reached the Ilidža turning on the Airport Road he pulled the car over onto the right fork. He guessed that Brad had been shaken by the explosion. He must have been pretty unsteady to give away his tip about the witness in Ilidža. Brad desperately needed a story like that right now.

Thinking this he became uneasy. When Brad had taken hold of him in the garage Baring felt it only decent to do whatever would be helpful. Brad didn't want this story to get away, but he'd opted to take little Miro to the airport rather than go to Ilidža himself.

Now Baring began to wonder.

Brad had heard from a secondary, now deceased, source that someone in Ilidža was willing to tell all to a foreign journalist about the minister's assassination.

The germ of a hideously unpleasant insight took hold. Baring felt the way he felt when younger journalists glanced at one another while he was in full flow, and he realised that they were making fun of him.

He was already in Ilidža but, obstinately, until he had resolved the sudden suspicion that he might have been tricked, and by a colleague for whom he possessed not an ounce of respect, he decided not to go to the Strand. He would stop and speak to one of his own contacts first. If Brad's supposed source really wanted to tell his story then the fellow would wait.

Baring's contact was an urbane and rather witty black marketeer who had just been appointed to the municipal defence council in Ilidža. His name was Mićo, and Baring believed that he was close to the Rebel leadership.

Mićo was fat. He wore an expensive cashmere sweater and smart blue corduroy trousers. 'What can I do for you?' he asked when Baring entered his second-floor office in the former Ilidža municipal building. Through diligent study of American television he had acquired a quasi-New Jersey accent. He had a hoarse, slightly high-pitched voice. Baring took out his notebook. 'The Airport Road,' he said dramatically.

'I have a statement from our military command,' Mićo said without much enthusiasm. He placed a single sheet of paper on the table in front of Baring. The statement was three lines long. It read, *The authorities welcome the announcement in New York that a special commission has been formed to investigate the fatal incident on the Airport Road. The authorities will cooperate fully with the commission.*

'What commission?' Baring was annoyed.

'They're sending some heavy hitters from New York.'

'When?'

'You'd better ask the UN about that, but I don't think it'll be for quite a while. The airlift is being suspended today.'

Baring remained calm. He hated, more than just about anything else in the world, looking clueless.

'I'd heard something about that,' he lied. 'Have the flights already stopped?'

'Round about now,' Mićo said, looking at his watch.

Baring knew then that he *had* been duped. While he wasted time on a wild-goose chase to Ilidža, Brad had an exclusive on a mercy dash to catch the last plane out of Sarajevo. That would top anything else that was filed that day. He guessed that Brad must have known about the airlift suspension. He guessed that Brad probably knew about the UN commission too.

On his way out of Ilidža Baring raced past the Strand, determined to get to the airport before midday. At the same time, a man stepped out of the café; he looked to his right and then to his left and after lingering for a moment he walked away.

41

'You OK?' Brad asked. He could see that she wasn't.

Anna looked at him and then she looked ahead. She was trying to adjust her flak jacket but she couldn't do it properly because her thick gloves, blue wool with a pattern of yellow triangles across the knuckles, got in the way.

'What's going to happen to Sanela?' she asked.

Brad slowed the Land Rover as they approached the first UN checkpoint.

He didn't answer. He thought about Wikram's mother, when Brad visited her two days after the ambush at Puttalam lagoon. In the shadows, in the large room with high windows, sounds from the garden echoing across the dark teak floor. The woman's patrician face was drawn. Brad's voice darted among the shadows; he was unable to say anything adequate or comforting, and when she looked at him he felt like Wikram's killer.

The French APC reversed off the track and let them pass. He drove the Land Rover slowly over the snow to the second checkpoint, covering the entrance to the airport.

Anna took off one of her gloves and rearranged the Velcro fastening on her flak jacket. Her thoughts darted here and there and she couldn't get them ordered. She tried to breathe deeply and calm herself but that didn't work. She could not reconcile herself to the image of a friend cut in two equal pieces.

Brad stopped the Land Rover in front of the APC, which blocked the end of the track on the edge of the airport compound. A sergeant emerged from the sandbag emplacement and walked towards them.

Anna knew then that they were going to be turned back. She took her ID card from her wallet. She tried to understand why she knew they wouldn't get the APC to move out of the way. Perhaps, she thought, they simply did not have the strength to move it.

They had fled from Otes; they were running, looking for help and they were no match for the APC and the power that lay behind it.

'What do you have in the back?' the Legionnaire asked.

'Two women and a small boy,' Brad said. 'They are being evacuated to London.'

The sergeant looked at Brad's ID and handed it back. Then he flicked his fingers lazily, indicating that he wanted to see Anna's card. She gave it to Brad and he gave it to the soldier. The man examined it and stood on tiptoe to see into the driving cabin and check that Anna's face matched the face on the card. He handed it back. The sergeant strolled to the back of the van. Brad got out and walked round the other side and opened the back door.

'Do they have documents?' the soldier asked.

Brad nodded to Terry. She produced her letter from the UNHCR and handed it over. She smiled at the sergeant and he looked back at her stony-faced. He glanced at the letter without reading it and said, 'You need a pass authorising you to enter the aerodrome.'

'They have permission to fly,' Brad said. 'They can't fly if they can't enter the airport.'

The man shrugged. 'They can't enter the airport without the proper documentation. Please reverse your vehicle and turn at the passing place.' He pointed to an area where the track broadened, about thirty yards away.

'This child requires immediate medical treatment,' Terry said. 'He must be put on the next plane.'

The soldier ignored her and moved back round the side of the Land Rover. 'Without the proper papers you can't come in,' he told Brad. 'Come back when you have authorisation.'

Brad climbed into the Land Rover.

'It's ten to twelve,' Anna said. 'They *have* to get in.'

Their path was blocked by solid steel. Brad began to feel the first stirring of rage. He'd promised to get them to the airport. Now the best he could do was to take them into the city, where they might wait for weeks. He hit the steering wheel and shouted, 'Fuck!'

Then the unimaginable happened.

The APC began to move. It shuddered, and its huge tyres ground into the ice and then it started to ease off the track onto a space beside the hut. A truck was coming out of the compound, a long white truck with a high canvas roof. The APC had reversed to let it pass.

'Fuck!' Brad said again. But this time he was elated.

He revved the engine and drove forward. The truck had stopped while the APC moved out of the way. It was just beginning to move again. Brad drove straight at it and swerved at the last second. He went off the track and felt the tyres rolling over frozen ruts. Then he swung round the truck and back onto the flat stretch of open ground inside the compound.

'Fuck!' Anna said, and he was pleased that they agreed.

In the rear-view mirror he could see the truck moving along the track and the APC reversing back into its original position blocking the entrance. The French sergeant had come out of his hut and skipped a few steps after the Land Rover before going inside to radio ahead. Brad accelerated past the warehouses at the northern end of the compound. Seconds later they pulled up outside the terminal building.

Brad and Anna jumped out. They ran to the back of the Land Rover. Brad opened the door and helped Terry and Mrs Pejanović to lift the cot out. Three people were walking from the terminal towards an RAF Hercules C-160, fifty yards away on the airstrip. It was four minutes to twelve.

He knew that that plane was the last, and he knew he would do whatever was necessary to get Miro on it. He thought about Zlatko and about Wikram. He wasn't going to let Miro share that fate.

They lifted the cot down and moved towards the plane. 'Let's go!' he shouted as Terry and Mrs Pejanović began to follow.

Brad looked down at Miro. The child blinked.

'They're coming!' Anna said.

A jeep moved towards them from the other side of the terminal building. When it reached the spot where they were carrying Miro, twenty yards from the plane, the sergeant shouted at them to stop.

It would have been comical, Brad thought, in different circumstances. It was like something from a Marx Brothers movie.

The jeep moved alongside and the sergeant shouted, '*Arrêtez!*' as they continued towards the plane.

Then the man barked an order to his driver and the jeep veered dangerously in front of them.

Brad swore. 'Take it round!' he told Anna.

They started to move past the front of the jeep.

The plane's propellers roared. The passengers had already climbed in, and the two forklifts that had been loading boxes on board had withdrawn. The rear entrance was closing. A crewman at the side door bent down to pull up the steps. He looked at the small party with the cot walking towards the plane and hesitated.

The sergeant jumped out of his jeep and strode up to Brad and said, '*Monsieur*, stop immediately.'

'Put him down,' Brad told Anna. Mrs Pejanović moved forward and crouched down to hold her son's hand. The sergeant began speaking but Brad walked past him and shouted up to the crewman standing at the back of the plane.

'We have an invalid child and his mother,' he yelled, over the noise of the propellers. 'The boy requires urgent medical treatment. He has permission to travel on the first available UNHCR flight. He's accompanied by a British doctor. I'm bringing them on now.'

The crewman looked doubtful, but he released the chain and let the steps drop back onto the ground. He disappeared inside the plane.

Brad returned to where the others stood. 'Give me the letter,' he said to Terry. She handed it to him. A second jeep with three French soldiers pulled up beside them.

The French sergeant shouted to the soldiers and they moved towards the cot.

'You are going back to the terminal building,' the sergeant told the group assembled around Miro.

A figure climbed down from the plane and walked towards them. Behind him two crewmen watched from the entrance.

'What's up?' the flight officer asked. He was a young man, late twenties. He had a clipped moustache and a thin face. He looked curious more than concerned.

'We have an invalid child and his mother,' Brad repeated. He handed the officer Terry's letter. 'The boy is being taken to London for urgent medical treatment. He's accompanied by a British doctor.' He pointed to Terry. 'And they have permission to fly on the first available UNHCR flight.'

The officer glanced at the letter and said, 'No problem. Bring them on.'

The French sergeant snapped an order and his soldiers lifted Miro and began moving away from the plane.

'Whoa!' the officer shouted. 'What's going on?'

'These people do not have permission to enter the airport terminal,' the sergeant said. 'They must go back.'

The soldiers began to carry Miro back towards the jeep. The pilot turned and made a small signal to the two crewmen at the door of the plane. They jumped out. Brad walked between the French soldiers and the jeep. They began to walk around him. Mrs Pejanović and Terry both stepped forward and got hold of the cot. The French soldiers tried to restrain them. The British airmen moved quickly and in seconds the cot was surrounded by six men and two women. Anna photographed the scene.

'These people are travelling with me,' the flight officer told the sergeant. 'If you do not order your men to desist, my crew will engage weapons.'

Anna's camera clicked and clicked again.

The sergeant looked at the pilot in consternation. '*Monsieur*, this is absurd!'

Two more airmen emerged from the plane. The sergeant stood back. The cot had been placed on the tarmac between the jeep and the Hercules. The flight officer marched forward and shouted at the sergeant, 'Order them to desist!'

The sergeant froze for several seconds and then he shrugged and jerked his head away from the cot, signalling the French soldiers to move back.

They let go of the cot and allowed the airmen to lift it and carry it to the plane.

The sergeant walked up to Brad and jabbed his index finger in his chest. 'You will be punished for this!' he said.

Then he got into his jeep and drove off.

42

Baring strode into the Movement Control Office and saw Jim Danby standing in a far corner of the room. Danby was speaking on the telephone.

'Yes?' The Argentinian officer on duty looked up from a sheaf of photocopies.

'It's OK,' Baring said. 'I'm waiting to speak to *him*.' He nodded in Danby's direction.

'Wait outside, please. This office is for UN personnel only.'

Baring looked at the Argentinian, who looked back at him with an insolent expression. Before Baring could respond, Danby replaced the receiver, walked over to the desk and told the Argentinian, 'I'll handle this.'

Baring didn't like the sound of that. He didn't expect to be handled, by Danby or by anyone else.

Danby motioned him into the office past the front desk. 'You were at Otes too?'

'How did you know?'

'I heard about what happened to your colleague.'

'My colleague?'

'The interpreter, the one who was driving Dr Barnes.'

'Ah.' Baring hadn't been thinking about that. He'd been thinking about being sent on a fool's errand to Ilidža while a story was breaking at the airport.

'Why weren't we told about the airlift closing down? Why wasn't *I* told?'

'You're among the first to know,' Danby said.

They were interrupted. The sergeant who had failed to prevent Miro's evacuation came into the office. Danby addressed him in French. Baring, who was proud of his language skills, listened carefully. 'You have exceeded your authority,' Danby told the sergeant. 'I've spoken to your superior. This is a disciplinary matter.'

The sergeant opened his mouth to protest but Danby stepped forward. He was beginning to get back in gear after a rocky twenty-four hours. He'd enjoyed telling Rocard on the phone that his airport troops were about to be made a laughing stock around the world. He'd enjoyed explaining to the major that if the major was very, *very* cooperative Danby might be able to minimise the damage. He gave Rocard a detailed account of French troops tussling over a sick child and capitulating to a British aircrew. Now he stepped forward. His face was very close to the sergeant's face. 'There *will* be disciplinary action!'

The Argentinian watched intently, until Danby glanced at him and the man looked quickly down at his forms.

'What's going on?' Baring asked.

Just then, Brad and Anna came out of a separate office and walked towards the front door. 'Thanks, Jim,' Anna said. She patted Danby's arm.

Baring didn't like to see press officers being thanked by other journalists. He hurried out of Movement Control after Brad and Anna.

'You knew about the airlift,' he told Brad.

Brad walked to the edge of the airstrip and Baring caught up with him.

'You knew about the airlift,' he repeated, 'and you sent me off with a cock-and-bull story about a witness in Ilidža.'

When Brad turned to face him, Baring was surprised by the altered expression on the other man's face. Baring wondered if he was drunk.

'What do you mean a cock-and-bull story?'

'You sent me to Ilidža because you wanted the airport story for yourself, the airlift shutdown and the little boy's evacuation. What was Anna thanking Danby for?'

'You went to the Strand?'

'No.'

'I told you to go to the Strand. There was a witness waiting there! He saw everything. He wanted to talk!'

'I didn't go to the bloody café. You sent me there to get me out of the way!'

Brad continued to look at Baring. Anna joined them on the edge of the tarmac and Baring glanced at her, anticipating support. She stood beside Brad.

'What the hell were you playing at?' Baring persisted. But Brad continued to look at him and Baring realised with a shock as powerful and unpleasant as a hammer blow that it was not a look of resentment or anger, but one of pity. As he grasped this, he understood that there really had been a witness; there really had been a scoop, and he had thrown the opportunity away.

Baring turned towards the terminal and began walking, slowly at first but then at a faster pace until he had almost broken into a run.

'We should go back too,' Anna told Brad gently. 'We should file.'

* * *

Ten miles to the west the Hercules secured a cruising altitude of 20,000 feet. The growl of the plane's engines was replaced by a rhythmic hum.

They had arranged the cot in front of Terry and Mrs Pejanović, and strapped it with canvas belts to the steel ribbing on the floor.

Mrs Pejanović looked down at her son and she knew everything was changed. 'I worry about the journey,' she said. 'This has been terrible for him.'

'He'll be in hospital in London tonight,' Terry said. 'He is going to get well again.'

Terry looked through the tiny porthole. Between clouds could be seen the tips of snow-clad hills, tiny hamlets dotting the winter landscape. Then she looked back at Miro. She bent forward and touched his forehead with the palm of her hand.

'Dobro,' Terry smiled. 'Everything is going to be fine.'

He looked at her, uncomprehending, and closed his eyes.

ACKNOWLEDGEMENTS

I am grateful to the people I had the privilege of getting to know in Sarajevo during the winter and spring of 1992/93, people who in many cases responded to the ugliness of conflict with extraordinary grace and courage. Among those who made this time memorable in the most positive way were my future mother-in-law and my late brother-in-law, and a host of their neighbours whose common characteristic in the face of shelling and shortages appeared to be a boundless supply of black humour. After I was wounded, my brother Gerry dropped everything to come and fetch me from a field hospital in the Balkans, and my sister Pat and her husband Jim gave me space to write the opening chapters of *The Longest Winter*, while letting me watch hours of a diverting but, alas, short-lived Spanish soap opera. Friends who have offered support and advice on this project include Dzemal Bećirević, Peter Maass, Jelena Sesar, Erika Paine, Alexandra Stiglmayer, Chris Bennett, Herbert Pribitzer and Marina Bowder. I am grateful to Peter Buckman at the Ampersand Agency for selling the manuscript and to Joel Richardson at Twenty7 Books for buying it; also at Twenty7 many thanks to Claire Creek, an assiduous and sensitive editor. Above all, I owe a debt of gratitude to my daughter Katarina, who resourcefully contends with the daily challenge of having parents who are writers, and my wife Marija, whose patience and fortitude made this book possible.